NORMAN HALL

GOOD GIRL

Cover image - Kristin Bryant
https://www.coroflot.com/kristinbryant

Copy-editor - Nicky Taylor
https://www.nickytayloreditorial.com

For Nicky

CHAPTER 1

Sujay Bahadur Gurung stood patiently on the edge of the trail, gaze fixed on the lone figure standing on a ridge a hundred metres away. He was weighed down by two backpacks: his own small daypack and the larger, heavier one belonging to his charge. It was not unusual for him to provide such assistance to foreign trekkers, as they invariably brought more than they could easily carry themselves, or usefully need. But he had been standing there a while and even his strong, broad shoulders were beginning to ache a little. He knew he faced the prospect of lugging both of them most of the way back, so he lowered the heavier of the two to the ground and checked his watch.

It was just after 5 p.m. and the sun was steadily going down behind Langtang Lirung, at 7,227 metres the tallest mountain in the valley. The light would deteriorate rapidly over the next hour and it would be dark within two. They had a three-hour trek back to the village where food, beer and a bunk in a teahouse awaited them, and although there was no inherent danger walking at night, he knew the temperature would drop dramatically.

He also knew that despite the weight of his backpack, his charge was not properly equipped for an extended walk in the Himalayan night air, even if it was downhill most of the way. But he had agreed to take the old gentleman to the place he wanted to go to – had insisted on going to – and despite his better judgement, he had felt obliged to take the job.

He hoped for, but did not expect, a big tip, his natural humility precluding any thought that it be taken for granted, and, even though his customer seemed like an honourable gentleman from England, he had been disappointed many times before.

But time was pressing, and he looked at his watch again: 5.09. He would have to call time soon. His experience taught him that staying any longer was going to make things difficult for them both; and, after all, the old gentleman had been up there for thirty minutes. What was there to see any more?

Sujay could envisage the view from the ridge down into the valley basin, but he had no need to go up there himself and take another look. He had seen it many times, both before and after the terrible events of April, and he wanted to remember it as it had been. Before. His charge was standing ramrod straight, binoculars raised to his eyes, slowly panning the valley below, left, right, up, down and back again. There was nothing there, Sujay knew. It was time.

Up on the ridge, the old gentleman peered intently down the barrels of his glasses, hope gradually receding that he might finally find some clue as to what he was looking for. The valley floor was four hundred metres below him, Langtang Lirung and the rest of the Himal range towering over it like giants, their forbidding and foreboding presence threatening, but currently benign and inert. And from Langtang Lirung itself, sweeping into the valley from two thirds of the way up its massive slopes, a continuous trail of scree and rock that extended right across the valley and beyond.

In the valley basin, there was little sign of life and no evidence of anything untoward or unusual; an otherwise natural scene, disturbed here and there by a random splash of colour, a red or yellow or white speck, a blue flash, incongruous in the brown and barren wasteland. Nothing, other than a solitary abandoned building, standing proud but forlorn, nestled up close to the base of the mountain. He didn't know what he had expected to see and had been told by those who knew better, his guide included, there was, in fact, nothing to see. But he knew he had to come here.

The guide had tried to talk him out of it, but he had been insistent, uncompromising; and eventually, as ever, money swayed the decision. After all, Sujay had a young wife and child and this was his job. A young wife and child, he thought with a sad irony. Now there's something worth fighting for.

He panned across the valley again and then up at the mountain to the north, a swirl of evening cloud around its peak. He could hear nothing but the chattering of birds and the faint rush of the breeze, a distant howl of wind as it swirled around the valley, and as time wore on, he sensed it getting noticeably cooler. The scene could be idyllic, was idyllic, and without the knowledge of what had happened here four months ago, uplifting.

New life was forming below him, replacing the old, the endless cycle continuing. Relentless. *Immortality is temporary, young man.* Indeed. The words came back to haunt him, had been in his consciousness for many years, and now stabbed him like a dagger to the heart. His concentration was suddenly broken by the sound of a distant voice.

"Colonel Peter, sir? Please, we must go now." The cry sounded plaintive, or perhaps it was just the accent.

Without turning, Colonel Peter Jeffries, Intelligence Corps (retired), slowly lowered his binoculars, although his eyes remained fixed on the scene below. Maybe it was the temperature together with the wind chill, or even the altitude, but his eyes were glassy and moist. There could be no other explanation. Dammit. Dammit to hell!

Reluctantly, he stood down. Involuntarily, his body sagged, his shoulders drooped and his head slowly tilted forward, eyes trying to focus on the blurry image of the dusty ground at his feet. The pain was almost overwhelming. It was over.

CHAPTER 2

Jess wiped her brow with a bare arm and returned to the task of trying to remove the stain on the carpet. Squatting on the floor, alone in the boardroom of Walkers Limited, suppliers of plastic mouldings to the furniture trade, *By Appointment to Her Majesty the Queen,* she dabbed at the dark patch on the carpet with her chemically doused sponge.

Clive had told her to carry out her usual vacuuming–washroom–bins–desks routine and then go into the boardroom and try and get rid of some nasty mark, coffee presumably, that the chairman's PA had reported. She had done her best, but it would take more than one application of cleaning fluid and a lot more dabbing if she was to avoid taking the colour out of the carpet as well, so she would report progress, such as it was, and try again tomorrow.

It was 7 a.m., nearing the end of her four-hour shift, and although she had no urgent desire to get home, she knew she had other tasks to perform today and needed to get on with them. She would text Clive and no doubt he would moan at her. She could only do her best, but for Clive her best was never good enough. Given a choice, she would tell him what to do with his job. She had no choice.

She packed away her cleaning kit in the storeroom, put on her coat and left the building, touching her key fob to the alarm panel as she left. The building was still empty, and unless some extremely diligent office worker wanted to get an early start, she usually worked there alone, which was the way she preferred it. The staff at Walkers would not be arriving for another hour or so, and she had neither the time nor the desire to chitchat with anyone, at any time. She had nothing to say and work to do.

She crossed the car park just as the industrial estate was coming to life, vans arriving at various warehouse units and the occasional sound of metal shutters rattling upwards, heralding the start of a new working day. She turned left out of the factory gates, hands in pockets, and set off on her thirty-minute walk home.

She could get the bus, and provided she didn't have to wait more than ten minutes for it, she would save another ten on the overall journey time; but that cost money, and money was something she just didn't have. She had plenty of time, though. Plenty of time before her next job, and she was content to walk in the cool morning air and see the new day unfolding.

The traffic was building up, many commuters trying to get a head start on the motorised mayhem that was a regular feature of life in Wellingford, as elsewhere. She knew nothing about cars, had never owned one and never driven. Her dad had had one once, she recalled, and she remembered it crammed with possessions when they had moved up from London, but it had been taken away many years ago.

She passed a parade of shops, all still closed apart from the newsagents and the ubiquitous coffee bars doing a brisk trade in takeaway cappuccinos and pastries. She loved the smell of coffee, and often thought she might indulge herself in the luxury of a latte or an Americano, whatever they were, but not today. Maybe another time.

The bus she didn't get overtook her as she passed the two giant gasometers bordering the cricket ground. It had been five minutes late and would still have been a slightly quicker option, but she had saved £1.60 and that was worth it. And she was in no hurry.

She was home by 7.30 a.m., back to her tiny two-bed terraced house in one of the myriad narrow backstreets, her quiet place of refuge, her open prison. She never left the lights on when she was out at work, she couldn't afford it, and so the gloom and silence she had left five hours earlier was still there to greet her return.

She closed and locked the front door behind her, shrugged off her coat, tossed it over the back of the sofa and then trudged straight upstairs for a shower. Normally she would only have a forty-five-minute turnaround before leaving for the office, but today was Tuesday so she had more time. She didn't start till 12 noon on a Tuesday and worked through till 8 p.m. – a concession generously granted by Derek, as he often reminded her, but an arrangement she knew suited him just as well.

She dressed plainly, as usual, in white blouse, black trousers. Office wear. Neutral, colourless, innocuous, anonymous. She wished she could be anonymous, wished she could simply disappear, disconnect, go off-grid, escape this miserable existence and the relentless flow of bad things that had haunted her continuously for the last four or five months. Existence was pretty much all she had, and she didn't much care for it.

Tidy as ever, she made the bed. A double, but only one side needed attention as only one side was ever slept in. She went downstairs into the tiny but spotlessly clean kitchen, and turned on the radio. For a twenty-three-year old, listening to Radio 4's *Today* programme would be regarded by most people as unusual, to say the least. But Jess had no desire to be bombarded by puerile, contrived banter and inane pop music. She would much rather be in touch with what was going on in the world, and, perversely, the incessant diet of doom, gloom and despondency – the health service, the railways, the police, prison service, teaching, the economy … you name it, it was in crisis – helped to put her own situation into some sort of perspective.

She put a cup of water in the kettle and flicked the switch. She opened the fridge door. Half a bottle of milk, half a white sliced loaf, a couple of yoghurt pots and a small piece of cheese. The fridge was never full; it didn't need to be. She didn't eat much, and she was on her own. She popped a single slice of thin white bread into the toaster and took a small jar of Marmite from the cupboard it shared with a half jar of marmalade, some tea bags and a couple of tins of baked beans.

She sat at her kitchen table, sipping her tea, her wet hair slowly drying, looking out at the back garden through the half-glass kitchen door. The radio burbled on in the background with an item about poverty.

"Define poverty," the presenter asked the lady from the Joseph Rowntree Trust.

"Poverty is when you don't have enough to get by, when you have to make a choice between heating and eating."

Jess heard the words but they didn't register. She didn't need anyone to explain. That was just for the ones who didn't know, so they could feel a rush of concern before they got back to their comfortable lives.

"The official definition is living on less than sixty per cent of the average income," she continued. Jess heard that one and looked at the radio with a frown. She was no maths scholar, but poverty as this woman had defined it sounded pretty good to her. She knew what poverty was. She had her own definition, and it had little to do with money.

Her eyes strayed to the framed photograph of a young girl, three years old, which sat permanently on the kitchen table. Long brown hair, big brown eyes, smiling, happy. It wasn't a complete picture as it only filled the left-hand side of the frame, a ragged edge the boundary between it and the black backing card. And on the little girl's shoulder, an adult hand. Large, brown-skinned, a signet ring and a fragment of gold watch at the edge, its owner invisible, expunged from the scene.

Jess often looked at the picture and thought about packing it away out of sight, or even throwing it away, but couldn't bring herself to. The picture was there, and it would always be there, a lesson from the past, for as long as she lived; however long that might be. Leila would stay with her forever.

Her attention was also drawn to the letter that lay on the table in front of the photo. It had landed on the mat yesterday while she was at work. She had read it once last night and much of the small print made no sense to her, but that didn't affect its meaning or her understanding of it. It bore the official seal of Wellingford County Court and the heading was unambiguous: "Notice of Eviction" addressed to "M Y Khalid and J A Khalid" as well as "The Occupiers", a catch-all in the event the owners were not the only residents of 14 Spencer Street.

She had received many letters over the past few months warning about non-payment of mortgage arrears, each stronger and more threatening than the last, but she had not been able to do anything about them. She knew it was simply part of a process, and she had no idea how long the process would take; but, inevitably, time was up. The bank had applied to the court and, according to the letter in front of her, she had to leave the house within four weeks with all her belongings; otherwise, they would be taken out for her and stacked on the pavement.

She scanned the letter again and gazed out of the kitchen window at her ramshackle back garden. This could have been a nice house – was a nice house – with a nice family, and things could have been so much better, but what little hope remained had dissolved in the text of the letter. It was final and there was no going back. Not for the first time in her life did she reflect on the fact that the actions of others had driven her to the edge of a precipice and were about to push her off. And not for the first time did she feel numb and impotent in the face of this latest adversity.

She put the letter down on the kitchen table next to the photograph of the young girl and went upstairs to finish drying her hair and prepare herself for the Tuesday morning ordeal. She looked at herself in the bathroom mirror and made a vain attempt to smarten her long brown hair, first tying it back with a band and then flicking out a few strands in an effort to counter the starkness of her pale, emaciated face. There was an attractive young woman under the ghostly pallor, but it was rarely seen.

When she had done all she could do, she returned downstairs to the sitting room. She heard the 9 a.m. pips on the radio. It was time to go. She switched off the radio, threw on her tatty black coat and, picking up a supermarket carrier bag containing her few personal possessions, let herself out of the house.

It was a forty-minute bus ride to Brinfield, and she sat alone on the top deck as the fields flashed by outside. It was turning into a bright and sunny day. She should be feeling good, she thought.

CHAPTER 3

Tracey Shepherd sat alone behind the reception desk of Debita Debt Management, opening the mail. Blonde, petite, bustling, and prone to being a little overzealous in the make-up department, she sliced open the envelopes with her paper knife and unfolded the contents one by one, sorting the paper into distinct piles for distribution.

The quantity of physical mail was steadily reducing in volume, but there were a number of established clients who still preferred the old method. Wellingford Borough Council was one of them.

Her employer was retained under contract by Wellingford to collect council tax arrears and ultimately, if necessary, take action through the County Court for the recovery of unpaid tax. Wellingford was a "Caring, Sharing in the Community" borough and its chief executive felt it unseemly, or more likely politically imprudent, to be seen to be harassing its citizens, especially the poorer ones, for unpaid debt, so preferred to outsource the dirty work to a third party. The mailbag, slight though it was, usually contained one or two letters from Wellingford formally advising of another miscreant council taxpayer, and there was nothing different about today's.

Except that today, one such letter had caught Tracey's eye and she studied it intently, wishing it were not true. She hoped there had been an error, a case of mistaken identity, but there was no doubt. She looked up into space for a moment and bit her bottom lip, pondering the implications, until she was distracted by the appearance of Derek's PA, Jane, passing through reception clutching a bundle of files.

"Jane?" she called out, and Jane turned and approached reception. Tracey handed over the letter. "I think Derek had better see this." Jane scanned the letter briefly and looked back at Tracey with the same expression of concern.

"Oh dear. Okay, no problem," she said before exiting reception through the glass double doors. Tracey sat back in her chair and sighed. She carried on with her work but within five minutes the reception phone rang. Internal call. Tracey pressed the button to answer.

"Yes, Derek?"

"Where is she?"

"She's on lates. She'll be in at 12."

"Tell her I want to see her the moment she gets in."

"Yes, Derek."

Oh no. Tracey couldn't help feeling guilty, somehow responsible for betraying her friend. But what could she have done?

CHAPTER 4

Jess finished the last 200 yards of her journey on foot, turning into a busy car park, the entrance to which bore a large white sign: "St James Nursing Home – Compassionate Caring For All." Tuesday. Her least favourite day of the week. But she had promised, and that was that.

She trudged up to the front door and rang the bell. St James had a primitive but robust attitude to security. No one could get in through the front door without a key, and keys were only available to staff. After a moment, the door opened and an Asian woman in a nurse's uniform greeted her fondly with a big smile.

"Oh hello, Jess! How are you today?" said Nisha, beaming from ear to ear as she held the door to let Jess enter the vestibule.

"Fine thanks, Nisha. Are you well?" replied Jess with as much enthusiasm as she could muster. She liked Nisha a great deal. She was always smiling and happy and courteous, and she seemed to enjoy her work, however traumatic that must be. Jess always wondered how anyone could be so unremittingly cheerful when confronted day in, day out by death and dying and hopelessness. It should put her own position into some sort of perspective, she told herself. But it didn't. Anyway, seeing Nisha again would no doubt be the highlight of her day and she should savour it while she could.

"I'm very well, thank you," replied Nisha, seeming genuinely grateful for the enquiry into her health and with that little side-to-side shake of the head that for Hindus signalled the affirmative rather than the contrary.

"How is he?" asked Jess automatically as she leant over the visitors' book to sign herself in. The same conversation each week. The same answer.

"Oh, he's okay," the word "considering" left unsaid, as always. But unusually, Nisha did have something to add. "But he has a mild chest infection, so the doctor has given him antibiotics."

Jess put down the pen and considered this new information for a moment. A mild chest infection in someone confined to a nursing home had a somewhat greater significance than it did for most people. Still, action was being taken, and that was no more and no less than she expected at St James.

"Okay, thanks," said Jess, then she exited through the internal glass doors.

Nisha dutifully maintained her smile as Jess left, but it quickly evaporated as she watched her walk down the corridor and turn left up the stairs to the first floor.

Nisha thought Jess a troubled girl, but she was very fond of her and was concerned. *So sad.* She was less enamoured with her father but then she had experienced abuse in one form or another all her life, from back home in Rajasthan to the moment she had set foot in Britain, and ever since. It was just something you got used to and had to deal with. *So sad to think Jess may not be visiting again.* The sound of the doorbell ringing startled her out of her thoughts, and the beaming smile returned.

***

Joe Butler was up and dressed but asleep in his chair. It was a fitful sleep punctuated by coughing, snorting and wheezing, interspersed by a vague and incoherent mumbling; confirmation, as if Jess needed it, that Joe was indeed a bit under the weather.

The room was warm and the spring sunshine streamed in through the side window, but despite this, Joe wore a string vest under his cotton checked shirt and his favourite red cardigan, a tartan rug covering his legs and lower body.

At six foot five, Joe had been a big man. But now, slumped in his chair, he looked sunken and shrivelled, vaguely cadaverous, his thinning grey hair unkempt, two days' stubble randomly speckling drawn cheeks and greying skin. Blue veins drew an incoherent map down the side of his nose and spread across his cheekbones under deep-set and dark eye sockets. His lips had a tinge of blue about them, too, with traces of mucus forming at the corner of his mouth.

The room itself was tidy and utilitarian and a not unpleasant place to be, but then Joe hardly ever left his room, which to him made it feel like a prison cell on death row. Nevertheless, Jess thought, it was better appointed than her own house, and that was ironic.

The room was dominated by a medium-sized, iron-framed bed and featured a small pine-effect wardrobe, bedside table and table lamp, two upright armchairs upholstered in faded green velour, and a chest of drawers on which sat two photograph frames. One held a picture of a schoolgirl of about eleven: Jess, looking smiley and self-conscious on her first day at high school. The other was an old wedding photograph: Joe and Madge on their wedding day back in 1975, Joe sporting a mullet and outrageously flared brown suit with a frilly shirt and red velvet bow tie, his bride similarly flamboyant in a white lace gown, her hair backcombed with ringlets down the sides, huge circular earrings dangling from petite ears and hands clutching a posy. Both smiling. Both happy. Together and in love on the best day of their lives. On the window ledge sat another, larger framed picture. Madge, alone, elderly, frail, but smiling stoically.

Jess laid her carrier bag quietly on the bed and took off her coat. She was reluctant to disturb him, especially if he was not feeling well, and the sleep might do him good. But she knew that was disingenuous and had to admit to herself that it was not the reason. She would rather he stayed asleep so she could fulfil her duty, carry out her promise, without any further effort or interaction. She had nothing to say to him of any importance, nothing she wanted to ask, no advice she needed. Nothing but idle conversation, and neither of them was any good at that. Not now.

She gazed out of the window onto a garden carefully tended with rose-filled flower beds, small patches of lawn and a bench for residents and visitors to use and take in the air; although few actually did. She leant against the wall, arms folded, eyes half closed in the glare of the sunlight, with her back to Joe, who continued to snuffle and snort restlessly behind her.

She wondered how much longer it would be before her duty was finally done. How many more times she had to come to this place to fulfil a promise, a promise she was forced to give but did so willingly out of love. Another complication she could well do without; as if that would make a difference. Maybe this would be her last visit. Maybe Joe would simply not wake up. Maybe.

As if he had read her thoughts, Joe spluttered and coughed and broke her train of thought. She watched him open his eyes wearily and try to focus on her. He adjusted his position in the chair and tried to sit up, a grimace of pain at the effort creasing his forehead. He took as deep a breath as his damaged lungs could manage.

"Hello, sweetheart," he said with a rasp and another wheezy intake of breath. "How long you been here?" A moment's hesitation.

"Just got here, Dad," replied Jess stiffly. She felt awkward and guilty but couldn't think of anything else to say, and she was in no hurry to make eye contact, so she decided to stay where she was. Despite his physical discomfort, Joe tried again with the pleasantries.

"Hmm. What you been up to, then?" Joe was originally from East London and still had the cockney twang and an economy of language which meant that participles, past, present or future, were usually foregone in the interests of brevity.

Jess sucked in her breath and exhaled slowly. She didn't want to have a conversation about herself, or anything else for that matter. She just wanted to go. Go back to her miserable world and leave her dying father alone in his.

"Oh, you know. Work and stuff," she said, just for something to say so as not to completely ignore him. Whatever she felt, she was not a rude girl. But then, chiding herself that she ought to try harder, half turned her head to catch Joe in her peripheral vision. "How you feeling?" she asked without conviction, stripping back the phrase to its bare essentials in a way Joe would understand.

"Shit," Joe declared, grimacing and then throwing his head back before launching into another painful coughing episode. Jess breathed in again.

"Oh," was all she could think to say in response. She didn't know what she had expected him to say in his current condition. Hoped vainly that perhaps he might simply join her in this forced and inane banter, with a "Fine, thanks." No chance. She turned her head back to the window. "Have you taken the pills?" Despite her best efforts, and to her continued discomfort, she could not conceal the lack of interest in her voice.

"Yeah, well, they ain't going to do nothing, are they?" Jess sensed the resignation and bitterness in Joe's voice. As always, he would find something to be angry about. Angry at his condition, angry at the unfairness of it all, angry at the missed opportunities, angry at her apparent lack of sympathy, and angry that, unlike him, she was blessed with youth, her future stretching out before her. *If only he knew.*

But maybe he was just afraid? She could empathise with that.

The coughing abated for a moment and he decided to get more than phlegm off his chest.

"You found that Paki waster yet?" he sneered, the mocking tone neatly conflating his racial prejudices and his disappointment in her dismissive attitude towards him.

Jess pursed her lips and closed her eyes. Here we go again, she thought. He can't resist bringing it up, finding a way to get it into the conversation every time. Doesn't he realise the pain? Of course he does. She was tempted for a moment to scream at him, throw something at him, walk out and leave him to his fate, the miserable old bastard. But she wouldn't give him the satisfaction. She just didn't have it in her.

"No, Dad," she said curtly, hoping that would be the end of it. It wasn't. Joe was onto his favourite subject and he wasn't about to let it go just yet.

"Nah. Told you he was no good. Told you not to get involved with them sort. That weren't never going to work." He shook his head. "I said to your mother, that'll end in tears, that will." Her dad had been right for once in his life, Jess thought, but she was not about to discuss it with him or admit it. It just wasn't worth it. He wasn't worth it.

"Play another record, Dad." She didn't much know what a record was – something music was played on in the old days – but she remembered her mother often saying the same thing to him and it had stuck in her mind. So she deployed the phrase when Joe was, as now, being boringly repetitive, and it was also language he would at least understand.

But she had already decided she would not be drawn into an argument and she hoped that, having said his piece, he would relent. Contrition didn't come easily to her father, but he sighed and softened his tone. Conciliatory and sympathetic. Well, almost.

"Ah, well. You don't learn nothing without making mistakes." He paused in contemplation for a second. "God knows I made a few." For a moment, Jess thought he might be about to launch into some sort of confessional, here and now, while he still had time, seeking absolution, but then realised there could not possibly be enough time for that. He coughed again. Jess turned and looked at him.

"Do you want a cup of tea?" she asked, hoping he would refuse.

"Yeah, go on then," he grunted without any enthusiasm.

"Digestive?" she said, reaching over and peering inside a tin which sat on a tray next to two mugs.

"Yeah, go on then."

Jess noticed someone had been at the biscuits since last week. One of the young girls who came in to clean his room perhaps, helping herself to one when he was asleep in the chair. Well, they were welcome to them, Jess thought. There had to be some compensations in the job, especially if every day you had to deal with a filthy, bigoted old sod like him.

"They're almost gone," she sighed. "I'll get you some more when I'm out."

"Yeah – you do that. Use me card. You still got it, ain't yer?" Joe had entrusted his debit card to his daughter for making incidental purchases on his behalf, like tea and biscuits. He had said he had no use for it, nor the meagre contents of his bank account. They were not going to make a difference. Not now.

"Yes, Dad," Jess said, irritated by the implication that looking after his debit card was not treated with utmost care and attention.

"You're a good girl," said Joe. It could have been a show of affection, or even contrition. But the words made her bristle and she felt the hairs stand up on the back of her neck. She suddenly had to get out of there, even if it was only to go and boil the kettle. She had to be alone for a moment. She did her level best not to react. She just stared at him for a second. He actually looked like he meant it. And that was what hurt her the most.

"Back in a minute," she said, turning away as Joe's head lolled forward and his eyes closed.

***

Joe Butler married his childhood sweetheart, Margaret Jamieson, in April 1975, when he was twenty-one and she had just turned twenty. They were a handsome young couple. They rented a council house in Lewisham, South East London, and after taking a succession of labouring jobs, Joe trained as a bus driver and got a steady job driving for London Transport. Madge had a part-time job in a newsagent which provided a bit of extra cash; that was all she needed because she and her new husband had planned to start a family, and soon there would be babies.

To their misfortune, Madge suffered two miscarriages over the next five years, and they began to fear they might never have children. Her GP counselled her to prepare for the fact that she might never conceive and suggested that they consider adoption or seek professional help with an emerging new technology he called IVF.

They were simple people, disinclined to seek professional help – that was only for rich folk – and felt that the adoption process was not for them. But in all other respects they were happy, and so their lives trundled on relentlessly with only the anniversary of each miscarriage to remind them of what might have been.

It was on their twentieth wedding anniversary that Madge visited the doctor, who informed her that against all odds she was three months pregnant. Six months later, Madge presented Joe with a beautiful baby girl who they christened Jessica Anne.

23

It seemed that their lives together had started all over again. Madge gave up work to care for Jess while Joe worked overtime to make up for the loss of Madge's income and the increased costs of family life.

Over the next ten years they were happy and contented, with Jess developing an easy-going and joyful disposition and Madge returning to work part-time so they could afford family holidays and other luxuries, such as a small family car. Joe and Madge doted on their only child and spoiled their daughter with presents on her birthday and at Christmas, and to their neighbours, they appeared to be the model family.

But the Butlers would soon face their biggest challenge. By 2004, London Transport had moved most of their fleet to larger buses, and this, together with the relentless growth of car ownership, resulted in fewer passengers, which in turn meant they needed fewer drivers. Despite long and loyal service, Joe was made redundant just before his fifty-second birthday, his bitterness exacerbated by the knowledge that other younger, mainly Asian drivers with fewer years' service had not been chosen instead.

Joe spent a difficult six months trying to get another bus driving job – it was all he knew – and while there appeared to be vacancies elsewhere in the country, the Butlers were Londoners born and bred, and to them it was inconceivable that they should move away.

But their savings were running out and they had to do something, so with much trepidation, Joe applied for, and got, a job in the Midlands working for a private bus operator in the market town of Wellingford. With heavy hearts they packed their belongings and left Lewisham for a new life in the country.

One advantage to living in the Midlands was that rents were much cheaper and so they were able to get a semi-detached council house with a small garden for the same price as their terraced house in London. Jess had just finished primary school in Lewisham so the timing was right for her, and she settled quickly into Wellingford High and made new friends, although to her they all seemed to have strange accents.

Joe had always liked a beer or two and he also liked his football. He never regarded himself as a heavy drinker, but back in Lewisham each Saturday afternoon, when his beloved West Ham were playing at home, he and his mates would go to the pub after the match and sink five or six pints while watching the highlights of the day's matches on the pub's massive new 36″ plasma TV.

As he didn't work on a Sunday, Joe had no qualms about enjoying a Saturday night out with the lads, sobering up the next day in plenty of time for his next shift on Monday morning. He took his job very seriously and never drank the night before a working day, which in any event was strictly against company rules.

He never managed to replicate this activity in sleepy Wellingford, but when England were playing a World Cup qualifier in Germany one Sunday afternoon, he told Madge that he would go to the pub with some of his colleagues from the bus company and have a couple of shandies.

England lost the match, and to drown their sorrows, he and the lads had a couple of pints before he made his way home at around 8 p.m. to find Madge and Jess slumped in front of the TV watching a costume drama.

The next day he started his shift at 6.30 a.m. as usual. At 8.45 a.m., on the High Street, a small car unexpectedly pulled out of its parking spot and the front of Joe's bus clipped the offside front wing. It was a minor accident in which no one was hurt and blame fell on the driver of the car, a woman in her sixties, who was mortified and profoundly apologetic.

However, procedures had to be followed and the police called. Both drivers were routinely breathalysed, and although falling far short of the legal limit, Joe was found to have traces of alcohol in his system, a legacy from the previous day's session in the pub. When his employers received the report of the accident, Joe was summoned to his manager's office and instantly dismissed without appeal.

This was not like redundancy. This was different, and there was no rehabilitation for a bus driver who had been caught with the barest amount of alcohol in his blood. At fifty-five he was unemployable on the buses and, in his mind, anywhere else. He made a concerted effort to find work but to no avail. Increasingly he found himself in the pub drinking ever-increasing quantities of beer and squandering his unemployment benefit.

At fifteen, Jess had grown into a beautiful and intelligent young woman and watched with increasing horror and dismay as her father descended into alcoholism and indolence; and as the money ran out, her mother fell into a desperate malaise, withdrawing into her shell, unable to cope with the transformation of her beloved Joe into a wretched old man.

***

Jess sat in the chair opposite her father, who had fallen asleep again. She had made him take some of the antibiotics with his tea and although his breathing remained raspy, the coughing had stopped and he was able to rest for a while.

She glanced at the clock on the bedside table: 11 a.m. She had been there an hour and she had time to spare before getting back on the bus to her next destination, but she needed to get out before he woke up. She didn't want to go through the motions of saying goodbye, and she would be back next week to do the same. Back to do her duty.

She turned her head to look at the framed photo of her mother on the window ledge. She leant forward and picked it up, bringing her mother's haggard face into sharp focus. Madge was clearly forcing a smile for the camera and the lines on her face belied her years. She had only been sixty when the picture was taken, but she looked ten years older and her face bore the stoicism with which she had tolerated her last few years. Jess could still hear her mother's voice, trembling, echoing in the dark recesses of her mind. *Jess, my darling, promise me you'll look after him. Look after him for me, Jess. Promise?*

She could still hear the pleading in the voice, the desperation in her last breaths, that she might yet elicit some semblance of reconciliation, something she couldn't do when she had been alive, and finally rest in peace. Jess was overtaken by a profound sadness. She had done her duty, but the reconciliation her mother wished for had never happened, would never happen. Madge may have been deluded, in denial of the terrible years in the run-up to her death, but remembering how it had once been was the only way she could face dying.

Jess was disturbed that she herself felt so dispassionate and unsentimental. She too wanted to remember her mother the way she had been when she was growing up. She had loved her mother, but in the end Madge had let her down, and she had had to put distance between them in order to save herself. *Who had been more selfish?* The separation had been forced on them, but in the end it had been the final straw and her mother had simply given up.

Jess replaced the picture and looked up once more at her father, who was breathing deeply and erratically. Without making a sound, she got up, collected her things and slipped out of the room.

CHAPTER 5

She arrived at her next destination at twelve noon precisely, exactly on time. She stopped to look at the sign outside the main entrance before pushing through the revolving doors of Debita Debt Management and approaching reception. The blonde girl at the reception desk was deep in conversation with someone on the phone.

"Yes, Mrs Wilson. Yes, I will give Mr Pemberton your message. Yes, I will. No, I won't. Yes, I will. Goodbye, Mrs Wilson," she said before putting the phone back on its rest.

"She never gives up, does she?" said Jess.

"Let that be a lesson to us all," declared Tracey as Jess removed her coat and hung it on the coat stand.

"Anyway, how is he?"

Jess suspected Tracey asked more out of politeness than genuine curiosity.

"Oh, you know," she said, "the same." She pulled her chair out from under the desk to take up her position next to Tracey, but before she could sit down, Tracey intervened.

"Oh, er … Derek wants to see you," she said, raising a mug of tea to her mouth with both hands in an awkward manner. Jess shot her a look and her eyes narrowed. Derek never wanted to see her. Derek barely passed the time of day whenever they crossed paths in the corridor. Derek was a charmless idiot and had very little good to say of anyone other than himself. But he was the boss, so he must have something to tell her, and it was not as if she had any choice in the matter. But she couldn't help feeling the stirrings of alarm and continued to stare sideways at Tracey, who was studiously avoiding her gaze.

"What about?" said Jess, perplexed.

"Dunno," replied Tracey, her voice muffled by the mug hiding most of her face.

Tracey knew exactly what it was about, but it was not her place to say so. Above her pay grade, as the saying went. She liked Jess; she liked Jess a lot. Jess was always on time. Jess always did her work without complaint. Jess covered for Tracey when Tracey needed cover, and Jess never got cross at anyone. In fact, Jess rarely showed any emotion beyond a pleasant smile for visitors, that disappeared the moment they had gone.

But Tracey and Jess weren't friends. Jess didn't have any friends that she was aware of, and Tracey knew nothing of Jess's family circumstances because Jess never talked about herself to anyone. Tracey only knew about Jess's dad being poorly because of their staggered work pattern on a Tuesday. But Tracey liked Jess, even though she thought she was a bit weird.

She watched from the corner of her eye as Jess smoothed down her blouse and headed for the double doors into the corridor, and when she got there, called after her. "He's in Meeting Room 1." Jess paused to take in the information and then proceeded through the doors. Tracey put her cup down and bit her bottom lip.

***

Jess had been sitting alone in Meeting Room 1 for ten minutes. Derek's secretary had said he was on a call and would be with her in due course, so best she wait for him in there. Jess doubted the veracity of this statement. Derek always wanted to control any situation, so it would have been unseemly for him to have responded to Jess's arrival immediately. It was pure Derek to make her wait for him.

Her eyes scanned the room, but little caught her attention or provoked any interest. She had only been in there once before when one of the other secretaries was away; drafted in to serve coffee and pastries to a director's board meeting, and being largely ignored by the assembly of self-important, boorish middle-aged males. She remembered the sweaty and corpulent finance director, Nigel, grinning at her lasciviously and telling her she had a nice figure, which had made her feel uncomfortable.

The room was empty and quiet, apart from the background hum of the air conditioner, the drinks fridge in the corner and the sporadic rush of traffic noise which penetrated the double-glazing.

She had spent the last ten minutes wondering what this could be about. Was she about to get a pay rise? Unlikely. Had she done something wrong? Had there been some sort of complaint from a client? She racked her brains to think of anything unusual that had happened recently. He knew she worked a late shift on Tuesday so it couldn't be that, not unless he was about to change the arrangement. That would be less convenient, meaning she would have to visit Joe in the evening or at weekends, but not insurmountable.

She had to wait no longer. The sound of the door opening abruptly startled her, and Derek strode in clutching a file of papers. Tall, skinny, bearded, Derek was an unprepossessing character with no sense of humour and an over-inflated view of his own importance.

She shifted slightly in her seat and glanced up nervously as he took his position at the table opposite her, flashing her a quick look of disdain before sitting down and spreading open the file on the boardroom table. No greeting, no pleasantries, no grace. This was pure Derek. Derek was always too busy with his extremely important and highly pressurised job to waste time in idle chat.

Jess was not alone in regarding Derek as a pompous, vain, fool. A middle manager with board aspirations that everyone but him knew would never be met. Charmless, graceless, arrogant. A prize arsehole, she had been shocked to hear someone say, but she thought that was harsh.

He flicked papers backwards and forwards in the file, affecting an earnest consideration as to their contents, a crucial precursor to his next big executive decision.

"How's your father?" he muttered without looking up. Jess was suddenly confused. Derek never enquired after her own health, or anyone else's for that matter, so it was unprecedented for him to enquire over the health of a relative. She didn't imagine Derek could know anything of Joe's condition, but then surmised office gossip had spread the word.

Derek was still rifling through sheets of paper seemingly at random in an attempt to look busy and diligent, though Jess knew neither of these descriptions applied. He was playing for time, she thought, ramping up the tension, and the casual, dismissive tone of his question merely proved to her that he was not remotely interested in the answer. Still, she decided, let's give Derek the benefit of the doubt for once. It's common courtesy, after all.

"He's fine, thanks," she said after a moment, without embellishment, gratitude or any desire to pursue the matter further. There was a pause so long she thought Derek hadn't heard her.

"Goooooood," he said, without looking up, and clearly without cognisance as the word stretched out to the length of a sentence. She could have said Joe had suffered a massive stroke, been savaged by a rabid fox, or even that his head had spontaneously combusted, blood and brain matter splattering the walls of his room, and Derek's response would have been the same. She stared at him as he stroked his beard and his eyes scanned one particular document that had caught his attention. She allowed herself an almost imperceptible shake of the head in contempt.

The door opened again and both Derek and Jess turned their heads towards the sound.

"Ah, Anne, come in. I've asked Anne to join us, if you don't mind," he said to Jess as Anne tiptoed over to the end of the table and sat down nervously. It wasn't so much a question as a statement and Jess didn't think a response was necessary, but she suddenly sensed something was wrong. Anne was personnel, and personnel didn't appear unless the matter at hand was personal and serious.

She looked nonplussed at Anne who caught her gaze briefly before turning her head away to open her notepad and ready her pencil, which signalled to Derek that it was time to start proceedings.

Jess's eyes widened and she felt a shiver of fear as Derek looked at her directly for the first time, his face affecting a patronising smile. He looked down at the sheet of paper he had been examining, puffed himself up and announced with gravitas:

"There's something I need to show you. A letter came in today. From the Council Tax Department. Another of its citizens hopelessly in arrears. Want us to collect." He sniffed, and slid the sheet of paper across the desk towards Jess. Anne looked down and squirmed.

Jess didn't react, her gaze fixed on Derek who had put both elbows on the table and lifted his hands so he could rest his hairy chin on two thumbs while looking at her intently. She knew instinctively what was in the letter and what it would say, and the irony of it struck her. Her job on reception, amongst other things, was to open the mail. She had been waiting for this one to arrive, but she wasn't there this morning so Tracey had opened the mail instead. If she hadn't gone to visit her beloved father, she would have opened the mail, seen this letter and then destroyed it. It would have only been a temporary solution to a long-term problem, and in due course the council would have chased up the lack of response, but it would have bought her a bit of precious time. Joe had done it again, albeit unwittingly, helping her slide further down the slippery slope to ruin.

She picked up the letter and gave it a cursory glance, speed-reading the salient words – "Mr & Mrs M Y Khalid … Arrears of Council Tax … £625.54" – before swiftly putting it back on the desk as if it were contaminated or about to explode, where it was gathered up by Derek's outstretched hand and laid back on top of the pile of papers in the folder. Derek sat back and launched into a speech he had no doubt prepared and rehearsed carefully.

"Now look, Jess, it's like this—"

"Am I being dismissed?" she burst in before he could get into his stride.

She hadn't meant to sound rude, it wasn't her way, but she knew what was coming and the last thing she wanted was a lecture from Derek. She felt a mild satisfaction that her interjection had appeared to throw him off balance, Anne too, who looked up in alarm, because Jess knew they all thought she was quiet and unassuming. Derek looked aghast at the impertinence and cut to the chase.

"We are going to have to let you go," he said, and as if to seek her understanding, added, "we can't have this, not here."

"Why?" she countered. "Am I not doing the job to your satisfaction?" It sounded overly formal but it was a good point. She knew she did a good job, was no trouble to anyone, and although she didn't make friends easily she was perfectly polite and efficient on the phone or when dealing with visitors face-to-face. She couldn't see how owing money to the council was incompatible with the way in which she performed her duties. She sat tight as a drum, rigid in her chair, defiant but also afraid. Derek looked at her, his patronising grin tinged with irritation. He sighed deeply.

"Unless it has escaped your attention," he proffered in a tone heavy with sarcasm, "*this* is a debt collection agency. It's highly embarrassing to be asked to collect a debt from one of our own employees. It's just not possible for you to

33

work here in the circumstances." And with a satisfied finality he returned to flicking pages in the document folder. "I have no choice."

Jess processed his final remark for only a second before batting it back in his face.

"You mean it's not your decision?"

Derek looked up in bewilderment. He seemed confused by her assertion and she wondered if he might be a little miffed that his authority was being called into question, especially in front of Anne. Wrong-footed, he blundered on.

"Yes, yes – it's my decision."

"Then you have a choice," she stated simply.

"No, what I mean is—"

"What you mean is," she hit back, taking control of the conversation, "because I'm struggling to pay my council tax, the obvious solution is to take away my income and any chance I have of paying it off."

Derek sat back in his chair tapping his pen on the table, sulking from the reprimand, while Anne tried to keep her head down. Jess looked at one, then the other, and thought she may have come across as too stroppy. *Yeah, well. I have a good right to be stroppy.* The pompous idiot was more interested in saving face than trying to help her out of a hole. She knew it was probably futile, but she softened her tone in an attempt to appeal to his human side. If only he had one.

"I need to work, Derek, I need to pay my bills." This was no throwaway line from Jess. She had inherited the work ethic from her mother. She had never borrowed anything and never asked for help. Would never ask for help. She didn't blame anyone else for her circumstances although she had every right to do so. She was in grave financial difficulty but was determined to dig herself out of it any way she could. Maybe, just maybe, Derek could see his way to steer her in the right direction rather than just throw the book at her.

He studied her closely and she could feel herself deflating. Any normal human being would have admired her pluck, but she knew Derek was not the type. She had to fight her corner, but she had turned it into a power struggle and now Derek appeared to be smarting from a couple of sound blows to his pride and his credibility. She knew he needed to win or else it would be all round the office. He couldn't even fire a low-paid receptionist without looking like an amateur, is what they would all say.

"What else do you owe?" he asked with seemingly innocent curiosity, although she was certain he already knew the answer. "Mortgage? Utilities? Credit cards? Payday loan?"

Jess's confidence evaporated as the words fell on her, one by one, like blows from a boxing glove. Derek raised his eyebrows knowingly and sat back with a look of satisfaction.

"Thought so. I'm afraid your contract does not allow for this. *You* are in breach of your terms of employment," he announced with ridiculous grandiloquence.

Jess was down but not out, and tried again. She needed to get him on side, appeal to whatever shred of decency he may have left and afford him as much respect as she could, because without this job, it was game over. She tried without much success to keep any hint of pleading out of her voice.

"Tell me what I need to do."

Derek was back in driving seat, so the patronising tone returned.

"Look, I know it's a shock …"

"It's not a shock," she sighed, fearing this was going nowhere.

"If I might offer you some advice?" Jess looked up, a glimmer of hope in her eyes, but one that would be quickly extinguished. "The best thing you can do is go through the bankruptcy process. Then, when you come out the other end, you might be able to apply for your job back." His disdainful

35

tone betrayed a belief in the utter futility of her pursuing this strategy. Jess could not believe what she was hearing. Was this supposed to be Derek's idea of help?

"Might?" Jess made no attempt to hide her scepticism at his dubious suggestion.

"Well, I can't make any promises, but I would have no objections. Would you, Anne?" They both turned to look at Anne, but she was staring into space and Jess realised she had not been paying attention. Suddenly startled, her gaze then darted back and forth between Derek and Jess, both of whom were now staring at her intently, waiting for an answer,

"No! No!" she blurted, shaking her head and wiggling her bottom on her chair. Jess tried not to snort in contempt.

"Oh. Well that's all right, then," she said, her tone heavy with sarcasm. Suitably put down, Anne dropped her head in shame. Derek sniffed and tried again.

"Look, I know it's hard. But you have to appreciate my position. This is very hard for me too." Derek was a master at condescension, but this was too much to take.

"Hard for you?" Jess could not believe what she was hearing and fought to conceal her contempt for a man who was trying to elicit sympathy for *his* predicament. She remained calm and said steadily, by way of admonishment, "You'll have forgotten about it tomorrow. Tomorrow it'll still be hard for me. And the day after, and the day after that." Derek's mouth twisted in rage and he thrust his head forward aggressively.

"I did not get you into this position!"

Jess was momentarily startled by Derek's petulance, and she saw he was too, as he glanced nervously at Anne, whose head was down, trying not to notice he had lost his cool. There was no sound for a moment while they all contemplated his outburst. He swallowed uncomfortably and slumped back in his chair, and folded his arms like a truculent child. Jess broke the silence. She could read his mind.

"I've only myself to blame." It was neither confession nor admission. Just a statement.

Derek looked pleased with himself. He spread his arms and gave her a knowing expression before sliding a brown envelope across the table towards her. He stood up and put out a hand.

"Anne will help you clear your desk." Jess picked up the envelope and stood, ignoring the outstretched hand. She turned abruptly without saying another word and headed for the door. But before she could get there, she heard a parting shot.

"Quietly, please." She halted, her back towards him. "We don't want to upset the others." She closed her eyes, and the knife in her back stung as she exited Meeting Room 1.

***

Tracey was away from reception, which Jess was pleased about as she hated emotional farewells. She didn't want to explain what was going on, even though she realised Tracey probably knew already.

She retrieved her coat from the stand, threw it over her shoulders and picked up her carrier bag, putting in the brown envelope Derek had given her. She headed for the revolving doors, but before she got there, she heard the clack of heels on tile and the plaintive voice behind her.

"Jess!" Jess stopped and turned as Tracey tottered across the reception area on her five-inch heels at as rapid a pace as they would allow. "Jess …" Tracey put her arms round her in an awkward embrace, more so because Jess remained inert and didn't respond.

"I just wanted to say goodbye, Jess, and good luck." Tracey stood back, arms outstretched on Jess's shoulders. "You're a good girl, Jess." Jess closed her eyes in dismay at Tracey's choice of words. "Too good for here," continued Tracey, oblivious to the irony in her own statement. Jess said nothing, and simply turned and walked out of the building into the greying afternoon.

She stood on the steps outside her erstwhile employer's office and looked around at the people going about their business, the cars and lorries and buses meandering along the road. Everyone had places to go, things to do, people to see. Apart from her, or so it seemed. She had no idea what would happen next, but she knew it was not going to be good. It felt like the end was fast approaching. But what she could not know was that this was not the end; it was the beginning.

CHAPTER 6

Jess was home just after 2 p.m., the house as quiet and gloomy as she had left it that morning. She dropped her coat and bag on the sofa and bent to pick up the mail. She took it into the kitchen, and although she knew there would be nothing other than more bad news, not least because she recognised the style and stamp on both, she ripped open the first of the two envelopes.

It was addressed to Mr and Mrs M Y Khalid and it was from Wellingford Borough Council, Council Tax Department, informing her that as previous demands for payment had not been met, they were assigning collection of council tax arrears of £625.54 to Debita Debt Management Limited.

She placed the letter on top of the Notice of Eviction, which was where she had left it earlier that morning, and opened the second envelope. It was from Northern & Midland Energy informing Mr M Khalid that due to his failure to respond to repeated demands for payment, the electricity supply would be disconnected on the twenty-first of July. Jess glanced at the wall calendar: tomorrow.

Her shoulders sank a little further, but none of this was a surprise; it had been inevitable and was simply the foreseeable consequence of events that had always been outside her control. The doorbell rang.

Without stopping for a second to wonder who might be calling at two o'clock in the afternoon, when she was almost always out, she put the letter down on the pile and headed back through the sitting room to the front door. She grasped the handle and pulled it open.

She recognised them immediately, but the shock of the unexpected visit made her gasp with fear, and in a blind panic she slammed the door shut and threw her back against it. She put her head back, eyes wide in fright and shock at the terrible image, but she knew straight away something was wrong. The door had not latched, but had bounced back against her with a crunching and splintering noise, and she could still hear the sounds of the street outside. With mounting fear and confusion, she slowly turned her head to her left, terrified at what she might see. It was worse than she had imagined.

A baseball bat was wedged between door and jamb, preventing its closure. The doorjamb was broken and pieces of shattered wood hung limply below the bat, which apart from a few chips and some sinister-looking stains, appeared unscathed. She shut her eyes again but knew there was nothing she could do. If they wanted to come in, all they had to do was push against the door, and she would have no chance resisting their strength; which meant that despite the extreme tactics, they intended no physical violence, at least not today. She slowly opened the door and stepped onto the mat.

Two men in dark suits, ties and black overcoats. One, five foot tall, bald, a clipboard cradled in his left arm, was smiling broadly at her. His associate, six feet five and eighteen stone, chipped and stained baseball bat resting casually over his left shoulder, stared directly at her, unblinking, with neither expression nor emotion, like a large fish. He sported a prominent scar down one side of his face; a scar that had never fully healed after the altercation with "Stanley Knife" Eddie five years ago, in which it was fair to say Eddie had come off worse. She had never decided which of them frightened her more: Bond villain "Baldie" or scarface "Gorilla Man", but together they were a formidable sight.

She knew them well. They came round every week, usually in the evening at about 6.30 and always on a Friday. Jess made sure she was always in because that way, their business could be conducted with as little friction as possible, and her windows stayed intact.

But she had been taken by surprise this afternoon. This was unprecedented. Perhaps they had been tipped off? Perhaps they had seen her coming home early? Perhaps they had just got lucky, or on this occasion decided to vary the time of their visit in order to catch Mo at home for once. Whatever the reason, they were here now and they meant business.

Baldie was clearly the boss, because his companion never said anything. Gorilla Man was bag carrier, protector, minder, intimidator and enforcer all rolled into one, and without him, Baldie could not possibly do his job successfully. The mere presence of Gorilla Man imbued Baldie with a power way beyond his physical capabilities and he had the arrogance to go with it, evident every time he spoke.

"Good afternoon, Mrs Khalid," he said, still beaming, unperturbed by the incident with the door and the baseball bat, and relishing the intense discomfort and fear clearly etched on the face of the young woman standing in the doorway. "Is your husband at home, by any chance?"

Baldie inclined his head casually, his mocking tone betraying the fact that of course he already knew the answer to the question.

Jess tried her best to appear unfazed and defiant in the face of the implied threat but made the mistake of glancing up at Gorilla Man, whose eyes simply bored into her, making her knees go wobbly. She fought back the urge to slam the door again but realised it would be futile and she would do better not to try their patience.

"No. He's out," she replied curtly. The same answer to the same question. Week after week, they went through the motions on the doorstep, the same choreographed routine, and although it was true, of course, it sounded disingenuous; not least because it was. Mo had been "out" for over four months now, but she was not about to explain his absence to anyone. Baldie looked at her like a fox assessing cornered prey in a chicken coop, and resumed his sarcastic tone.

"He's out a lot, isn't he? Not very considerate, is it?" he went on, "leaving his young wife at home to deal with his" – he paused for emphasis – "business affairs?"

Jess looked at him, although she sensed Gorilla Man's attention remained fixated on her. She had no choice; she had to tell them.

"I haven't got it," she said in as matter-of-fact a way as she could. What else could she do? It was true. It wasn't a cold day, but Jess sensed a sudden deep chill in the doorway and she tightened the grip of her arms around herself to maintain her composure. Gorilla Man didn't flinch.

Baldie's beaming smile dissolved as his eyes narrowed, his jocular expression supplanted by a frown which signalled a combination of surprise, confusion and disappointment as he morphed seamlessly from cheery conversationalist into Bond villain.

"Why. Not?" The 't' snapped like the spring of a mousetrap.

"Get paid Friday," said Jess, her fear rendering her incapable of constructing a proper sentence.

"It's. Due. Today," he said helpfully, each word distinct, articulated slowly and deliberately to ensure there could be no misunderstanding, no doubt of his disapprobation, no doubt of the menace.

"I'll have it Friday," countered Jess, with a growing panic that a situation she already knew was out of her control – had always been out of her control – was nevertheless spiralling further downwards.

Baldie considered her statement for a moment and performed some mental arithmetic. Jess shot a glance at Gorilla Man, who remained motionless, unmoved but focused on the prey. She turned back to Baldie who addressed her calmly and gently, like a lawyer who might advise a client of the potentially disadvantageous consequences of taking a particular course of action.

"It'll be an extra fifty by then," he advised. Jess's bottom lip quivered. She couldn't help it. She wanted more than anything else to be brave, to be resilient, to be strong and fight back, but she had nothing left. She swallowed, and mercifully the tears that had been welling up inside her subsided. She hadn't cracked.

Perhaps sensing she was on the edge, Baldie's earlier charm returned. Had he spotted an opportunity to have some sport, or perhaps something even better? He smiled at her playfully, slowly looking her up and down as if he were assessing a candidate for a modelling assignment and about to pass judgement on her appearance. When his eyes reached her middle, he ventured, "or maybe ... we could negotiate a" – with eyes wide and brows raised, he met her gaze with his triumphant conclusion – "discount?"

Had she been in any doubt what he was alluding to, she had to look no further for confirmation than Gorilla Man, to who, having sensed some movement, she had involuntarily returned her attention. Gorilla Man had teeth, she noticed for the first time. Yellow ones, through which the tip of a purple tongue could be seen protruding. The scar, also purple, had creased up his face and his bloodshot eyes narrowed, piercing her with a lascivious glare.

This tipped her over the edge. She sucked in a huge breath which added two inches to her height, and with all her strength leapt back into the sitting room, arms flailing desperately, reaching to grab the door to her left while knowing that within a fraction of a second the bloodied and bruised baseball bat would be deployed quicker than she could possibly react, knocking her back into the house and onto the floor, after which she would surely be at the mercy of these two hideous monsters and be, who knows, entirely at their pleasure?

43

But then, remarkably, the door slammed shut. She fumbled for the lock and hastily turned the key. She waited for the inevitable reaction. The predictable resort to violence, the shouting, banging, crashing, breaking glass. But nothing happened. Just silence. Then, as she held her breath, she heard two sets of footsteps slowly receding. Baldie and his gorilla, off to see their next client.

She pressed her forehead to the door, closed her eyes and gathered her composure. Another crisis averted. No, postponed. Another reason. How many did she need?

CHAPTER 7

The minicab's tyres crunched on the gravel driveway on the approach to Chalton Manor, an eighteenth-century Georgian pile nestling in four acres of rural countryside in a village bearing the same name.

From one of the upstairs windows, Iveta Kalnieks watched the car swing round in an arc to the left of the wide expanse of the drive and ultimately disappear from her view as it pulled up outside the entrance portico below her. He was back.

She had monitored his progress on Flightracker, and although the flight had arrived ten minutes early, a miracle given the distance, the journey from the airport was bound to be less predictable. So she had arrived an hour ago, just to be sure, as she didn't want to miss him on her last day.

She turned away from the window and approached the large mahogany chest of drawers, giving it a rudimentary wipe with the duster she held in her right hand. It didn't need dusting but she wiped it anyway, then turned to the large bed to adjust cushions that didn't need adjusting and smooth a bedspread that didn't need smoothing. Satisfied everything was as perfect as it could be, she made her way around the bed towards the door, stopped to take one last look at the large bedroom and let herself out the large panelled door for the last time.

Downstairs, Colonel Peter Jeffries, rucksack over one shoulder, pushed open the grand main entrance door to Chalton Manor and staggered into the large hallway, dragging a wheeled suitcase behind him. He dropped the baggage by the oak reception table and threw his hat and keys down next to a pile of letters.

He had shrunk in height since his days on the parade ground, and to his enduring dismay was rarely able to stand upright to attention anymore, one of the many debilitating aspects of the ageing process. But even at seventy he retained a good shock of hair, albeit silver, and a fine moustache that, to his mind at least, passed daily inspection in the bathroom mirror and afforded him a modest degree of personal dignity.

In contrast, of course, his girth had expanded over the years as his exercise regime declined and he had gradually succumbed to the pleasures of fine wine and, when someone provided it for him, good food.

But age was telling now, as was his condition. Traipsing halfway around the world used to be routine, part of the job, but he rarely travelled now and when he did it was only to mooch up the river on *Carician*, so the combined effect of airports, jet lag and, on this occasion, unusually strenuous walking at altitude had taken its toll.

He looked up and around the hallway as if visiting the place for the first time. There were several oil paintings hanging on the walls, a large standard lamp and, as well as the oak reception table, a chest of drawers upon which sat a large eighteenth-century French clock and a couple of Meissen porcelain figurines. To the right of the door stood a large grandfather clock, ticking languorously, next to a deep container made from cane which held numerous umbrellas, walking sticks and tennis rackets.

He had lived here for the last ten years, although it had always been the family home, his father's before him and his father's before him and so on. Peter had grown up there, but now he felt completely detached. The house had become a stranger to him now that everyone had gone. It needed people, a family with noise and activity to breathe life and vibrancy into its crusty and decrepit interior. Now he was alone, it felt alien to him, and oppressive, as if he didn't belong, and he wondered what the future now held him for them both.

He looked down at the pile of mail and instinctively picked it up to scan the bundle of letters that had accumulated over the last three weeks, but he was not interested in any of them. He gave the first two or three a cursory glance and dropped them back on the table. Cup of tea is what was needed, he thought, and hobbled down the hallway to the kitchen, aged legs aching with every step.

Before he had reached halfway down the long kitchen, with its large central table capable of seating a family of ten, his mobile phone rang. Without breaking step, he fished it out of his inside jacket pocket, examined the display and, with a nod of recognition, put the phone to his ear. He stood at the window over the kitchen sink, looking out onto the back garden.

"Michael. Good morning to you." He tried but failed to keep the weariness out of his voice and said it with as much enthusiasm as he could muster. But then Michael Goodman was a good friend of his, he was pleased to speak to him and genuinely grateful that he had called.

"Hello, Peter. I wasn't sure what time you'd be back." Michael had been Peter's lawyer, friend and confidant for over thirty years, and together with Michael's wife Emma, just about the only people in the world he could call family.

"Just walked through the door," said Peter.

"And how are you feeling?"

"Ah well, you know what these long flights are like." Peter was not in the mood to explain his state of mind, or body, for that matter, but he knew Michael was not purely interested in his friend's health.

"And were you able to get any information?"

"Yes, I did." He tried, without success, to keep any sense of resignation out of his voice. "But I'm afraid it's not very good. I just don't know what else to do." He felt close to despair.

"Well, I think you should take some time to rethink the options. I have some contacts out there who might be able to continue where you left off. But in the meantime, don't let it drag you down." It sounded trite and simplistic to Peter, but he didn't blame his friend. He meant well, but what could he say?

"No, I won't. But it's very hard," said Peter. "I have never felt so despondent." The word said it all. The once garrulous, bombastic, humorous, confident, supremely able Colonel Peter Jeffries, emotionally and physically drained in a way he could not recognise and had never experienced before. He wished for inspiration, something to ease the pain.

"We're thinking of you, Peter. We're thinking of you both. Call me in a couple of days when you've settled back in and we'll have chat."

"Thanks. Bye now." Then quickly, before Michael had hung up, he said, "Oh, and love to Emma," courteous and thoughtful as ever.

He pressed the cancel button just as an unfamiliar sound from behind startled him, and he turned to see what or who it was, realising immediately there was no danger.

"Ah, Iveta, it's you." He took a few steps towards her and they met halfway down the kitchen. "I didn't expect you here today," he said gently. Iveta stood looking mournful and uncomfortable and wearing her coat, which to Peter meant she had either just arrived or else was just leaving. Iveta stretched out a hand that held a small bundle of keys.

"I just came to bring you these," she said in her heavily accented English. Reluctantly, Peter took the keys from her and pulled himself together.

"Good luck in your new job," he said with as much warmth as he could manage.

He was greatly saddened Iveta was leaving, but fully understood her reasoning. It could not have been a whole bundle of laughs living with a miserable old fool like him in a tired old house like this for the last few months. She was young, mid-twenties, and no doubt craved a bit more variety and personal interaction in her work. She had been offered a job with a nice professional couple who had two small children and it was an opportunity she couldn't turn down. There was nothing here for her anymore, and he knew it. But she had been a very good housekeeper, diligent, industrious and uncomplaining, and although she had a brusque and businesslike character and often failed to laugh at his merry quips, she was unquestionably honest and reliable, and he would miss her.

Iveta smiled ruefully. "Colonel," she said, and he could see the sorrow in her eyes, "did you find anything?" He appreciated her concern, which he knew to be genuine, but was in no mood to explain.

"No," he said. Iveta pursed her lips and looked away. She hesitated a moment, then returned his gaze.

"I am very sorry for you." The Latvian intonation made her sound officious and unfeeling, but he managed to smile at her and she thrust out a hand, which he shook gently.

"Goodbye," she said with finality and turned away. Peter watched her go out of the kitchen and listened to her receding footsteps on the stone floor in the hallway.

"Bye, Iveta," he said out loud to himself as he heard the main door open with a creak, then close with a distant clunk that echoed around the entire house that was Chalton Manor.

CHAPTER 8

Jess rarely slept well. Too many things rattling around her head, many of which she could do little about, but she always tried to focus on the things that she could, few as they were.

She felt sanguine about the events unfolding around her, and because she was alone, she was spared the burden of worrying about anyone else; which, perversely, was a good thing. The only good thing about being alone, she thought, was that it made things simpler.

She had gone to bed as usual at around 9 p.m. because she would be up again at 2.30 a.m., when she would throw on some jeans and a sweatshirt and get herself down to Walkers for the 3 a.m. start. Maybe Clive would have some more shifts for her so she could at least partially make up for the loss of her day job at Debita, but the pay wasn't as good; and even if it was, she would have to work twice the hours she did at Debita to earn enough to keep afloat.

But it seemed that no matter how much she paid the men in black coats, the debt kept rising. She had been given a mountain to climb, and although she was climbing higher and higher, the gradient got steeper and steeper. She should have realised long before now that she was pushing water uphill, and that was probably exactly what the men in black coats intended. The debt was never to be meant to be repaid; it would forever be out of reach.

But tonight, she couldn't get to sleep. Things were moving rapidly and now she had a deadline to meet. Friday. If she didn't do something by Friday, the thugs would return, and she had nothing to give them other than the meagre contents of her house – and herself. She had no illusions that she was anything other than of limited and temporary value, and the thought chilled her to the bone. But eventually, sleep came.

***

She's in her room and she's reading a book because she has to do it in English tomorrow and it's very hard to understand because it's William Shakespeare and he uses funny words all the time but there's a noise downstairs and someone is shouting and it's her dad and then her mum shouts, "Joe, no!" and something's happened and she drops the book and leaps off the bed and she's frightened to leave her room but there's more shouting and she tiptoes to the top of the stairs and then there's a crash with some crockery or something and then a sound like a slap and another cry and she goes halfway down the stairs and she's gripping the balusters looking through and Mum and Dad are fighting but Dad has Mum's hair in one hand and she is screaming and then he punches her in the face ... "No!" she screams and he looks up at her in fury and lets go of her mum and she drops to the floor sobbing and Dad puts his jacket on and walks out and slams the door and she's sobbing ... and she wishes he was dead.

***

She woke with a start and heard someone cry out. She half sat up in the large bed, wide-eyed, alert, and noticed the time on the bedside clock: 1.45 a.m. Forty-five minutes to go. Still time for a snooze, and she needed it. She sat and listened for a moment. There was no sound to be heard other than the distant rumble of a solitary car in the road at the end of her street. She laid her head down again and quickly dropped off.

At 2.15 a.m. her mobile phone rang, but she had fallen into a deep sleep and it took her a moment to come to her senses. Her phone never rang at night, so she was perturbed, but then suddenly remembered the reason she always left it on. Just in case. She quickly reached over to the bedside table for the increasingly agitated device and peered at the display in anticipation. St James Nursing. She was immediately deflated.

"Hello," she said.

"Mrs Khalid?" said the disembodied voice down the line.

"Yes?"

"It's Cindy, one of the night staff from St James."

Jess said nothing.

"It's Jess, isn't it?" said Cindy cautiously preparing the ground.

"Yes."

"Oh, Jess, I'm really sorry, but I'm afraid your dad has gone."

"When?" said Jess without intonation, without emotion.

"About half an hour ago." Jess glanced at the clock. *Half an hour ago. 1.45 a.m.* "We went in to check on him and he'd passed away in his sleep. We did what we could and called in the paramedics and they came straight away, but it was too late. I'm so sorry."

Cindy was used to piling on the solicitude even when it wasn't required, but she could never be sure how the person she was talking to was going to react. Jess said nothing, so Cindy continued.

"Would you like to come in and see him? He's resting peacefully now."

Jess hesitated.

"Yes … thank you." She turned off her phone and pushed back the covers. Another reason.

CHAPTER 9

She couldn't afford the minicab, but she had no other way of getting there. The buses didn't run at that time of night and she couldn't wait till morning. She wouldn't wait till morning. She kept a tin of small change and a few loose notes in the kitchen cupboard, which she'd emptied into her coat pocket. It would be enough to get her there, and she would worry about getting back later. Anyway, she could hang around until the buses started running again. One step at a time.

She sat in the back of the moving minicab as the streetlights of Wellingford gave way to open countryside and then to the brightly illuminated dual carriageway which formed the route to Brinfield. The driver was, not surprisingly, Asian, and had a strong Birmingham accent which, Jess decided, made him at least second or third generation. British born and bred. She was instantly nervous the moment she saw him pulling up outside the house and the irony was not lost on her, but as soon as he opened his mouth, she somehow felt more at ease. Irrational, maybe, but she had no choice. She wondered if they even existed, white British cab drivers prepared to work all hours.

She soon found out what sort of a character he was because from the moment she climbed into the back seat and the car left the kerb, he started to chat and never stopped for breath. A Bangla pop song was playing loudly on the radio, which meant that he had to raise his voice to compete. Jess wondered why he just didn't turn it down but did her best to ignore the noise.

Her mind was buzzing anyway and she found him difficult to understand, so her ears filtered the combined noise to a dull echo in her brain. The absence of any response or reaction from his passenger appeared to be of no consequence to him and she wondered whether he talked to himself when there was no one else there. Undaunted, he launched into yet another minicab anecdote.

"So I picks up this next bloke, right? All booted and suited, like. Businessman out on the razz. Had a few, like …"

Jess continued to stare out of the window at the scenery flashing by. She was aware the driver was talking but he and the accompanying Bangla music sounded like they emanated from the dark recesses of a cave or the bottom of a deep well. She wasn't taking in anything he said. Her mind was still reeling from the implications of the late-night call.

"'Why don't you just fuck off back to where you came from', 'scuse my French. I said, 'What, Birmingham?' Ha! You should a seen the look on his face."

She could see little in the dark, other than her own reflection in the glass. She thought about the last eighteen hours. It seemed like everything was happening at once, an uncontrollable sequence of events propelling her remorselessly to some indeterminate destination.

"You know, I'm a human being and I got feelings. If you prick us, do we not bleed? That's an old Muslim proverb, that is …"

She was powerless to stop it. It was totally out of her control, so why did she not feel panic? Maybe it was just meant to be. One step at a time. She never regarded herself as an eternal optimist, but she had endured so much in her short life, surely some good would come out of this?

"So next day I goes down the cop shop, right, and makes a complaint for racial abuse, and you'll never guess what? He's only the bleedin' chief constable! The geezer in the cab. He's a top copper. I'll tell you what that is. That's the drink. That's what the drink does to people. Brings out the dark side."

The mention of alcohol and the dark side somehow penetrated the aural fog and reached into her consciousness.

She twisted her head to look up at him in the driver's mirror. Until then, everything he had said had been a barely audible blur, but this had struck a subliminal chord. He carried on relentlessly, oblivious to her sudden attentiveness.

"I mean talk about Jekyll and Hyde, dyanotamean? Now my mum says—" He broke off suddenly. "Oh, here we are, love. St James Nursing Home."

The announcement snapped her out of her thoughts, and she watched out of the window as the grim four-storey Victorian building loomed up at them. The cab halted outside the front door and the driver switched off the radio, the Bangla music mercifully falling silent. He looked puzzled.

"Er, funny time for visiting, innit? Are they open?" he said to her through the mirror. Jess didn't answer. He turned in his seat and looked at her. "Or are you the night shift?" He chuckled loudly but then seeing her lack of reaction, stopped, looked back at the building, and as the penny dropped, so did his head. "Oh … I'm really sorry, love. Got a big mouth."

Jess was unmoved and actually felt sorry for him, but was in no mood for more chatter.

"How much is that?" she said.

"It's nothing, love. It's on the house. You mind how you go."

"Thank you very much," said Jess, touched by the man's generosity and humanity. If only he knew how hard up and therefore how grateful she was. But she was not minded to prolong the incident, nor argue about it, so she opened the door and climbed out. Before she had gone three paces, she heard the front passenger window slide down and a voice call out.

"'Ere!" She turned back to the cab and leant over to look through the passenger side. "How long you gonna be?"

"Dunno … about half an hour?"

"I'll wait for you."

She nodded, smiling lamely, and then turned back to approach the front door.

CHAPTER 10

Jess sat in one of the upright chairs facing the bed. The only illumination in the room was a dim lamp on the bedside table to her right, which bathed the room in a gloomy reddish-brown glow. The body was stretched out on the bed, head propped up on a pillow, stripy pyjamaed arms on top of the covers, one hand over the other, a small primrose pressed between the fingers. Joe's head was tilted back, mouth slightly open as if he was still taking in breath, but there was no movement. He was utterly inert. Life extinct.

Jess had always wondered how she would feel when the day eventually arrived. She had been expecting it for some months now, but when the call finally came, she was not prepared for it and now she struggled to come to terms with her own feelings, or more accurately, the lack of them. Where were they? No distress. No sadness. No pit of the stomach grief and no fighting back the tears. Nothing. She looked at this greying shell of the body of a man who had once been her father. Once.

Way back, when they were a family, they did family things, celebrated each other's birthdays, wore silly hats at Christmas, and went on day trips to Southend. When Madge cooked Sunday roast for a treat and they sat on the couch together watching *Only Fools and Horses* on the TV and laughed out loud when Del Boy fell sideways through the open bar top in the pub. Once. But they were both gone now, and although she had wept and wept at her mother's bedside as she slipped away and wept again for weeks afterwards, here there was nothing. Just finality. A closed chapter. Another reason.

She struggled to remember her father when she was young and he was fit and healthy. There must have been some good times, she thought. It couldn't always have been so awful and so tormented. She glanced at her parents' wedding photo on the chest of drawers. They looked like kids; even younger than she herself was now. She tried to imagine their lives. How happy they looked and what hopes they might have had for their future together. The boundless optimism of youth and a new, exciting world unfolding before them, theirs to take with both hands, joined forever by their marriage vows, a bond of mutual love.

She was insanely jealous of the young couple. They had had everything to live for, but ultimately the opportunity had been squandered. And she was bitter. She had never experienced happiness like that; it had been denied her. And although she thought she had got close once, it had all turned to dust, leaving her worse off than before. Her youth had been stolen from her and it would never come back. She was truly alone now, the last link severed.

She stared at her dead father again, and as she did so, her mother's voice floated into her consciousness from the dark recesses of her mind. A voice weakened by illness and enfeebled by a profound sadness, but at the same time energised by as much strength as she could gather in these, her dying breaths. The sound echoed in her mind and it was if her mum was there, next to her.

"Jess, my darling. Promise me you'll take care of him. I don't know what's going to happen to him now. He was always useless at looking after himself. He loves you a lot, you know. We both do."

Jess blinked back the tears and felt her jaw tighten, but she could not respond; didn't respond then, couldn't respond now

"And I loved him too … once. He was well handsome. I still love him. Despite everything he did."

Her mother's words. Slow, deliberate, thoughtful, regretful. *Despite everything he did.* The purple bruise below her mother's eye, her cheekbone covered with excessive make-up, the split lip caked in scarlet lipstick, the premature crow's feet around the eyes and the greying hair of a sixty-year-old who looked more like someone in her seventies, and, above all, the utter exhaustion of someone for who the fairy-tale romance had long since died, and who, through stoicism, stubbornness, eternal optimism and a misplaced sense of loyalty, remained in perpetual denial. The ultimate self-delusion that love – yes, love – could forgive everything.

Jess remembered the noise, the shouting, the sound of breaking glass and crockery flung across the room, and the slaps and the screams stifled lest they travel upstairs to her room but which had been as clear as a bell, even with her fingers in her ears and the bedcovers over her head. The tears in her eyes, the rocking and swaying, arms tightly folded around her chest willing it to stop. Praying to God it would stop. He would stop.

And then, the next day, life carrying on as normal, as if it were nothing but a bad dream. Breakfast served, clothes washed and ironed, packed lunches prepared, and being sent off to school, her father kissing her mother goodbye as he set off in search of work, again, her mother wearing rather more make-up than was necessary for a Wednesday morning. And so it went on.

She remembered the world becoming hostile, and turning in on herself. Turning away from her relationships at school, recognising subtle shifts in friends' demeanour, attitudes fostered by gossiping neighbours passed on through their own children developing into bullying, hatred and ostracism.

Turning away from life at home, where she spent all her time alone in her room, unable to live with the constant fear of further attacks, her mother's acquiescence and the contempt for her that grew from her capitulation, her absolute submission.

Learning to spot the signs early, recognising the flash points and making herself scarce. Her father's sorties to the pub, drinking money they didn't have and returning in a rage, ranting about the unfairness of it all; and the conduit for his anger was always there, waiting dutifully for him. The woman he loved. The voice of the woman he loved was still pleading with her daughter.

"Your dad ain't a bad man, Jess. He didn't mean you no harm. He just can't help it."

Jess swallowed deeply. *He didn't mean you no harm.* She felt her chest expanding with the involuntary intake of breath and the pressure in her heartbeat which began to resonate in her ears. The memories were coming back and she couldn't stop them tormenting her.

She's fifteen again. She's in her room, in bed, listening to the sounds of the night. It's almost midnight on a Saturday and she can hear the front door latch, as she does the same time every Saturday night. Last orders at The George plus a bit, plus the stagger home, dodging the traffic, kicking empty bottles down the street, shouting and swearing at neighbours complaining about the noise. The slow, lumbering trudge of feet on the stairs, the thunderous waterfall of urine into the pan, the flushing of the toilet, the cack-handed wrestling with her parents' bedroom door and its careless closure, and the muttering and arguing and oral recriminations which would eventually give way to loud snoring. And then, only then, could she sleep.

But this night, the toilet flushes, and … nothing. Nothing but silence, and in the silence her eyes darting around the ceiling, ears straining. Something's different. The scuff and a snort outside her door, the familiar creak of the spring in the door handle and the squeak of the door hinges, yellow light pervading the darkness in a growing strip along the wall. Anxiously turning on her side to face the window away from the door. The squeak of the hinges again, this time in reverse, and the click of the latch and the fading of the yellow light. And the voice, familiar, gentle, whispering, comforting. "Jessie? Jessie? Are you awake, Jessie? Where's my little girl? Where's my good girl?"

Then the rustle and movement of the bedcover and duvet she is gripping tightly around herself, her body contracting and curling into an ever-tightening ball, his weight tilting her mattress backwards and the sweaty, stale tobacco and boozy stench of his breath close to her neck. The arm under her head curling around her neck, clasping her shoulder, pressing her body to his, his free hand reaching under the duvet, straightening her leg and resting on her knee.

And then, amidst the trembling fear, fear that his dormant rage will suddenly erupt and she will surely die, silence and motionlessness. Silence apart from the laboured breathing and the snuffles pre-empting the inevitable snore. She holds her breath. She will slide out when she can, and go. But where? Anywhere.

Then he's snoring, asleep. She waits an interminable time, five minutes. She's trying to slither out from below his arm but it's too heavy. He snuffles and the snoring stops. She freezes. The right hand moving slowly up her leg taking her nightdress with it until, under the duvet, her leg and thigh are bare, and his hand is on her hip. He is awake again and the fear intensifies "You're a good girl, Jessie, A goooooood girl." The hand leaving her hip and his fingers sliding across her belly. She can't move. She can't breathe.

And so it began.

"Look after him for me, Jess. Promise?"

Jess opened her eyes again and felt the sweat on her brow and realised she was back, here, in this room, with this thing who is, was, her father.

She recovered herself and stared at his corpse, at his gaunt, grey, lifeless face, and she thought for a moment she could sense the faint smell of decomposition, the stench

61

of putrefaction, and they were strangely familiar. She had done as she promised. Despite everything. *Rest in peace, Mum.* Without a further look, she got up and left him for the last time. Another reason.

CHAPTER 11

A shaft of sunlight streamed through a gap in the living room curtains and onto the sofa where she lay, fully clothed, under a blanket.

The kindly cab driver had brought her home, free of charge, the return journey conducted in complete silence; out of respect, she assumed. She had been moved by his kindness even though in her case it was misplaced, and the irony was not lost on her. An Asian cab driver, who looked and sounded like many of the others she had had the misfortune to encounter, yet worlds apart, a true gentleman, one of life's givers.

Mo had been like that in the early days, but Mo had wanted something in return, and soon his true character and motives had become terribly apparent. The driver didn't want anything other than to help her in any way he could. Lesson learnt. Don't judge people for who or what they seem to be, or say, but for what they do.

Once home, she had neither the energy nor the will to climb back into bed and at 4.30 a.m. had simply crashed out on the sofa and, for once, slept soundly.

Jess stirred and squinted as the beam of light caught her eyes and she manoeuvred herself into a sitting position, the blanket still wrapped round her waist and knees. She thought about last night and wondered why, after she had got the call from St James, she had even made the effort. They weren't to know, of course, and would have thought it very strange if Joe's only relative had refused to go and pay her last respects, even at the dead of night. But that wasn't the reason. She had to go and see for herself. She had to be certain that this was not just another bizarre trick, a cruel joke played by her father to punish her for her apparent lack of concern. Or perhaps the staff at St James had made a terrible mistake and she would turn up and find that, against the odds, either they had managed to revive him or he had miraculously recovered. No, she had to see him, to be sure, because from that moment on there would be no going back.

She reached for her phone, which was still on, and to her astonishment she saw that the time read 10.10. She had been asleep for almost six hours. The phone had been on mute all night, and she noticed that someone had left a message. She pressed the button, put it on speaker and got to her feet to pull back the curtains and let in the sunlight.

"One new message," came the automatic announcement, "seven twenty-seven a.m."

"Jess!"

A disembodied voice bellowed at her, violating the silence in her small sitting room. Jess bristled and put her head back to listen to the tirade. Clive was not happy.

"Where the bloody hell were you this mornin'? You was supposed to be on the three till seven at Walkers! I had to go in there meself and sort it out. Client was well pissed! Yeah, well ... I ain't happy. So consider yourself sacked!"

She put both hands to her head as the phone clicked off abruptly and the message ended. She had forgotten, of course. The phone call at 2.15 a.m. from St James – a mere fifteen minutes before her normal alarm had been due to go off – had changed everything, emptied her mind of all other matters. Her dawn shift at Walkers, the only paying employment she still had, should have been of paramount importance to her.

Had she rung Clive, even at the last minute, to tell him of her circumstances, she would surely still have a job. But the more she thought about it, the more she realised it would have made no difference. Clive would not have believed her and, even if he had, he would have used it as an excuse to get rid of her.

She had once made the mistake of suggesting to him his pay rates were below minimum wage, which immediately marked her out as a troublemaker. So she had not made herself popular and there were plenty more slaves out there who would do the job without complaint. In fact, she was one of them. Another reason. However many did she need?

She climbed the stairs, got into the shower and stood there for a while under the cascade, eyes closed, wishing the warm soapy water would wash away the last vestiges of her miserable existence. Not much left now. Soon things would be different. They already were.

With no work to go to, she dressed in jeans and a light sweater. Clean hair tied back in a band, she went into the kitchen and made herself a cup of tea and a slice of toast. There were only three slices left in a loaf that had lain in the fridge for three weeks now, so she had certainly made that last. Good timing, perhaps. No waste. When they came to turf all her belongings out onto the street, it would be better if the fridge was completely empty, rather than just almost.

She had the entire day to herself, she realised. No cleaning. No office. No bosses. No men in black coats. No husband. Her eyes settled on the framed picture of three-year-old Leila. No school. She felt herself swallow and fought back the tears.

She sat back in the chair with her mug in her hand. *No way, dammit. No way.* Jess had never asked for help in her life and was not about to start now. However many tiny insignificant steps, turns, decisions, errors or omissions it had taken to bring her to this precise moment sitting at the kitchen table, looking at a picture of her lost daughter, she could not say. But here she was, and there were thousands more tiny steps to take before she would give up.

She picked up the three threatening letters on the table and flicked through them again, wondering whether there was any scope for appeal, any ambiguity in their meaning, or whether she had simply understood them correctly.

There was no ambiguity. Derek had taken the last of her pay and settled the council tax bill. She felt a perverse comfort in the fact that one of her long-standing debts had been expunged, but he had just paid Paul and robbed Peter. The men in black coats. That was their money and they were coming on Friday to get it.

The men from Northern & Midland Energy would arrive at any moment with their pliers and cut off her power, and there was nothing she could do about it except plead with them to give her more time. But she had already done that, giving them £10 now and then to keep them at bay, but word had spread, data exchanged, and the vultures were descending to get the pick of the carcass. What would it be like with no power? No kettle, no fridge, no light, no hot water. No water at all when Midland Water got in on the act. But power or no power, water or no water, she still had a roof over her head. Until such time as the bailiffs came to move her out, take the keys off her and kick her out onto the street. In eighteen days' time.

But long before then, the men in black coats, expecting, on Friday, the latest instalment of a debt that could never be repaid. Armed and dangerous and unassailable, the complete antithesis of her. She didn't have a penny to give them; and even if she did, it would only keep them satisfied for seven days, then they would be back for more. Cash or payment in kind.

And when she was out on the street, homeless, bankrupt, on benefits, they would still find her, hound her until she had been bled dry, and then some more. She could never escape them. Yesterday she had two jobs and even that wasn't enough to keep her head above water. Today she had no jobs and now, no income, and even if she started looking immediately for another job, it would take time and her debts would spiral further out of control.

She spread her arms out in front of her on the kitchen table and rested her forehead, seeking inspiration, redemption, help, knowing at the same time there was none.

She sat still for a moment and emptied her mind, shutting out everyone and everything, and then, without warning, it came to her. Of course, she thought ruefully. The answer was obvious, had been staring her in the face for months, and if the events of the last forty-eight hours had not all come together, there would have been no catalyst. No fuel. No spark of ignition. No energy.

She was not religious, and for a moment something made her think there were forces at work here and that this had been predetermined for her. But then she remembered school and her English teacher once philosophising to class, and the words had stuck in her mind ever since because they rang true.

> "… there's no such thing as fate. Wherever we end up is simply a combination of actions and events, planned, contrived or random, controlled or otherwise, lucky or not. Don't seek an explanation or reason for everything. Just accept it happens and move on."

She sat up, taut, bristling with energy, adrenalin coursing through her veins. There was no one but her. She had her brain and her arms and her legs and her spirit, and she would not let anyone take them away. She knew at once what she needed to do, and no one could stop her. She was in control now and she felt liberated, invigorated, exhilarated. She swept the letters off the table and marched up the stairs.

In the bedroom, she foraged around in the back of one the drawers and found a battered leather-covered ring box where it had lain since her mother died. She sat on the bed and looked down at it for a moment, hesitant, guilty, nervous and confused. But her mother would have approved. Given her blessing. She opened the box. In the lid sat a small card with an inscription in Joe's shaky hand.

"To Madge from Joe, with all my love."

Her mother's sapphire and diamond engagement ring and her nine-carat wedding band nestled in the slot in the base. They were modest pieces, bought with love and little money, but all the money he had at the time. Childhood sweethearts fulfilling a destiny they had been planning for over ten years. Priceless yet probably worthless. Jess had no idea what they might be worth, but they would be worth something. There was a jeweller in the town and a pawnshop and any number of cheque/cash/gold converter shops too. One of them would give her cash for these, surely?

Before the pangs of guilt had time to take hold and give her cause to change her mind, she rushed back downstairs, grabbed her scruffy black coat and let herself out the front door.

Outside, her elderly neighbour Joan was sweeping her front porch as Jess slammed the door shut and set off up the path without stopping. Joan always liked a chat, but the old girl had been slow on the uptake and Jess was well past her before she had a chance to speak. "Oh hello, dear," she said to Jess's back. "How's your dad doing?"

Jess pretended she hadn't heard and kept going, out the gate and up the street. Joan was well meaning but an incorrigible gossip, and she had no intention of engaging in conversation with her or anyone else. Jess took neither questions nor orders nor gave answers to anyone now. She was in control; although control of what, she didn't quite know.

CHAPTER 12

Jess pushed her way through the front door of her tiny terraced house, laden with her purchases from the Outdoor Shop. A large rucksack, pop-up tent, self-inflating mattress and two carrier bags full of clothes and equipment. She locked the door behind her, took her purchases upstairs and threw them on the bed. She would sort it out later. First, she had work to do, and time was of the essence.

The cupboard under the stairs was the depository for a range of domestic items: ironing board and iron, dustpan and brush, dusters, washing basket, spare light bulbs and various cleaning materials. Right at the back, she found what she was looking for. An old single-sheet shredder Mo had bought a while back to get rid of surplus paperwork and receipts but hardly used. She managed to find it buried under some black sacks and dragged it out, took it into the living room and plugged it in.

She had a file of papers, all the correspondence relating to the mortgage, loan account statements, interest certificates, statutory notices from the Crown Court in respect of eviction proceedings, the increasingly threatening letters from the council, reminders and disconnection warnings from Northern & Midland Energy, as well as letters of appointment from her erstwhile employer, Debita Debt Management, payslips, documents from HMRC she didn't understand, and letters from the Home Office and the Foreign Office that she did. Letters from St James about Joe's treatment and care, funeral bills and death certificates for her mother, birth certificates for herself and Leila. It was sobering how it had mounted up so quickly, especially in just six months, before which she had hardly seen any paperwork at all. Mo had never let her open any mail and she guessed he must have shredded most of it himself while she was out at work.

She opened the file at the beginning and, cross-legged on the floor with the shredder in front of her, she put the first sheet into the slot. It burst into life with a loud whine as soon as it sensed the first page, gobbling it up in a few seconds. She tried to do multiple pages but quickly realised the cheap shredder was not capable of taking more than one at a time without jamming, so she went slowly and methodically, page by page, file by file. She had just got into a rhythm when the doorbell went.

The shredder went quiet and she looked up at the front door. It couldn't be the men in black coats. They wouldn't come back until Friday, she was certain, and no one else usually called; but then how would she know? She was always out at work. She got to her feet and opened the door.

Two men in uniform. Dark trousers and blue polo shirts sporting the motif "Northern & Midland Energy", ID cards dangling from their belts: older one at the front, fifties, balding, glasses; younger one behind, small toolbox in hand. The older one had a moderately pained expression on his face.

"Mrs Khalid?" he enquired politely. She looked him straight in the eye without answering. He continued. "We're from—"

"I know where you're from," she said, stopping him in his tracks, and before he could say anything else she had whirled around, leaving them at the open door, and taken up her position on the floor in front of the shredder, where she resumed her work one page at a time.

The older one looked round at his younger colleague and, giving him a nod, stepped tentatively into the hallway and open-plan sitting room, followed nervously by his assistant. Jess continued to feed pages into the shredder and was suddenly aware of the terrible noise it made, but tried to ignore their presence as they took up position on the other side of the sofa that separated them. The older one cleared his throat to indicate his presence but was drowned out by the noise of the shredder. He raised his voice a little.

"Mrs Khalid?" Again, a little louder. "Mrs Khalid?" Jess stopped what she was doing but remained on the floor, staring at the now silent machine. "Mrs Khalid," he went on apologetically, "unless you or your husband settle your account immediately, or at least make the minimum payment, we're authorised to turn off your supply?" The sentence ended like a question. Did she understand what he was saying? Jess understood. Without hesitation she started again, feeding a sheet of paper into the machine which roared back into life, gobbling, chomping. Destroying.

The older one gave his sidekick a look of consternation and decided it was pointless to continue negotiating. He nodded towards the kitchen and they left her alone in the sitting room on the floor, concentrating on the shredder, her expression fixed in quiet determination at the task in hand.

It only took them twenty seconds. Halfway into the jaws of death, one of the pages halted as the shredder abruptly died and simultaneously the lights went out. Jess froze for a moment and then tipped her head forward onto her chest.

The men returned to the now gloomy sitting room, the only light coming in from the open front door and through which, in the unlit room, the street sounds seemed curiously amplified. Jess sat immobile, staring at the inert machine and the piece of paper stuck halfway in, halfway out.

"Mrs Khalid?" said the older one, again a hint of apology and sympathy in his voice. "We've terminated your supply." Jess could not think of a suitable response to this, there being no doubt why her home was now silent and in darkness, but he went on, fingering and waving a business card at her. "If you would like to ring this number and make the minimum payment, we can reconnect you." They both knew it was futile, but she assumed the company had laid down procedures that he had to follow and he was just going

71

through the motions, delivering a speech he had to make several times a day. He laid the card gently down on the back of the sofa. "We'll see ourselves out," he said, and she thought she could sense some sadness in his voice, but she ignored him anyway. He nodded to his companion who followed him out of the front door, closing it behind him.

Jess sat still on the floor as the sounds of the street dissolved and the gloom deepened. All she could hear was the sound of her own breathing, a heartbeat thumping deep in her chest and a distant hiss of static in her ears caused by the unholy silence that enveloped her. The machine was dead and so was her house. Deprived of the oxygen of electricity, it was nothing more than a shelter from the wind and rain, a lifeless shell that would now begin to decay and one day slowly return to earth. She had already considered how debilitating the absence of power would be. No cooker, no microwave, no fridge, no fire, no washing machine, no TV, no kettle, no hot water, no light. But now it had actually happened, it took on a whole new meaning.

She had a radio and a torch, both good until the batteries ran out, and her phone, whose battery would die in due course, never to be recharged.

She looked at the single sheet of paper, stuck in the jaws of the shredder, and sucked in a deep breath. She was suddenly calm. She didn't know why. Was it the calm before the storm? She should be collapsed in a heap, curled up in a foetal position, rocking and moaning, wailing and crying at the succession of blows that had rained down on her in the last couple of days, taking the last traces of her existence and leaving her with nothing other than the clothes she was wearing.

From a happy and conventional family life eight years ago to this precise moment where she sat cross-legged in the gloomy silence; she wondered how she had got here. What sequence of steps had brought her to this moment in time? She knew, of course, but never imagined it would come to this. Jessica Anne Khalid had finally been vanquished, destroyed, wiped out by the actions and, often, the inactions of others, and she had borne it all, spiralling downwards, little by little, without realising what was happening.

But the adrenalin kicked in again and she reminded herself who she was. She was someone else now, and that someone else lifted her head up in defiance, fuelled by a strength and determination she didn't know she had. She was finally free. Free from the abuse of her father, free from her ignoble, cold-hearted bastard of a husband, free from the worthless, futile jobs she did simply to fulfil obligations that were not hers to fulfil, and free from the insensitive men who called themselves her employers. Free from the men in black coats and free from the threatening letters demanding another piece of her. Free from her cold, miserable, pointless existence. Free from everything.

Not quite. She looked again at the sheet of paper forlorn in the shredder and, with a flourish, tore it off, slapped it into the file sitting on the floor and jumped to her feet.

She found matches in one of the kitchen drawers and then hurled open the door to the tiny, paved area at the back of her house, retrieving a metal bucket that sat next to the bins. She set it down with a clatter, scrunched up the torn paper and threw it inside. She fumbled for a match and when it caught, applied the flame to the corner. It was reluctant to start, but start it did, igniting with a puff of white smoke as she reached into the file for the remaining documents.

One by one, she dropped them into the bucket, and as each one caught, the smoke cloud grew and billowed out across the backyard. The letter of dismissal from Debita, the council tax demand, the electricity bills, the letters from the County Court, the letters from the Home Office, the bills from the nursing home, the letters from the bank, the eviction notice – all went up in flames, leaving an ever-growing pile of grey ash in the bottom of the bucket.

And finally, the last document. She stopped to read it. A birth certificate. Hers. Jessica Anne Butler, girl, born 1 October 1995 at Lewisham General Hospital, father Joseph Albert Butler, bus driver, mother Margaret Doreen Butler, shop assistant. The last record of her entry into this world and her existence in this place. She looked at it again, hesitant, and then slowly fed it into the dying embers of the tin bucket where it caught immediately and was quickly consumed. Jessica Anne Khalid, née Butler, no longer existed. She was free. And tomorrow, she would start all over again.

She sat on the floor in the sitting room, in front of the coffee table, scissors in hand. A candle flickered in its holder, projecting dancing shadows on the wall, the only light in the house apart from the sporadic sweep of headlights as a car passed by in the street outside.

The radio was on, playing something soothing, but the batteries were old so the volume undulated as reception became increasingly crackly and erratic. An empty takeaway pizza box lay open on the table next to the remains of a bottle of cheap sparkling wine. The last supper. She snipped through the last of the credit cards with the scissors, although almost all were useless and had been stopped, and reached for the bottle, tipping the last inch or so into a tumbler, glugging it back messily and swallowing deeply.

She had remembered the bottle and retrieved it from the back of a kitchen cupboard where it had lain unopened for the last four years. The handwritten label was still tied round the neck: "Something to wet the baby's head! Love, Mum and Dad xx" it said in her mother's block capitals. Cause for celebration, she had thought, and had then phoned Papa John's to order in a pizza, something she had never done before even though she had passed the shop hundreds of

74

times, wondering what it was like to enjoy a luxury like that.

She had used the last of her cash to do it, but she felt like celebrating her new status. She still had Joe's debit card which she had used earlier that day in the Outdoor Shop, and she would go to the cashpoint tomorrow to withdraw what was left, if anything.

She knew his pension payment would be credited in a few days and had considered waiting until then, but Joe was dead and she knew his pension would stop on the day he died. Even though the pension company would not be aware of it and the payment would most likely go through as normal, the money didn't belong to her; and no matter how much she needed it, she wouldn't take it. She would not start her new life owing money to anyone.

She drained the tumbler and leant over to switch off the radio. She hadn't drunk anything for years so the alcohol made her feel especially woozy and lightheaded. She blew out the candle, and the darkness and silence enveloped her. Time for bed.

But she wasn't tired. Her mind was buzzing. She lay awake in bed in the dark contemplating, planning, anticipating. She wanted the morning to come. Now.

***

A misty rain drizzled down on the back streets of Wellingford, the puddles forming on the roads and pavements reflecting the sparkle of streetlamps. Sixteen-year-old Jess could sense the patter of raindrops on the hood of her anorak, and feeling the odd one splash on her cheek when she lifted her head, pulled it forward to keep dry.

It was 1 a.m. and she felt it was time to go home. It would be safe by now. There was always the possibility that

Joe would wait up for her, but more often than not, his drunken, weary body would succumb to the need for rest and would soon overcome both his yearnings and any frustration he felt at finding his daughter absent from her bed. Again.

She had once got back at 12.30. Too early. From the top of the stairs, she had heard him in in her room, moaning to himself, bedsprings squeaking, breath heaving as if running an indoor marathon, reaching a crescendo before blurting out her name in a gasp and sigh of relief. She had quickly retreated down the stairs and, huddled in the stairwell, watched his shuffled return to his room, head bowed. Only after another twenty minutes did she carefully and silently enter her room, do her best to clear up the mess and get to bed.

Her new regime had evolved over time. His visits were irregular but almost always followed a drinking session and had become more frequent. He had also become more demanding, as if it were not already distressing and repulsive enough, and while she developed an ability to shut each experience out of her mind, she could see where it was going and it frightened her. She knew that there would come a point where she had to resist; and if he was drunk, he would react badly.

So her normal routine on a Saturday night, as well as any other night she knew her father would be in the pub, was to slip out at 11 and not get back till after 1 a.m., just to be on the safe side. Her mother knew what she did and pretended not to notice. Madge judged it the lesser of two evils and a cruel irony that her daughter's safety was probably better preserved at midnight out alone on the streets of Wellingford than in the sanctuary of her own home.

The morning after, she would have breakfast quickly and quietly, not a word exchanged with her mother, her father still languishing in bed sleeping off his hangover, before grabbing her bag and setting off for school. Madge would kiss Jess goodbye and wish her well for the day. Their eyes rarely met, but when they did, Jess could see the darkness that lay within, the utter sadness and despair, a reflection of the desolation she felt herself. And when she got home and her father was in the chair watching afternoon TV, he would greet her fondly, ask about her day, what she had been up to, and invariably told her that they would all go out for a picnic at the weekend. Nice as pie. Normal, loving, concerned and considerate. Sober. Her dad. Then she would go to her room and stay there till morning; or 11 p.m., if he went out.

At sixteen, Jess was already a woman – her father had seen to that – but she remained naïve in many ways. She didn't mix easily with people, didn't engage with strangers, however benign they might appear, and felt safer in her own company. She became increasingly insular, observed the world through hooded eyes and looked over her shoulder at every turn. The people she used to call friends had turned against her. Girls her own age at school, primed with gossip from their parents, neighbours with whom she once exchanged day-to-day pleasantries, all now regarded her with contempt and suspicion, as they did the whole Butler family, all three of them.

There was little in long rows of terraced houses that folks didn't know about other folks. They knew what went on behind closed doors in the Butler household, knew there was no smoke without fire, knew that acquiescence in domestic violence was every bit a crime as violence itself. She heard them talking in the street to her back as she walked past on her way to school, loud enough for her to hear, knowing she wouldn't challenge them.

"It's disgusting, what they do, them Butlers. I bet she enjoys it, the little tart. She'll be on the streets in no time, mark my words. At least that way they'll be earning and not sponging off the government. And if 'er indoors had any bottle, she'd clout him back. If my Brian ever tried that, God help him, he'd get a blunt knife to his balls and the fat end of a frying pan, he would."

77

Jess never regarded herself or her mother as victims, but by no stretch of the imagination could they be regarded as willing participants. So she found it extremely difficult to rationalise the attitude of those people who criticised her, despised them both for allowing it to happen. She formed the view that perhaps the cruelty inflicted by others was as much to do with concealing the inadequacies in their own lives, deflecting attention from themselves, a moral deficiency laced with a large dose of good old-fashioned gossip.

It seemed to her that in the absence of an escape route, the only way she and her mother could tolerate her father's behaviour was to manage the situation as best they could, and maybe, just maybe, he might get a job and their lives might then take on some semblance of normality. Jess was out tonight, managing her situation.

She decided she would get to the end of the street, turn back the way she had come and then take the shorter route home past the gasometers and the all-night petrol station. The rain was easing off now, and as she approached a crossroads, the intersection of four streets of terraced houses, she stopped to lift her hood and let the cool night air flow around her long brown hair.

She could see no one and almost all the house lights were off, but she thought she could hear people laughing and talking animatedly, voices lowered and raised, as if a party was going on somewhere nearby. But there was no one around and she was puzzled that she couldn't determine the source of the revelry.

The street to her right was notable for a large gap in the row of terraced houses where three of them had been demolished following a fire and gas explosion two years previously. The front was still boarded up with corrugated iron sheeting which over time had begun to rust in the weather and buckle from a series of minor collisions, accidental and otherwise, and which at one side had become detached from the wall of the adjoining house. The laughing, no, giggling, was coming from behind the corrugated iron barrier.

Her immediate instinct was to walk away, mind her own business, but something compelled her to approach the gap and peer through into the darkness of the waste ground beyond. Twenty yards distant, she could see eight or nine men arranged in a semicircle, some standing around, one sitting on an upturned oil drum, one on a wooden crate, another on a white plastic patio chair, each with a bottle in hand, gesturing and provoking each other in accented English. And standing before them in a small group, three girls, twitching and squirming, giggling at the crude humour of the men until one of them would turn to her friends and let out a shriek of laughter.

One of the men passed the taller of the three girls a wine bottle which she raised swiftly to her mouth and took a long swig before falling back, spluttering and coughing, to the hilarious reactions of all those present. She then passed it to her friend who repeated the trick, and finally, the third one, who managed the task without incident, eliciting loud praise and applause from the men. A small plastic bag was being proffered by another of the men to each of the girls, sweets perhaps, which they took and giggled in delight as they put them in their mouths.

Jess thought if this was a party it was not a very good one. Many of the men were middle-aged, one or two as old as her father, while others were maybe in their twenties or even thirties; whereas the girls were no older than she was and probably even younger, maybe fourteen or so, and one of them perhaps no more than twelve.

She stood for a moment, fascinated but unnerved, so didn't hear the two men behind her until one of them spoke and made her jump. "Good evening, miss." She turned swiftly. Her instinct was to run, get away, but one of them was blocking the path to her right, the other the path to her left, a parked white minicab blocking the third way out into the narrow street. "Is you looking for someone?" he said with a relaxed smile.

He was Asian, Indian, Pakistani, whatever; she couldn't tell the difference except for those guys who had brightly coloured bandages around their heads, Sikhs, and he wasn't one of those. Middle-aged, maybe fifty-something like some of the men she had been watching, with a thick head of greying hair and a bushy moustache, white shirt, sleeves rolled up and black jeans. She glanced at the other one. Also Asian, but much younger, fresh-faced, big shiny watch on his wrist, two shirt buttons undone revealing a heavy gold necklace clearly visible against a smooth bare chest. He looked familiar. The older man spoke again.

"Is you looking for a friend?" She turned back to him. "Or maybe you want to have some fun?" he asked, hands on hips, smiling, revealing a full set of white teeth. Jess said nothing, just looked at him, fear and trepidation rising steadily. She shifted her weight from one foot to the other, unsure of what to do. She rarely saw anyone on the pavement during her midnight walks, and if she did, she would cross the street or hurry off in a different direction, always choosing a well-lit street over parkland or industrial estates. The guys did not look threatening, but she was still afraid.

"No," she said quickly. "I'm just on my way home." She attempted half a step but the men adjusted their positions to compensate and she froze. The older man went on gently. Still smiling.

"Oh, now that is big shame, cos we is just going to have birthday party at my place with lots of nice young people there, and music and lots of drink, and pakora and samosa. Do you like pakora and samosa?" he asked pleasantly. She had heard of them and thought it was food of some sort but had never tried them. Joe was not going to have any of the foreign Paki muck in his house.

80

"Do you want to come? I have my minibus here," he said, pointing up the street. She turned her head to see a van with windows, sliding door open to the pavement, lights on.

"So, transport is provided and we take everyone there, and when we finish, we take everyone home." He raised his arms in a gesture which said, how could you refuse? "Please, come to my party and have some fun, then, when you are ready, we run you back home again."

She hesitated. They seemed nice enough, and although she just wanted to go home, something in what he said sounded strangely alluring. Or maybe it was his younger companion who intrigued her. She never went to parties because no one ever invited her, and it was ages since she had mixed with people her own age. She was two or three miles from home and didn't know anyone in this part of town, so no one would know her and no one would be horrid to her. She thought it might be fun and it would certainly be different. And tomorrow was Sunday; she could be back before breakfast and her parents would be none the wiser.

The older man could see she was thinking it over and became slightly more serious, almost fatherly. "And if I may say so, I don't think a young lady like you should be out alone at night by yourself. You meet lots of strange people these days, and you never know," he said with a concerned expression and a wag of his finger. The younger man said nothing. "I think it best if we take you home in my minibus. But even better if you come to my birthday party!" He beamed again and spread his arms wide.

She smiled and looked at the younger man, who had an awkward expression. He said something in Urdu to the older man. "*Mein usay jaanta hon.*" I know her.

The older man responded and the conversation became animated. Rapid, argumentative, remonstrative and unintelligible, punctuated with arm movements and hand gestures. Jess's head swung back and forth between them as they argued out whatever it was they were arguing

81

about. She felt uneasy again. They stopped. The older one made a dismissive gesture with his hand and a hissing noise between his teeth, and without another word, strode past Jess, who turned and watched him pass through the gap in the corrugated iron barrier into the waste land beyond.

"You're Jess, aren't you?" said the younger one. She turned back to look at him, puzzled, wondering how he knew her name, but now he looked more familiar. "From Pickering Street?" He knew where she lived, too. He went on. "I'm Mohammed Khalid. I live across the road from you, about ten doors down" His English was perfect, virtually unaccented, as it would be for a second-generation Pakistani, born and bred in Wellingford. The penny dropped. Yes of course.

"Oh. Yes. Hello, Mohammed," she said, not knowing what else to say but relieved that there was probably nothing to be afraid of. After all, he was a neighbour, of sorts. They had virtually grown up together and been to the same school, although he was much older than she was, perhaps even twenty-one, and she had seen him and his family many times over the years, although they had never spoken before. Her dad didn't approve.

"They come over here with their hundreds of kids and their filthy old folk and there's ten of 'em in that house and they stink the street out with their curries and then they're allowed to build a bleedin' mosque and go there shoutin' Allah Oo Akbar *or whatever and then they take all the jobs so decent people can't get work. It's a fuckin' disgrace. I tell you what I'd do, I'd pack 'em all in a big ship and send 'em back, that's what I'd do, or bloody sink it, more like. This country's for British people, not a bunch of lazy fucking Pakis. The place is overrun with 'em and one day there'll be no room for any of us decent folk. Don't you go near 'em, you hear? So help me God. And when did you see a white person driving a bus – never! They got it all sown up, the bastards."*

"Mo" he said offering his hand, which she took limply. His flesh was warm and soft and he hung onto her hand for longer than necessary, but she had no desire to pull it away. It was a nice feeling. "I told my uncle that I knew you," he explained, "and that it might be better if I took you home now as we both know your father wouldn't approve of you going to my uncle's birthday party. And also, they might be getting worried about you."

He smiled, and she smiled back. She was a little disappointed but also a little relieved. He went on: "I'm not going to the party as I have to take some people to the airport early tomorrow, so I'm going home now in my cab." He gestured at a white Passat behind her. "Can I drop you off? We live in the same street, and I'd be a bit worried about leaving you out here by yourself."

Jess thought about this for a moment but decided she could trust him, and something inside her wanted to stay with him a while longer, party or no party.

"Okay," she said and smiled, and he guided her past the open minibus to his car and like a gentleman let her into the passenger side, closing the door after her. She was flattered and pleased by this modest act of chivalry and watched him as he swaggered in front of the car. But her attention was drawn to the corrugated iron barrier where they had been standing a moment ago.

She could see people spilling out from the gap in the barrier. Four men with one of the girls, the older one, unsteady on her feet. The girl clambered into the minibus followed by the men, and Jess was sure one of them had helped her up by placing a hand on her bottom. A second group followed, but this time the girl had her arm around a man's neck and he had an arm around her waist. He deposited her head first into the doorway of the minibus where outstretched hands grabbed her under the arms and she was hauled inside, followed by the other men, still swigging from beer bottles and laughing.

Finally, Mo's uncle appeared, carrying the twelve-year-old in his arms. He handed her into the bus, slid the door closed and climbed into the driver's seat. The minibus pulled away from the kerb, passing Mo's Passat which Mo then guided out of its space, heading in the opposite direction.

Jess was a little confused about what she had just witnessed. The girls seemed too tired or too drunk to go to a party, and there were no Asian women or white men there either; just three youngish girls and a bunch of Asian men. And why were they out so late? Why was a birthday party starting after midnight? Maybe it was one of those all-day things and they always started at very beginning of the day. She felt she needed to say something to Mo to break the silence.

"It's very kind of you to run me home."

"It's no problem." He smiled at her. "But don't tell your father about it. I know he's not very keen on people like me, especially the men." he said without rancour. How true was that? she thought. Joe would go mad if he saw her in this car with this man. "And he would be very, very unhappy if he thought you had gone to an Asian celebration," he said, smiling again. She looked him and judged he must be at least twenty-one. An adult. His teeth were white as snow, especially set against his dark skin, and he was very handsome, very charming. She felt a stirring inside her that she had not experienced before.

"You know him, then?"

"Let's just say, I know what he's like. He's not the only one. There are lots of English people round here who don't like us, don't like what we are or what we do, or how we look, or how we dress. I understand that. I can see it from both sides. I'm English and my brothers are English, but our family is from Pakistan and we're Muslims, and that's difficult for some English people to accept. People just don't like those who are different from themselves. It would be the same in Pakistan if an English family went to live

84

there. They would find the same problem." Jess didn't respond. It sounded reasonable, but it didn't excuse her father's behaviour towards them or anyone else. That was the drink.

At half past midnight it took only ten minutes to get across town to Pickering Street, whereas it would have taken her an hour on foot. But as Mo pulled the Passat into her street, Jess spotted a familiar figure, swaying and weaving along the pavement, dishevelled in open brown raincoat, hand reaching for support from every parked car he shuffled past. Joe. Without thinking, she put a hand on Mo's left arm.

"Keep going!" He looked at her hand and then her animated face, eyes tracking the pathetic figure on the pavement. "Drive past. I can't go in yet." She looked back at him and saw him smiling, and quickly removed her hand, feeling suddenly awkward. He did as she asked and slowly guided the car to the end of Pickering Street and turned the corner.

"What's the matter?" he asked, appearing concerned.

"It's my dad," she said, and thinking quickly, "he mustn't see me" – and then as an afterthought – "with you." It sounded lame but was partially true, and she was merely repeating what Mo had already said. All he had to do was stop the car around the corner and she could walk back. But that was no good, either.

"Can we wait here for a few minutes?" she asked, sitting back in the seat. She knew she would have to give him fifteen or twenty minutes, thirty to be really safe, before he had got through the door, climbed the stairs, checked her room, done whatever he wanted to do there and then fall into his own bed. She would have to get out and go for another walk.

"Yes, of course." Mo pulled the car over to the kerb, engine still running.

"I'm sorry," she said awkwardly, "I'll get out here. You have to go and get some rest for your job tomorrow." She reached for the door handle.

"Wait!" he said, but she was already getting out. "Jess!" She turned and looked at him through the open door. "Can I see you again?" He was smiling broadly, teeth, watch and gold necklace gleaming in the streetlights. Very handsome. She didn't know what to say. But she would continue her midnight meanderings in the future, for as long as it took, and at least he might be someone to chat to.

"Er, yes, if you like," she mumbled. But she didn't know when or how, "But …"

"Tomorrow night," he ventured. "I'll wait at the bottom of your street, on the corner of Telford Road. Ten o'clock?" She nodded and closed the door.

She headed back the way they had come and she listened to the car pull away. She got to the corner of Pickering Street and saw it was deserted. She looked down towards her home. It was too soon. She crossed over and walked away along Spencer Road. She would give him thirty minutes.

But a wave of exhilaration returned when she thought again of her encounter with Mo. He was wearing a musky scent, too, a male perfume of some sort, and some of it had rubbed off on her when she touched his arm. She put her hand to her nose and she could still smell it and it made her tingle.

***

Mohammed Khalid put his foot down and turned on the radio, his hands drumming on the steering wheel to the beat of the Bangla pop music pumping out from the Asian channel. The moment he saw her in town he had to say something to divert her attention. She may not have recognised him immediately but it was only a matter of time before she did, and that would do none of them any good. Best she was well out of it, for all their sakes.

And she was very good-looking too, he thought, not one to be wasted on those other animals. Maybe she could be of some use to him. His business career was beginning to gather momentum and it would afford him a semblance of respectability to have someone so pretty on his arm.

On top of that, he had his own place now and he could do with someone not only to keep house for him but also satisfy his pleasures as and when he wanted them, rather than rely on this dangerous nonsense his Uncle and his mates were involved in. Yes, he would pursue that one and see what came of it. Her father was a complication, but she would probably jump at the chance to get away from him, and he would never find out where Mo lived. Only his family and his mates knew that, and even if there was trouble, he had no shortage of contacts who could deter or deal with a sad old drunk like Joe Butler.

Mo sang and tapped the wheel. Still time to get to the party, he thought. *I hope "Uncle" has kept me some dessert.*

CHAPTER 13

Peter Jeffries stood in the study of Chalton Manor, looking out onto the back garden. He must get out there and do some deadheading, he decided, otherwise the cosmos would stop flowering, and he loved the riot of colour they would continue to produce all summer if they were treated properly. The garden was huge, of course, and he couldn't possibly manage it all, but he liked to tell the few people he knew that most of it was a "conservation area", which fooled no one, but they all enjoyed the joke.

Janica would have loved it, he thought, and a wave of sadness swept over him. Her framed picture stood on his desk, standing proud and tall and beautiful, long dark hair pulled back and tied in a knot on her head, smiling broadly, her body canted to one side and supported on one hip, their beautiful Lisa, three years old, bright-eyed and wondrous. He could barely bring himself to look at them, his family, and now he was the only one left. It was said time healed everything, but he couldn't see how that might happen, or how long it might take. *Oh Janica, Lisa. How I miss you.*

He had been in many difficult situations during his career, life-threatening situations, in which some of his colleagues, his best friends, had been lost. He remembered escaping from *HMS Aries* after she had been hit in San Carlos Bay, and days later, the battle of Goose Green, where Captain Jeffries had successfully led his company's assault on the enemy positions and many men on both sides had died, some at his hand. Only afterwards did the full horror of what they had been through become apparent, and the fight to deal with the trauma had been almost as difficult as the fight itself.

But deal with it he did, and he went on to other areas of conflict and saw much the same thing time and time again, wondering what it was all for. Who was it all for? A tiny number of extremists and despots in positions of power. Men, intoxicated by and addicted to power, holding sway over the lives of millions, until the threat of losing it to other men drives them to irrational and unspeakable cruelty. It was ever thus.

Peter had always thought he was doing something noble, something honourable and just, fighting for the cause of freedom and justice against tyranny and oppression, and he had paid a heavy price, physically and emotionally. But nothing had affected him so profoundly as the events of the last three years, and had he been remotely religious, he would surely have lost his faith overnight. But as he had always said to others who sought his advice, and he was never slow to dispense it, get a grip. There are no guarantees, ever.

But he now knew his own advice to be fatuous and simplistic. Philosophy was not his strong point, and he was too old to start changing now. He also knew that his time was limited, necessarily curtailed, and he was at least sanguine about that. Surprising, he often thought, having dodged bullets successfully for so long, that he would eventually succumb to the enemy within. And that made him think, if there is a God, show yourself now, because I could do with a bit of help once it's all over. *Bit late for that.*

The grandfather clock chimed ten o'clock, and the sound resonated around the building like a church bell in a huge cathedral. And then it stopped, and the sounds of silence returned, reminding him how alone he was now, and he didn't know how he could continue to bear it. He picked up the picture, opened the top left drawer of his desk and carefully placed it inside, face down. He closed the drawer and raised his head to look again out of the window. What would his father think of him now? He had made such a mess of things.

Sir John Jeffries had expected his only son and heir to follow him into the family business, just as he and his father had done before.

Established in 1735 as a firm importing silk from the Far East and then engaged in manufacturing all types of cloth, Arnold Jeffries & Son had grown over two hundred and fifty years to be one of the most highly regarded firms of its type in the country, if not the world. Even after production had long since ceased in England and inevitably transferred to South-East Asia, the company had diversified into design and had become a supplier of premium grade cloth to high-end couturiers in Europe and the US.

Knighted for services to the textile industry, Sir John was also a philanthropist, benefactor and patron of several charities, and together with Lady Caroline, whose own charity work was legendary, became a pillar of the community. So it was with some dismay and consternation that they received the announcement from their recently graduated only son, Peter, that at the age of twenty-one he intended to break with family tradition and join the army. The ensuing family rift which persisted for over twelve years almost healed at the premature death of his mother, when Sir John finally acknowledged that his son, now thirty-four and having risen up the ranks to be a Major in the Intelligence Corps, may have actually made a success of his life.

Whilst Peter's military career had been exemplary, his personal life had been less so. At twenty-three he married the Honourable Phoebe Torrington, only daughter of Sir Arthur and Lady Torrington. Sir Arthur was a senior civil servant in the Ministry of Defence and Peter had met Phoebe at his Sandhurst passing out parade. He was smitten. They made a perfect couple and a grand wedding was organised, there being no shortage of resources from either side of the family.

The intention was to start a family immediately, but three years passed without issue, and with Peter away for months at a time, the opportunities to procreate were limited. Furthermore, Phoebe, unprepared for the privations and disruptions afforded by army life, found herself increasingly bored and alone in army accommodation, however comfortable and relatively opulent that might be for a senior army officer.

Without children to keep her occupied and a regularly absent husband, she inevitably found solace in both the gin bottle and the arms of Second Lieutenant Jack Anderson, a young subaltern in the fourth regiment of the Royal Dragoon Guards. Peter and Phoebe divorced on their sixth wedding anniversary.

Peter threw himself back into his career, serving in Northern Ireland and then the Falklands, and by the time he was in his late forties, he was a full colonel serving with the UN Protection Force in Yugoslavia, with special responsibility for intelligence gathering and interrogation.

There, he met a young Montenegrin interpreter, Janica Simovic, twenty years his junior, with whom he worked closely interrogating suspected Serbian terrorists. He became entranced by this tall, dark-haired, stunningly beautiful young woman and she, overwhelmed by this dashing English army officer almost twice her age, agreed to his proposal of marriage without hesitation.

Fifteen years later, Sir John Jeffries, a widower since 1984, died leaving his entire estate to his only son. Peter had no interest in the family business and promptly sold the three-hundred-year-old company to a Hong Kong-based conglomerate. He retired from the army, and moved into Chalton Manor with his young wife and fourteen-year-old daughter.

***

The grandfather clock chimed once for a quarter past ten, and Peter snapped out of his thoughts. He had to get away for a while, clear his head. The sun was shining and it was a perfect summer's day. He would take *Carician* out for a few days. Disappear up the river, see the world from a different perspective; something he always found whenever he was on the water.

She hadn't been out at all this season, what with the distractions of the last few months and his visit to Nepal, and she may need coaxing back into life. He turned with a new purpose, threw on his floppy hat and set off down the garden towards the riverbank.

CHAPTER 14

The shower was cold, of course. No electricity, no hot water. Jess squirmed and shrieked as the chilly water tormented her body's senses and she hopped animatedly from foot to foot in the bath, twisting and turning in an attempt to mitigate the discomfort.

Mercifully, the weather was fine and the house temperature ambient, so she soon got herself dry and slipped into her new outdoor gear: white tee shirt and black cargo pants. There was no means of making a hot drink nor any chance of toasting some stale bread, so she simply had a glass of water and returned upstairs to pack her rucksack. She didn't expect the men in black coats to return until Friday, but she could take no chances. She had to get out of the house as soon as possible, to slip away while no one was looking.

She emptied the contents of yesterday's shopping onto the bed: sleeping bag, two more tee shirts, another pair of trousers, three pairs of heavy socks, underwear and a micro fleece. Gas canister and microburner, knife, fork, spoon and tin cup, small torch and matches, tea bags and a few sachets of packet soup. She also had a medium-sized towel, a face flannel and a plastic bag containing items from the bathroom: toothpaste and toothbrush, hairbrush, soap, a small bottle of shampoo and a half used roll-on deodorant. It wasn't much, the bare minimum, but she felt somehow liberated by the lack of possessions; and in any event, she had to carry all of them on her back for the foreseeable future, so the lighter the better.

She gathered up the rucksack, self-inflating mattress, an unopened shoebox and her red waterproof jacket, and lugged them all downstairs to the sitting room.

Like everything else, her walking boots were brand new and she hoped they would not take too long to break in, but then they weren't expensive and so probably softer than the better-quality ones she could not afford. She slipped her feet into the boots and laced them up tightly, finished closing up her rucksack and strapped the mattress to the top. Finally, she put on her red jacket, loaded up the rucksack on her back and slung the circular pop-up tent, her new home, over her shoulder.

It was time. She had everything she needed, except for one thing. In the kitchen, she picked up the framed photo of Leila, ripped off the back and extracted the torn photograph from the frame, placing it in the inside pocket of her jacket.

She didn't stop to check the house. Everything there now belonged to someone else, and even if there was anything she might like to keep, she couldn't carry it. Anyway, she didn't want any memories; everything she now owned was brand new and she was either wearing it or carrying it. The only constant in her life would be Leila, and she would never give her up.

Jess opened the front door for the last time and stepped out onto the path, turning instinctively to close and lock the door. Then she stopped. What was she doing? Why was she locking the door? She shook her head to clear the mist that was fogging her thoughts and retracted the key from the lock. She pushed the door open again and with a flick of the wrist, tossed the keys into the house where they landed with a clatter on the thin, rough carpet. You want your house? she thought. Come and get it. She turned and strode off down the path.

As ever, Joan was out front, bent over plucking the odd weed from the gaps in the paving slabs, and she bobbed up from behind the fence as Jess walked by, as if she had been waiting to ambush her.

"Hello, dear. How's your dad?" she asked, and Jess felt she could not simply ignore the old dear.

"He's fine, thanks," she said. Joan nodded, looking curiously at the rucksack on her back.

"You off on holiday, then?" she said, inquisitive as ever.

"Er, yes," said Jess. There was some truth in it.

"Oh well, have a nice time. Going anywhere nice?" Jess fidgeted about on her feet; she just wanted to get away.

"I'm not sure. Just going away," she replied, but she knew it sounded odd. Joan frowned.

"Oh, okay. See you when you get back." Jess smiled at her, turned and left through the gate, disappearing from view.

Joan turned back but saw Jess's front door, left wide open, and then she spun around again to raise the alarm, to call her back, but she had gone.

***

The morning sun was warm and the birdsong loud and varied in the graveyard of St Mary's Church. Jess's rucksack and equipment lay propped up against a wizened old pine tree as she knelt in front of a small plaque set into a stone base, a bunch of wild flowers she had picked from the meadow in her hand. She had been there for a few minutes and was not quite sure why she had come. Another thing for her to do for the last time.

"He's gone, Mum. I've left him there. I expect they'll sort something out." She was apologetic about that, but there would be no recriminations, at least none that she would hear about. "There's nothing more I can do. I've got nothing left." The spoken admission sounded strange, but it was true, she thought. *I have nothing left.*

There was never the possibility of her being able to pay for a funeral for Joe. She simply couldn't afford it, and neither could he. And in any event, she had done her duty.

She loved her mother and she had carried out her wishes, however misguided they may have seemed. She thought back to that time, her mother weakened to the point of extinction by an illness the doctors could not diagnose, pleading with her daughter to take care of her husband, her father. The man her mother had once loved but who had turned into a monster, lashing out at everything and everyone, wreaking havoc in their lives, destroying them as he slowly destroyed himself. He didn't deserve compassion or consideration or care, he just deserved to die.

She never understood why her mother should be insensitive to her daughter's feelings, so insistent that she be left with the responsibility of looking after him. Jess could only imagine that her mother prayed that there could be some reconciliation for them, some contrition on his part, some return to the way it was, even though she herself would not be alive to see it. To the end Madge remained in denial about her husband, her childhood sweetheart, vainly expecting that one day everything would be all right again, the way it was. Forgiven and forgotten. The doctors couldn't say for certain what took her, but after Madge had slipped away, it all became clear to Jess. Madge had died of a broken heart.

"I have to go now. I probably won't be back. Love you, Mum," she said, and gently placed the already wilting flowers in front of the plaque.

***

She stood on the road bridge, arms resting on the parapet overlooking the river, and stared into the distance where the water meandered its way eastwards out of town. She had no idea which way she was headed nor where she would end

96

up, but for some reason the flow of the river appealed to her senses.

There would be fewer people to meet along the riverbank and no cars to bother her. She wanted to get out of town and into the countryside. She wanted to breathe air free of traffic fumes and noisy trucks, hear the birds and the trees rustling in the breeze. Above all she wanted to be alone, and there was more chance of her being alone on the river than anywhere else.

Also, she thought, the river was on a journey to somewhere or other and would not stop till it got there, and that much they had in common. She felt a wave of exhilaration. There was no one to tell her what to do. No one to control, threaten or intimidate her anymore. The men in black coats would never find her, the credit card companies would write off their debts, as would the electricity company, and the bank would sell the house and perhaps even get their money back; and she would be forgotten. The men in black coats had already been repaid three times over, so they wouldn't waste time tracking her down once they realised she had disappeared. And they could then turn their attention to another victim, and so it would go on. After a while, no one would even remember she had existed. One of the forgotten people.

She walked along the bridge, the traffic loud and pervasive on the road beside her, and when she got to one end, descended to the riverside footpath via some stone steps and a long, winding ramp. But as she reached the water's edge, her new-found anonymity and serenity were suddenly shattered by the sound of the mobile phone ringing in her jacket pocket. She was momentarily confused. *Why did I bring this with me? There's no way of charging it and it's the only thing in the world that links me to my previous life.* Habit. That's why. She had slipped it into her pocket instinctively, the way she always did. *That was her old life*. She thought about ignoring it. After all, it would not be a well-wisher.

She fished it out of her pocket and stopped in her tracks to look at the screen as the phone continued to wail ever louder. "St James Nursing" it said on the display. Of course. When she left there the other night, she said she would start making arrangements. She had lied and felt badly about it, but then what else could she say? She had no intention of making arrangements, no money with which to make them. No doubt they would be apologetic about bothering her, but they had another corpse on their hands and wanted it taken away, not least to release the bed for the next patient.

The phone in her hand connected to the home where her father's body lay, a gossamer thread linking her to a life she wanted to forget. She started walking again and with a flick of the wrist, tossed the still-ringing phone into the river, barely missing a pair of ducks who quacked and flapped their wings in protest at the sudden assault.

The phone hit the water with a loud plop and fell silent. She was now officially off-grid. She strode off down the riverbank path and into her new world.

CHAPTER 15

The narrowboat *Lady Braunston* chugged its way along the canal, its slow-revving diesel engine beating out a steady rhythm synchronous with puffs of black sooty smoke from its exhaust. It meandered past The Navigation Pub and Restaurant which sat serenely on the canal-side, patiently waiting to welcome the first batch of customers of the day.

It was too early to consider a lunchtime pint, so the old boy holding the tiller on the *Lady Braunston* would not have given the pub a second glance had his attention not been grabbed by an angry exchange of unintelligible words emanating from the pub. He turned his head to see what the commotion was, but his narrowboat cruised on inexorably, the moment passed, and the sound was lost in the throbbing rhythm of the engine.

The side door of The Navigation flew open and a young blonde woman with a large leather holdall stormed out of the pub, a fierce expression on her face and muttering under her breath. She marched angrily down the path towards the car park, where a black Mercedes Benz was waiting, engine running. Before she got there, a dark-haired woman exited the pub in a similarly frantic fashion and in hot pursuit.

"Katya! Katya! Wait! Katya!" she shouted to the back of the rapidly receding figure in front of her.

"*Vas manzel je kreten!*" Your husband's an arsehole! Katya shouted back without turning round or breaking step, thrusting the middle finger of one hand in the air, leaving no doubt as to her attitude to the woman behind her. Trish didn't speak any Czech so couldn't fully understand what Katya was saying, but given the furious tone, she could hazard a guess.

Katya wrenched open the car door, threw her bag in, climbed into the passenger seat, and the car sped off without delay. Trish stood for a moment, forlorn and helpless as the car disappeared. Suddenly filled with rage, she about-turned and stomped back into the pub.

Dave was in his usual position behind the bar, flicking through *The Sun.* He knew what was coming but he wasn't bothered. It was only ever going to be her word against his, and now she had walked out in a strop there would be no argument about what had happened.

Pity, he thought, she was a looker, that Katya, and he had a thing about Eastern Europeans; their accents and mannerisms appealed to him. He'd been working hard on her for a while but had got a bit impatient by the lack of response, so had decided to escalate matters a little. She's only playing hard to get, he thought, and they all need the money, so a little enticement can go a long way. It usually worked. Usually.

Unfortunately for him, or perhaps fortunately, he was standing right behind her when she unexpectedly bent over to pick up some rubbish from the floor. He had taken no evasive action and her buttocks had collided with his crotch, so he had to grab her by the waist to steady them both and then had used the opportunity to tell her what a nice arse she had. Big mistake. Ah, well … plenty more fish, he thought, and continued to flick the pages until he got to the sports section, his favourite. He heard the sound of heavy footsteps but declined to look up until his wife had drawn level with him on the opposite side of the bar.

"You tosser!" said Trish with unmistakeable contempt.

Dave swung his head around, looking in vain for the object of his wife's anger, and then feigned surprise, expertly combining shock, confusion and innocence in one expression.

"Whaaat—?"

"You know very well what," continued Trish, arms outstretched and rigid on the bar, looking at her husband with visibly rising anger. "You just couldn't help yourself, could you?" *Deny, deny, deny. That's always the best strategy.*

"I didn't do nothing!" complained Dave, continuing the pretence and looking his wife directly in the eye for effect.

"I know what you're like, Dave Morley," she said with exasperation. Dave decided it would save time if he just cut to the chase and got it over with. It wasn't the first time and it wouldn't be the last.

"I never touched her," he said returning his attention to the paper, a hint of truculence in his tone.

"Ah, okay" said Trish, nodding. He had inadvertently opened the door of truth a little, and knowing her as he did, he was certain she would get her toe in and prise it open a bit more. "So, what did you say?"

"Nuffing," wailed Dave, and then, backtracking a little, "just passing the time of day." And then, as there was always a little bit of truth in every lie, "complimenting her on her appearance."

"Here we go," she said in that superior tone he knew only too well.

"It weren't nuffing," Dave assured her with a weary shake of the head, "just a bit of banter."

"Banter?" she barked back at him

"Yeah – she was just a bit … well, sensitive … no sense of humour, these foreigners," he huffed, returning to flicking the pages.

"Oh, yeah. I know you and your humorous banter when it comes to young blondes. There's laws against sexual harassment, you know. You better hope she don't know what they are," she continued, jabbing a finger in his direction.

"Don't get paranoid," he said. *There she goes, overreacting again.*

"I'm not paranoid!" she said through clenched teeth. "I'm just sick to death of you and your disgusting little obsessions."

"Didn't bother you back in the old days," said Dave with a satisfied chuckle and a hint of reproach, forgetting that his wife did not like being put on the defensive.

"Yeah, well ... back then I was young and impressionable and lovestruck," – Dave raised his eyebrows as she went on – "and you, were slim, funny and good looking." He furrowed his brows and his expression turned quizzical.

"And your point is ...?"

"Aargh," said Trish in exasperation. "No time for that, there's work to do so you'd better get your bloody marigolds on!" And with that, she stormed off into the kitchen.

Dave watched her go with a pained expression. *Cleaning? Not on your Nellie. That's women's work.* He returned his attention to more important matters and flicked back to the racing pages.

CHAPTER 16

Jess woke to the sound of a cockerel crowing in a nearby farmyard. She had no idea what time it was, having no watch or any technical means of telling the time, but it was light, and it was June, so she guessed it must be around 5 a.m. Not that it mattered. The clock no longer ruled her life. No place to go, no place to be at any particular time. Nobody waiting for her and no chance of being late. For anything. That in itself was liberating, and for the first time in many years, she woke without fear, without anxiety, and without the stress that today she had to perform some task she hated and all for no conceivable purpose.

She had decided long ago she was chronophobic, a word she had invented and was quite proud of. Like most people, the clock had ruled her life and its tyranny had a debilitating effect on her. Being rid of it was a blessing she could not have imagined. But then her circumstances had been forced upon her. She may never have had the courage to get away and start again if there had been a realistic alternative.

Had she been thrown out onto the street and declared bankrupt, the council would have been forced to provide housing for her, and with benefits she might have been able to eke out an existence of sorts on the bottom rung of the social ladder. But the men in black coats would have found her and so it would continue until they had bled her dry again, or worse. Jess knew that there could be no compromise on that score, and the only conceivable choice was to disappear and start again. Reboot. As someone else.

However, she was not so naïve as to think she wouldn't encounter a new set of challenges and problems along the way. Paradoxically, she had more money now than she had had for a long time. She had used the proceeds from the sale of her mother's rings together with her father's debit card to buy her tent and equipment and then, before she left town, emptied his account of what remained: the princely sum of £70. She had then bent and twisted his card and dropped it down a drain.

In the last fortnight she had burned through half of it buying food and water, so she knew how much longer it would last; and that assumed she had no need to buy anything else. The small gas canister she had brought with her to cook packets of soup and make tea would run out soon and she couldn't afford to replace it. And stopping off in public lavatories to clean up as best she could was not a sustainable option.

In any event, for the time being at least she preferred to avoid civilisation, only venturing into villages and petrol stations to use their facilities and buy the cheapest food she could. She wanted to be alone for a while. She didn't want to be hurt. She wanted to be safe. But she did have to eat and she knew she would have to sacrifice her independence at some point if that was going to happen. She had planned to get as far away from Wellingford as possible, to somewhere she could not possibly be identified, not possibly be found, and eventually get a job and a place to stay. Quite a simple plan, really.

The riverside path she had followed out of town soon petered out and she had been forced to go inland across fields, following footpaths where possible, but crossing open country where necessary if there was no obvious path, or even just because she liked the look of it. And if she had to make a choice between two paths, she took the more obscure route.

She had remembered from school the English teacher making them read *The Road Not Taken* by an American poet named Robert Frost and she had been fascinated by its premise that one should go one's own way and not follow the crowd. Now she actively avoided the crowd, although one day soon, she knew she would have to re-engage with the human world, with society, a society that had done her no end of harm. But for the moment she was calm and confident in her own company. Her life had only just begun and this new independence was precious to her. It was pretty much all she had.

The cockerel crowed again so she unzipped her sleeping back and crawled out of the tent to greet the day. The field she had slept in looked bigger in the morning sun. She had picked a discreet corner away from the road or any gates, and as there was no farm in sight, felt confident that she would not be disturbed. She realised she was probably trespassing, but she meant no harm and would leave the place as she had found it.

She stood and stretched and looked around her. Her two-man pop-up tent (she had decided to go for the bigger one to accommodate both her and her rucksack) had been easy to erect. In fact, it was automatic in that as soon as it was released from its circular bag, it exploded into shape, and all that was needed were a few pins to fix the guide ropes. Having built her home, she had assembled the gas canister and microburner. There were no instructions, but it was fairly obvious that the burner screwed to the top of the gas canister and metal legs needed to be teased out to form a platform to hold her tin cup. It needed no matches either, igniting instantly with a press of the trigger, and for supper she usually boiled up some powdered soup from a sachet with bottled water.

Although erecting the tent could not have been simpler, getting it back into its bag on the first morning had proven to be a challenge almost beyond her wit. Despite examining the diagram and the reading the instructions, clearly written by an English-speaking Chinaman, she had been completely flummoxed. There was no doubt that she had to end up with a disc-shaped tent to fit a disc-shaped bag, but she could see no possible way that the dome-shaped frame could revert to being circular, despite her certain knowledge that what came out of a circular bag must somehow go back in.

It had taken her an hour, during which she almost despaired of ever succeeding, before she finally learnt the technique, and like a magician performing an impossible stunt, turned and twisted the frame until it conformed to the required shape and it could be stuffed into the bag before it could explode again.

This morning, as most mornings, she would boil up a cup of water on her portable micro-stove, using up more of her precious gas, and make a cup of tea with one of the three remaining tea bags she had brought from the house. She had the remains of a packet of cream crackers she had bought in a petrol station, and a couple of these plus the last banana from the same place would comprise a handsome breakfast. A robin chirped at her from its perch on top of her tent, no doubt hoping to share in the spoils, and she felt at one with the world. She felt at home, and share her modest meal she would.

Within an hour, she was packed up and ready to go. She gauged the direction from which she had come from the rising sun and turned her back to it. If she had any fears it was that she might lose her bearings and go round in a circle to end up where she started, so she had determined to guide herself by the position of the sun. She set off west. She would find a river again, if possible, and follow it. And she needed a shower. She had no idea how that was going to happen, but if she found a river then that would do. That would be her work for the day. She had an apple for lunch, a packet of soup for dinner, and two bottles of water replenished yesterday from a drinking fountain in the park, so she had supplies, meagre though they were. One day at a time, she thought.

***

She didn't find a river but she did find a campsite, and late in the afternoon, tired and weary, she stood with her arms on the five-bar gate looking into a small field adjacent to a large cottage.

The site was a modest affair with half a dozen caravans, most of which looked like they had not moved in years. But the sign outside offered toilets and, most alluringly, a shower. She hadn't washed properly since she had left Wellingford and that must have been at least ten days ago, and she felt intensely grubby. She would do anything for a shower, and she could take the opportunity to wash her dirty tee shirts and underwear at the same time.

She opened the gate and stepped into the field, and immediately a woman appeared from one of the caravans to greet her.

"Hello, love." It was the first time she had engaged in conversation with anyone for a while other than exchanging the odd pleasantry with people out dog walking. But before she could say anything, the woman said, "Do you want a pitch?"

"Er, yes please, if that's OK."

"No worries, bags of room. That'll be five pounds for a single tent for the night, then." Jess was momentarily taken aback. She hadn't thought for a minute that she would have to part with her precious cash, and five pounds would make a big dent in her reserves, but she chided herself for being stupid and fished around in her trouser pocket, pulled out a crumpled fiver and handed it to the woman, who in turn slipped it into her shirt pocket.

"Shower and toilets over there by the house," she gestured, "and there's drinking water from that standpipe over there. You can stick your tent opposite that other one." She pointed to a large tent and gazebo in the corner of the field with an estate car parked alongside. "If you need anything else, just come up to the house and ring the bell."

107

"Thanks," said Jess, and wandered over to her pitch.

Within ten minutes she had set up, and sat outside her tent to enjoy the late afternoon sunshine.

The large tent opposite belonged to a middle-aged couple who were pottering about outside, the woman setting up table and chairs and the man assembling a portable gas stove, presumably in preparation for cooking the evening meal. Food, thought Jess. She didn't have any and she was hungry, but it wasn't the first time and she would manage. First things first. Get washed and do the laundry.

She rummaged in her rucksack and pulled out her towel, soap and shampoo, her dirty underwear and a clean tee shirt which she had saved for the occasion, and set off in search of the showers.

Twenty minutes later she was back in position, brushing her wet hair, clean, refreshed, skin tingling from the good scrub she had given it, and her clothes, laundered with shampoo, hanging over the tent to dry. She couldn't afford the five pounds it had cost her, but as luxuries went it was right up there with the best of them. But she was hungry and wondered whether the campsite owner would sell her some bread, or anything for that matter.

She sat cross-legged in front of her tent as her hair dried in the gradually setting sun and looked across at her fellow campers. The man was hard at work in front of the stove frying something, and the sound and smell travelled across the twenty-five-metre gap between them to where Jess was sitting, pricking her senses and exacerbating her hunger. The torment was almost unbearable and she couldn't shut out the aroma, which was slowly driving her insane with hunger. She lifted her knees and rested her head on her arms, turning away from the sight and sound of the man unwittingly taunting her, and closed her eyes, attempting to think of something else.

And then, after a minute, she sensed a movement which startled her, and she looked up in surprise to see the woman camper standing over her, smiling, hand outstretched, wrist adorned with a number of colourful bangles. The woman said nothing and nor did Jess, but the meaning was clear. Jess hesitated for a moment and reluctantly held out her hand. The woman pulled her up onto her feet and led her across to the gazebo opposite.

***

Jess lay in her sleeping bag as the sounds of the night filtered through the cool evening air. They had been a delightful couple and Jess felt humbled by their generosity, the kindness of strangers. She had tried to offer them payment for her dinner, the first proper meal she had had in ten days, but they would have none of it. It had been a long time since anyone had shown her such consideration and she only wished she could reciprocate in some way.

They had tried to quiz her on her background and situation, and she felt guilty about being unforthcoming, but there was no way she could explain, and she thought they might want to help her some more and she wasn't ready for that yet. She had to find her own way. So she simply told them she was backpacking for a couple of weeks between jobs, and there was at least some semblance of truth in that.

She felt warm and replete but couldn't sleep. Tomorrow she had to find some more food, and as she only had about twelve pounds and some loose change left, she knew that sooner rather than later she would need to find a way of earning something. She closed her eyes but sleep would not come, and inevitably her mind turned to the things she missed the most. And as always, one thing, one person, one little girl, who was always on her mind, night and day, and who was lost to her forever. She felt the damp forming in her eyes and bit her lip to stop it trembling. *Leila. Where are*

*you? I hope you're safe and well, wherever you are. I love
you.* And then she was asleep and the sounds came back to
her, as they did time and time again.

*"Mummy, Mummy," whispering quietly, secretly, not
wanting anyone else to hear, just between them, a delicious
secret to be shared. "Mummy, Mummy!" with more urgency
but still a whisper. Trying to attract her attention. "Mummy,
Mummy!" There's someone at the door and then Jess is
wiping her hands on a tea towel and standing in the hallway,
Leila tugging at her pullover, Mo and four other men
jabbering away in a strange language, then quiet, then Mo
looking serious, "Go upstairs! Take Leila," hesitation, Mo
shouting and stepping forward menacingly, "Go now!"
picking up Leila, who's starting to cry, Mo looking angry,
men watching her, running up the stairs, people at the back
door too, coming into the kitchen, then she's in the bedroom,
slamming the door shut, turning the key, hugging, nursing
and rocking Leila on the bed, chatting to her, kissing,
smiling, consoling, but anxious and terrified, then quiet.
Downstairs, murmuring, laughing, bottle, glasses, more
strange language, more agitated, more laughing, getting
louder, new voices, girls voices, men shouting and jeering,
on and on, an hour, two hours, three hours, getting dark,
one girl crying, men shouting, a slap, a squeal, another girl
crying, wailing, men grunting, primeval ... and then
eventually doors slam and it's quiet and she's nervously
opening the bedroom door, carrying Leila asleep to her
room, putting her into bed and tucking her in and going
downstairs very slowly and seeing the kitchen strewn with
glasses and bottles and half-empty takeaway cartons and
food smeared on the worktops and table and the sitting
room, furniture all displaced, cans and bottles and sofa
cushions on the floor and the stench of stale beer and sickly*

cheap perfume and the stains and patches on the sofa and the carpet, sticky, wet, repugnant ...

Jess, wide-eyed and awake, sweating in her sleeping bag. She fumbled for the zip but it was tight and wouldn't move, and as she twisted her body, the bag tightened around her, pinning her arms like a strait jacket. She wrestled herself free and sat up and reached for the zip at the front of the tent, pulled it up sharply and thrust her head outside in the cool night air, gasping for breath.

The stars were out, blinking at her in unison, and the full moon in the east shone brightly, bathing her face in a silvery glow. She breathed in the pure night air and felt grateful for the day ahead.

CHAPTER 17

Jess had still not found the river. But she had found the canal, and in some ways that was better. The canal had a towpath so she could walk for miles without having to make a decision about which way to go, and although she knew she was travelling mainly south rather than west, the route was still taking her further and further away from her previous life, which was the main thing.

The canal also passed through towns and villages where she could buy food, and there was plenty of free drinking water from official water stops. These were normally locked and needed a specially supplied key to access the tap, so she got used to waiting for a boat to come along, fill their tanks and then ask if she could fill her bottle before the tap was locked again. No one minded helping the young lady, bedraggled and scruffy though she may have appeared.

But she was hungry again and dirty, and this time she had almost run out of money. She had camped overnight by a flight of locks and the continuous trickle of water over the gates was soothing in the cold night air, but it had started to rain and when she woke the skies were grey and rain fell in a persistent drizzle.

She stayed in her tent most of the day waiting for it to stop, and through a gap in the front cover watched a steady procession of narrowboats navigate the locks, their crew replete in waterproof gear, wielding their cranking handles or "lock keys", she heard someone say, before continuing on their way up or down the canal.

The drizzle eventually subsided so she packed up her wet tent. She was now an expert at folding it and could get it back in the bag within twenty seconds. She set off downstream but she was tired and her feet dragged as she trudged along the towpath. The optimism and liberation she had felt in the first two weeks had gradually dwindled and the bare facts of her situation were becoming increasingly apparent. She needed to eat. It was still summer, but soon it would be autumn and the weather would only get worse. She needed to find somewhere, and it needed to be soon.

By late afternoon, the rain came back in earnest and she hastily threw up her tent behind a hedgerow in a field that bordered the towpath. She guessed it was only 5 p.m. or thereabouts, but she was going no further that night. She didn't have the energy or the motivation and that alone gave her cause for concern. It would be fine tomorrow, she told her herself, this was just a bad day at the office. But she had nothing to eat. She had finished the cream crackers, banana and the last packet of vegetable soup the previous day, had not come across a village or canal shop since, and it had been almost forty-eight hours since the meal in the campsite. She would have to go and forage when the rain subsided, but for what?

After a couple of hours, she decided that given a choice between hunger and being wet, the latter was the lesser of two evils, and she could wait no longer. She crawled out of her tent and set off in the drizzle along the hedgerow bordering the field looking for berries, but the blackberries were not yet ripe and still inedible. She reached the end of the field and looked out over the gate at a field where a number of sheep grazed, oblivious to the rain. And then, to her right, she noticed a large patch of nettles and she remembered she had once seen a recipe for nettle soup.

She knelt down to pick a few from the base of the stalk and was immediately stung on the back of the hand. She squealed in pain and put her hand to her mouth, sucking on her injured knuckles and cursing herself for her stupidity. She felt a wave of hopelessness and suddenly wanted to cry.

But then she noticed some large dock leaves in the same patch, so she carefully picked two, wrapped her right hand in them and used them as a glove to pick the nettles. She managed to assemble a bundle of nettles enclosed in the safety of the dock leaves, but not without the vicious weed fighting back and stinging her again.

Eventually satisfied she had enough, she returned to her tent and assembled her stove in the entrance, gently feeding the nettles one by one into her tin cup of boiling water. She had read that the nettles' stinging hairs were neutralised by boiling. To her relief, it proved to be true. Partly.

***

She's gone to the school at the usual time. No one talks to her, not the mothers or the fathers or the children, but they all steal a glance and when she catches their eyes, they look away and shepherd their children away and give her a wide berth and then when the playground is almost empty she ventures in, looking, searching and Miss Hicks is coming out with her bag and some papers and because she's nice she asks her and she says, "Oh, I thought you were off for a picnic," and she says "Picnic?" and she says, "Yes, your husband asked if Leila could leave early, said you were all off for a picnic. Watch out for those nettles!"

"Leila!"

She was sitting up, feverish, hot with sweat but cold from the damp, shivering and frightened and confused. Leila.

She screwed her eyes tightly closed and clenched her teeth. She could hear her heart beating in her ears and her head pounding and feel her pulse twitching in her neck. She took several deep breaths to calm herself down and sat leaning forward, her heads supported by her hands, trying to compose herself.

114

After a while, she swept her hair back and put her hands behind her head and finally lay back, pulling her feet up towards her and tucking the sleeping bag under her legs to try and insulate them from the cold. She pulled the sleeping bag over her head and bathed in the warmth of her own breath.

Alone in her silent dark cocoon.

CHAPTER 18

She couldn't tell how far she had walked along the towpath, and although she had been walking slowly, she had set off early so she must have covered a few miles at least. She had nothing but some hot water inside her, having decided the nettle soup, or tea, more like, was not worth the bother. She was tired, thirsty and hungry.

She was dirty, too; her trousers and jacket streaked with mud and grass stains, her hair greasy and matted and her fingernails broken where they weren't black.

If she had had a mirror, she would have been alarmed at her drawn features, the dark shadows under her eyes. She instinctively knew she was a mess, so she kept her head down when she came across the odd runner or dog walker, avoiding eye contact and saying nothing.

Her head was down when she approached a large canal-side pub with three or four narrowboats moored alongside, so she didn't see it until she was almost upon it. The Navigation loomed into view and she looked up at the swinging sign and the proud boast: "Cask Ales, Fine Wines, Home Cooked Food and Free Moorings".

She fished in her trouser pocket and brought out some loose change. It was all she had. But she had no choice. Maybe she could sweep up for them outside, or collect glasses in return for a sandwich? It was late morning and there seemed little activity, but she headed for the entrance door facing the canal and stopped when a sign in the window caught her eye. To the right of the door, a handwritten sign read: "Cleaner/Bar Staff Required". Her heart lifted. *Maybe. Just maybe?*

***

Trish was behind the bar pouring a pint of Guinness, a long and slow process that took a degree of concentration. It wasn't yet twelve noon, but already one or two boats had pulled in and their occupants were anxious to get started on the booze.

The Navigation boasted two separate bars: one that serviced an informal seated area where customers could simply enjoy a drink and a snack, and the other, the main bar servicing the fifty-cover restaurant.

Even without looking up, Trish noticed the shuffling, dishevelled figure enter the bar area from the canal-side door and tentatively sidle her way towards her. Trish was not in a good mood. Dave had been lazy and useless as usual, and she and Jade had had to do most of the cleaning, again. He was currently glad-handing the odd punter coming into the restaurant, playing "mine host", the thing he enjoyed most, swaggering around like the big swinging dick that he was, while she and everyone else ran around like headless chickens, trying to do ten things at once.

She was getting too old for this game, she thought. Twenty years ago, running a pub and restaurant was vibrant and exciting, and she had been full of optimism for the future. Then a vivacious, raven-haired young waitress, she had fallen for the charms of the handsome, quick-witted and cocky assistant manager, Dave, who got the GM's job when old boy Trevor had retired. They became an item and soon married, the pub providing them with live-in accommodation plus a reasonable salary as the brewery owners became increasingly happy with the pub's performance.

But that was then and this was now. Time and work, never-ending graft, had taken its toll on Trish, who, at forty-six, was probably past her prime. She still took care over her appearance, if only to avoid frightening the punters, and according to her supremely gracious husband, "scrubbed up well". But she had recently overheard a garrulous old geezer, a regular drinker of theirs, talking about someone who "used to be a looker but she has let herself go a bit," and she was left in no doubt who he was referring to.

And Dave had shown himself to be a less than ideal husband, getting worse as he got older, lazy and complacent and heedless of the pressures of running the business, letting Trish and others do all the work while constantly eyeing up and harassing the female bar staff and waitresses with his unfunny innuendos and embarrassing jokes.

Trish often felt like a prisoner in this poxy pub, hitched to this feckless idiot, and wondered how different things could have been and where they went wrong. One day she would just walk away, she told herself, but she wasn't sure she was brave enough. One day.

Jess shuffled up to the bar and stopped, wondering whether she should say something and interrupt the woman who was clearly concentrating on the job in hand or wait till she had finished. The decision was made for her.

"You all right, love?" said the woman without taking her eyes off the trickle of black liquid that slowly filled the glass.

Jess was suddenly not sure what to say. She hadn't spoken to anyone for three days and her mouth felt dry through a combination of hunger, thirst and apprehension. When she did open her mouth, the words came out in a croak.

"I wondered … hmm …" – she had to clear her throat before continuing – "I wondered if I could speak to the manager, please?" The woman was frowning and her expression fierce, even though it was still directed at the beer.

"That'll be me. What can I do for you?" she shot back sternly, eyes fixed on the Guinness level as it finally reached the top of the glass. Jess felt discomfited. She already felt she was being put under pressure and, not having had a sensible conversation with anyone for several weeks, was struggling to find the few words she needed to explain why she was there. She swallowed and gulped.

"Er, you've got a sign by the door." Her head swung backwards involuntarily in case the woman didn't know where the door was. "About staff?" The woman had been turning the beer glass in a swirling spiral in order to paint a shamrock on the froth and, having examined her handiwork, put it down on the bar. She looked up at Jess.

"Got any experience?" She looked forbidding.

"Er, what sort of …?"

"Done anything like this before?" Trish said, clearly with mounting exasperation.

"Um … office cleaning and reception work," she offered hopefully. The woman said nothing, but looked Jess up and down, taking in her unkempt appearance, dirty face and fingernails, crumpled jacket, and turned her head in recognition of the rucksack on her back.

"On yer holidays?" she said mockingly, raising her eyebrows.

"Er, no." Jess felt deflated again.

"Gap year?" Again, a hint of torment in her tone.

"No," mumbled Jess, feeling that the interview, if you could call it that, was not going well.

"Runaway?" said Trish. The woman had hit the target.

"No!" blurted out Jess a little too quickly, and then, by way of explanation, "I just need a job and a place to stay." There it was. It was out. There was nothing more to say, and for a moment she stood awkwardly, feeling the woman's eyes bore into her.

Trish examined this wretched young girl for a moment and felt a pang of conscience that perhaps she had been too harsh, less than friendly, just because she was in a bad mood. She didn't know where "runaway" had come from, but then realised, yes, she did. It had been on her mind and here she was, confronted by someone who was doing exactly what she herself was incapable of.

The girl clearly looked distressed, physically and mentally, and probably needed a bit of help. Well, she wasn't the only one. Trish softened her tone but stopped short of forcing a smile.

"You look like you could do with some food inside you. Go and take a seat over there and we'll have a chat when I'm off," she said, gesturing to a small table by the window. Jess nodded her head slowly and did as she was told.

Trish watched her trudge over to the table, unload her rucksack and slump dejectedly into a seat with its back to the wall. There was something wrong there, she thought. She would have to find out what it was.

Jess was not sure whether to run or to stay put. The woman had appeared fearsome and daunting but hadn't chucked her out, so maybe there was a possibility that something might come of it.

The pub was warm and bright inside and there were intoxicating smells emanating from the kitchen. She was in no hurry to depart but hadn't ordered anything to eat and the hunger pains continued to torment her. Before she had time to decide what to do, the woman was back and she sat up, almost to attention.

Trish put a cheese sandwich and glass of water on the table in front of Jess, who looked up in surprise. "How much is that?" she croaked, suddenly panicky that she didn't have enough money to pay.

"Don't worry about it. Give me half an hour," said Trish, and strode off to the restaurant area, leaving Jess alone. Jess took one look at the sandwich and then grabbed it with both hands, taking an almighty bite out of the crusty bread. Nothing had tasted that good for a long time.

Forty-five minutes later, Trish returned, mopping her brow, half-full cup of coffee in one hand, and sat down at the table opposite Jess with a loud exhalation. Jess sat up straight again, anticipating an interrogation.

"Okay, love. What's your name?" Trish's schoolmistress tone had returned. Jess somehow had not prepared for this, the most obvious of first questions, and she hesitated. She didn't have a name. She used to have one but it wasn't hers anymore. Jess was no more. She looked to the floor searching for inspiration and then to the bar, and then the mirror behind the bar. A looking glass.

"Alice," she blurted without looking at Trish, and then, when there was no response, couldn't help looking up, her eyes meeting those of the woman opposite. Trish was staring at her. The silence said it all.

"Are you sure about that?" she said finally.

"Yes," insisted Jess. Trish's doubts had already been confirmed, but it was consistent with the runaway theory, so she decided to play along.

"Okay. Where are you from?" Another impossible question, or rather one that had an impossible answer.

"Nowhere, really."

"Where do you live?" said Trish, evidently with growing impatience, but Jess didn't have a reply. She didn't know how to explain. She opened her mouth as if to speak but no words came out. Trish cut to the chase.

"I knew it. Who're you running from? Husband? Old bill?"

"No!" pleaded Jess. "I just needed to get away for a bit."

121

"And why's that, then?" The woman was not going to give up. Should have known better. This was like her old life. People harassing and haranguing her, demanding, controlling. Why couldn't they just leave her alone? This was the reason she left in the first place, to get away from everyone making life difficult and telling her what to do. Her first tentative steps back into so-called civilisation were becoming a re-run of the nightmare of the last seven years. She had had enough. She reached for her rucksack.

"I'm sorry, I've been wasting your time. How much for the lunch?"

Trish knew she had gone too far. "Sit down, love." The girl stopped at Trish's command and there was a moment's silence. There would be time enough to find out who she was and where she was from, but for the moment, Trish desperately needed another pair of hands. And she had seen something in the girl that her years of experience told her was all right. The girl was frightened and vulnerable and, whatever her problem, Trish was disquieted by it, and her concern persuaded her to cut her some slack. She had seen it before, the hunted look, the repressed torment, troubled by something she couldn't speak of but would eventually, when the time was right. Trish broke the silence and tried her best to sound conciliatory.

"Okay. I need some help and you need a place to stay. It's minimum wage, two hours cleaning, bar, restaurant, toilets, windows, three hours serving lunches, five hours serving dinners, one day off a week; except for cleaning, which is every day unless I say otherwise. You get a four pound daily food allowance; anything above that comes out of your wages."

Jess's head swirled and she nodded mechanically as the facts and figures were thrown at her like darts at a board, but without any real comprehension other than it sounded positive.

"You need a place to stay?" Jess nodded shyly. She understood that part and it was by far the most important thing she had heard. "We have a staff room you can rent. It's not the presidential suite, but it'll do. We'll take it out of your wages until you can find somewhere else." By now, Jess would have agreed to anything.

"Start now, okay? Alice?" Trish's emphasis on the last word made it clear that as names went, this was a working title.

"Okay," said Jess, relieved. The interview was over. She had no idea what would come next, but she would make the most of it while she could and then, when the time was right, she would hit the road again. If nothing else, it would be a welcome, if temporary respite from the privations of outdoor life. She could regain her strength, get some regular food and sleep and be able to clean all her clothes, as well as have something useful to do. The woman was smiling at her for the first time, welcoming almost, and she was thankful.

"Bring your things, I'll show you up."

Jess nodded meekly. They both stood, and while Jess was gathering up her rucksack and tent, she noticed the woman was conversing with a middle-aged man standing behind the bar.

Trish leant on the bar, looking directly at her husband whose eyes were focused on a spot over her left shoulder.

"Who's that, then?" he whispered conspiratorially.

Trish gave him a piercing look. She knew exactly what was going through his mind and she didn't like it. *Have to nip this one in the bud.*

"Another waif and stray looking for sanctuary," she whispered back. He raised his eyebrows and lifted his bottom lip over the top one. She gave him a steely look. "Don't even think about it."

"I can look, can't I?" he protested.

"As long as you don't touch. I swear to God ..." The threat was unmistakeable.

Dave watched his wife and the girl with the rucksack disappear through the door marked "Staff" and felt pleased with life. He liked a challenge.

***

Trish opened the window shutters and light flooded into the room.

"This is your new home," she announced, and Jess followed her in, eyes taking in the surroundings.

The floorboards were exposed apart from a threadbare mat by the foot of the single bed with pillow and rolled-up duvet, a small bedside table with lamp and clock, two shelves and a writing table and chair. The walls were cracked, the paintwork chipped and grubby and a single bulb with shabby lampshade hung down from the middle of the ceiling. It was basic, to say the least, but compared to her pop-up tent, it might have been a room at the Dorchester.

Trish was rattling out further instructions at a rapid pace.

"You'll find towels, soap and stuff in the store along the corridor, next to the bathroom. Here's the key. Keep it locked." Jess took the key from the woman's outstretched hand. "In there as well, you'll find staff uniforms: white blouse, black skirt and apron when you're serving, black tee shirt, trousers and apron when you're cleaning. To be worn

124

at all times on duty. Your job is to keep them clean and presentable. Washing machine's in the cellar. All the restaurant linen goes in the main laundry which is collected once a week." Jess nodded profusely, trying to keep up.

"Right," – the woman looked at her watch – "it's three now, I'll give you till five to settle in and smarten up, then see you downstairs for a quick tour." She moved to the open door, stopped and looked back at Jess. The woman's body relaxed and she gave Jess a big smile. "Oh, I'm Trish, by the way. The gormless one is my other half, Dave."

"Thanks, Trish," croaked Jess, her voice failing her again. But she was feeling better already.

"You'll be all right here," Trish said gently, nodding, and softly closed the door behind her.

Jess dumped her rucksack and tent and sat on the edge of the bed staring out of the window that overlooked the car park. She was smelly, filthy and exhausted, but she took a deep breath and closed her eyes. A new chapter was about to start for Alice, however brief it might turn out to be.

***

She made her way back downstairs just before five. She had showered, washed her hair for the first time since she had left the campsite and was dressed in the requisite items of uniform she had taken from the storeroom.

The pub was quiet, lunch long since over, and serving would not begin again until 6.30 so other staff were either in their rooms or had gone home for a brief lie-down between shifts.

She entered the main restaurant hoping to find Trish, but the only person there was a middle-aged man, sitting at one of the tables with a coffee and a newspaper. She recognised him as the one she had seen earlier behind the bar talking to

Trish. *What did she call him? The "gormless one".* He must have been in his late forties, she judged: short-sleeved shirt, jeans, stubble on both head and chin, thin gold chain around his neck and heavy watch.

Dave heard her coming but pretended not to notice until she got closer. He had been waiting for her. He looked up. *I knew she'd scrub up well.* He stood up, cocked his head to one side and gave her a wide toothy grin, like a predatory cat sizing up his next prey.

"'Allo, 'allo, you must be Alice." He held out a hand. "I'm Dave," and to make sure she was in no doubt of his status, added, "the boss." The girl looked momentarily confused.

"Oh, I thought Trish was ..."

"We both are." Dave's grin was fixed and his eyes bored into her. "But, well, I'm in charge."

She took his hand and he held on to it softly, still grinning, but was suddenly distracted by the sound of footsteps on the oak floor.

"I see you two have met."

Dave snapped his hand back and his head to his right to see his wife giving him a look of disdain. "Come on, Alice, let's get started." Dave's eyes followed them both as they went off to start her induction.

***

She lay on the bed under the duvet, warm and comfortable. The bed was soggy and creaky and the duvet thin, but it didn't matter. She was back in the land of the living. The last four weeks had been liberating and stimulating, but arduous and at times frightening and, she had come to realise,

126

unsustainable. But somehow she had achieved her objective. She had successfully abandoned her old existence and was exhilarated by the start of her new one.

She had quickly acclimatised to being called Alice, and for the most part everyone had made her feel welcome, even though there had been no time for idle chat with a busy pub and restaurant to service. She was relieved that she had not had to explain herself to anyone yet and decided she must cobble together a story with enough truth to make it honest and plausible, without revealing or reliving the horrors of the past.

She was exquisitely tired. But her mind was still buzzing from the adrenalin, the frantic running around meeting the demands of customers, and she was pleased that she had got through her first shift without dropping anything, spilling anything or being generally useless. Jade had helped her a lot. The Australian was very experienced and direct, and she obeyed every command without question. There was still a lot more to learn, but she had made a good start and was determined to become proficient in her new role as soon as possible.

She had to be up by 7 a.m. tomorrow to start the clean. What a luxury! A positive lie-in. She was still thinking about how she would organise her cleaning regime when she drifted off without realising.

***

It's 9.45 and she's slipping out of the house. Her mother's in bed, Joe's asleep, snoring in the armchair in front of the TV, still on. She shuts the door and pulls her hood over her head. It's dry but cold. She gets to the end of the road. Mo's car is there and he's in the driver's seat holding a phone to his ear, gesticulating silently with the other arm, chunky gold watch sparkling in the light of a street lamp. He notices her and smiles, hangs up. She gets in the other side. She can smell his musky cologne again, sweet and spicy at the same time with a faint scent of peppermint. They move off. They talk. They laugh. He has big brown eyes and white teeth and she likes him. He's twenty-one and it's time he left home. He has the keys to a flat he wants to rent. Does she want to see it? Yes, she would love to see it, and it has modern furniture, glass and chrome and a nice bathroom and a big TV and she sits down, they have some wine and it gives her a warm feeling and her head goes fuzzy so she soon begins to feel like she is floating and forgetting about home. They talk and they laugh some more. He says when she wants to go home he'll take her, but she doesn't want to go because it's nice here with him and it's not nice at home. He sits on the sofa next to her and takes her hand and pulls her gently towards him, smiling. He kisses her gently and she doesn't resist. She doesn't want to go home ...

CHAPTER 19

Jess settled into life at The Navigation as if she had been born to it. She was up at seven every morning to start her cleaning regime before anyone else surfaced, and in this role she had plenty of experience. She wiped down the bar tops, vacuumed and mopped the floors in all the public areas, cleaned and replenished the toilets and, once a week, cleaned the inside of the windows.

She didn't have to worry about the kitchen – the KPs did that themselves – nor any crockery, cutlery or glassware, which was routinely loaded into the machines for washing at the end of each session, but there was always a stray item on the floor or in a strange place which needed washing up by hand. She was always done by 9 a.m. and so could have a quick breakfast and go for a walk along the canal before her next shift started at 11.30.

The staff had been generally welcoming and she had a new best friend, Jade, who had shown her all the workings of the bar and restaurant: laying tables, clearing tables, taking orders, understanding the meal tickets and the "pass" in the kitchen, and learning how to use the electronic point of sale system and the espresso machine. The girl called Alice had rapidly become adept at waitressing and curiously warmed to people, staff and customers in a way Jess never could. Within a week she was an established member of the crew.

It was Friday morning and Jess and Trish were in the office. Trish was pleased with her and was smiling broadly. Her new waif and stray had been a godsend, vastly exceeding her expectations. She had someone reliable to do the cleaning – the girl actually enjoyed it! – and after rent had been deducted for occupying the scruffiest room in the building, she was very cheap. Alice would have tips as well, of course, and as she had no expenses, she should be perfectly content with her pittance of a wage. Everyone was happy. She handed over a brown envelope.

"Here you are. Tips in there, too. You done well this week. I'm impressed." Jess burst into a big smile and took the envelope. Trish lowered her voice and leant forward a little.

"Look. There's no payslip. You're off-grid. Thought you might prefer it that way and it suits me too. Just don't mention it to anyone, okay? Shouldn't do it really. Check you're happy with the money."

Keeping her off the books was not strictly legal, but she knew Alice was not her real name and demanding a National Insurance number might precipitate a crisis that she wanted to avoid for now. Her priority was to keep the place running smoothly, and not only had Alice proven herself to be highly capable, she seemed to be enjoying her job. The brewery would not be happy if they knew, but because turnover and profits were on or above target, she and Dave were left alone to run the place as they saw fit; and if that meant cutting a few corners here and there, Trish was sure they would turn a blind eye to what she regarded as a minor transgression. Anyway, all pubs and restaurants needed a bit of casual labour from time to time. It was the only way some of them could stay alive.

Jess peered in at the contents and her eyes widened at the bundle of cash.

"Thanks!" she gushed. Trish was genuinely happy for her, it seemed like the ideal arrangement, and within a week Alice had transformed from the shambling wreck of a girl who had walked through the door into an enthusiastic and bubbly member of staff. But she knew there was potential for danger and felt compelled to ask.

"Well, week one over and done. How're you getting on with Dave?"

"He's nice. Everyone's nice."

Trish was relieved to hear it but couldn't help herself. Alice needed to be warned.

"Well, watch yourself. Wandering hands ..." Jess's smile began to drop. "Wandered over me, once," said Trish, reminiscing momentarily before getting back to business. "Go on, then. Work to do!" she said with mock severity and Jess turned, smiling again. Trish watched her go. *Nice girl. I wonder what story she has to tell. We've all got one, that's for sure. Thank God Dave is behaving.*

***

It was a warm Wednesday afternoon. Jess was sitting by the canal watching the boats go by, seemingly lost in thought. Trish was thoughtful too. She stood at the window looking out at the girl sitting on the grass, wondering what was going through her head. She sensed someone slide up behind her and look over her shoulder and knew immediately who it was. "Strange girl," she said out loud to no one in particular. Dave scratched his nose.

"Yeah. She's definitely got a hang-up or two."

"She don't say much. Never gives anything away."

"You'll have to get to the bottom of it."

"Not yet. Don't want to freak her out."

"I could have a word," he said casually

"You, will leave her alone," snapped Trish, and although she didn't have eyes in the back of her head, she could tell Dave was making a face.

***

Jess was busy stacking bottles in the saloon bar fridge. It was 11.30 a.m. and the pub was coming to life. There was the usual clattering of pots and pans and excitable chatter wafting out from the kitchen, and Jade was in the restaurant with two other girls, setting up for the lunchtime session. Dave appeared from around the other side of the bar and shuffled forward to where Jess was crouched in front of the bottle cabinet.

"Y'know, me and Trish are well pleased with you, Alice," he said. She stood up and smiled at him, looking slightly embarrassed. Compliments had always been few and far between for Jess.

"Thanks, Dave, I'm grateful to you and Trish for giving me a chance." It sounded lame but it was true. She was still a little apprehensive about being around Dave. She didn't know what it was about him, but she always felt like he was looking at her strangely, making her ill at ease. Maybe it was the way hc smiled at her, which always seemed forced or unnatural. Or maybe he just thought that he had to maintain a sense of superiority over his staff. She wasn't the only one to feel a little unnerved; some of the other girls did too. It was irrational, she knew, but above all she didn't want to say or do anything that might antagonise him.

"Yeah, well. It's hard to get good staff. Especially English ones." Dave was nothing if not patriotic, but evidently felt he had to explain himself.

"Don't get me wrong, there's nuffing wrong with yer Poles and yer Slovaks and that. Good workers. Knows their stuff. But they can be a bit bolshie, if you get my drift. Always pickin' on this and that, moaning about the wages and the tips. And no sense of humour. Don't get me wrong" he said again "nuffing against them as such, but they're just not like us, are they?"

Jess always tried to agree with Dave as it was the safest option, but on the subject of the relative merits and work ethics of different nationalities, she had no view. Instinctively she thought his sweeping generalisations misguided, to say the least, and she was unsure how to respond to this, but mercifully, his rant was largely rhetorical and he went on, turning inquisitive.

"Whereas you … you're a bit of a mysterious enigma, you are. Wouldn't say boo to a goose. Just gets on with it. I like that. More to you than meets the eye, I reckon."

Jess was suddenly nervous about where this one-sided conversation was going. Dave seemed to be showing an interest in her for the first time, and if she were to draw up a list of people to whom she might open up, he would probably be somewhere near the bottom. She smiled meekly and tried to busy herself around the bar.

"Thing is, I ain't seen you have a proper laugh yet, Alice. Is there anything up? Anything I can help you with?"

It sounded innocuous, but there was something in the tone of his voice she found disturbing, as if he already knew something about her and was simply waiting for her confirmation, playing with her, provoking a reaction for no reason other than to see her react. Jess shook her head and shrugged. The last thing she wanted to do was discuss her past, and he was the last person she wanted to discuss it with.

"Nothing's up. I just keep myself to myself, I suppose." Dave studied her closely and she felt a chill of discomfort she hadn't felt for several weeks. He took a step closer and she had to fight the urge to flinch or step back. He put one hand on the bar, leant in towards her and lowered his voice.

"Well, if anything's bothering you, if you ever want to talk about anything, private and confidential, like," – he touched the side of his nose with one finger – "talk to Dave. Ain't no problem that can't be solved. Seen 'em all in this business. Nothing's going to shock or surprise me," he announced with certitude, brushing past to get to the reservations book at the other end of the bar, but so closely she had to breathe in.

He flicked the pages and ran his finger down the list. "Now then. Party of twelve coming in for lunch today. British Legion Annual reunion. Oh dear, oh dear. Bunch of old geezers," he scoffed. Jess wasn't sure what he meant. "Now you watch yourself with them." He wagged a finger at her. "One of 'em 'll try and touch you up."

She couldn't quite believe what she was hearing. Was he really warning her to be vigilant in case an elderly customer made advances, or worse? She frowned and, for a moment, looked alarmed; not at the threat itself, but at the warning and the way it had been delivered.

"I'll be watching," he made an attempt to reassure her, "but tell me if you get any hassle – I'll sort 'em out." Jess decided it was time to go and fill the ice buckets.

***

MV Carician was moored close to the Biddington bridge, swaying gently backwards and forwards in the current as the river flowed south or as another boat passed by. The weather was warm and sunny, the trees were green and the sound of birdsong jostled with the lap of the water against the hull.

Peter sat on the rear deck, reading yesterday's *Times*, a glass of white wine on the table before him. He had been out for a few days and his old lady, a Bates Starcraft of forty years vintage, had not let him down, so far.

Once he had charged the batteries and got the twin Volvos throbbing back to life, he had stocked up on provisions, locked the old house and taken off upriver. He didn't know how long he would be away, but it didn't matter. He just needed to escape. Clear his head. Think about what he was going to do next.

He hadn't given it any thought so far; he was too busy doing nothing, as the saying went. His biggest task was deciding what he would have for supper. In the absence of a decent hostelry at his evening moorings, it would be beans on toast. Again. No matter. He slurped a mouthful of Sauvignon Blanc and put down his glass next to his phone. It rang. *Bugger. Should have switched it off. Probably another PPI call or some other crank.* He looked at the screen. Michael Goodman. He smiled and swiped the green blob with his index finger.

"Michael! How the devil are you?"

"Very well, thanks, Peter. Are you fit?"

"Yes, thanks, couldn't be better. Just messing about on the river, as it happens. Thought I would get away for a few days in the warm weather."

"Lucky for some," mused Michael, and Peter could imagine him sitting at his desk, surrounded by papers and folders, and decided to have a poke at his old friend.

"Perks of retirement, old boy. You ought to try it sometime," he scoffed.

"Some of us still have to prop up the economy, old boy. Earn a crust, pay for those little necessities in life," said Michael with mock weariness. Peter latched onto it immediately.

"Ah yes, there is that. And how is the lovely lady then? Still spending your money?" He enjoyed being provocative, but they had known each other for long enough and he knew Michael would see the joke. Michael and Emma were his oldest friends. Perhaps his only friends, and he loved them as family. "Well, give her a big hug from me. We must get together sometime." There was a pause before Michael answered.

"That's actually why I was calling. Since you got back from Nepal," he said carefully, "I have been looking at your

135

situation and I think it's time we had a review." Peter's smile dissolved as Michael spoke, and the dread came flooding back.

"It breaks my heart to think about it," he said, trying to keep the sadness out of his voice, "but in the circumstances, another look might be in order. You're right, Michael, as always." He sighed.

"When do you expect to be home?"

"Early next week, I suppose. Rather depends on the weather. I'll call you then and we'll set up a meeting."

"Okay. Have a good trip, Peter, bye for now."

"Bye. Oh, and love to Emma."

***

The old soldiers and sailors from the British Legion were charming. They came dressed in their berets and regimental blazers adorned with medals. They were polite, disciplined and respectful of their surroundings and all the young waitresses who served them their three-course lunch. They drank modestly, conducted themselves with good humour, and Jess enjoyed serving and chatting to them all over the course of the afternoon.

One or two of them were veterans of WWII and to her that may as well have been ancient history, like the Romans and the Greeks she had read about at school. But she felt at ease with this group of old gentlemen, more so than she had ever thought before, and she couldn't understand why Dave had been so disparaging about them.

The oldest member of the group was well into his nineties, and although he walked with some difficulty and needed a stick, he insisted on getting himself back to the bus without resorting to the wheelchair they had brought with them for emergencies. Jess could see he was unsteady on his

136

feet and she took his arm as they walked slowly down the sloping path to the car park where the bus was waiting.

The old boy climbed the steps to the minibus and, raising his stick in triumph, received a rousing "Hurrah" from his comrades. The driver slammed the sliding door shut and the bus moved off, Jess smiling and waving a fond farewell. She turned and strode back to the pub, pleased with herself. The pub and restaurant were largely empty now and she found Dave leaning against the bar, looking decidedly grumpy.

"That went well," she said, still buzzing from the excitement of it all and the pleasure she had got from the many compliments she had received. Dave was not so happy.

"See, Alice. Was I right, or was I right?" he said truculently.

"What?" She was genuinely puzzled. She had no idea what he was talking about and feared she may have done something to displease him.

"I saw old squadron leader whatshisname with his arm round you, having a good feel, randy old bastard," he grunted. Jess was a bit shocked but relieved; it was just a misunderstanding.

"Oh, no, he has trouble walking. I was just helping him on the bus."

But Dave was having none of it.

"Don't give me that," he sneered, "he can walk, all right. He tried that with Olga when she was here, and she didn't half slap him one." Jess's smile had vanished. "Had to let her go, of course. Can't be having that, slapping the punters."

Trish appeared from behind him.

"Ain't that right, Trish? That Russian girl Olga gave old Douglas Bader a poke in the eye last time he was here." Trish seemed to take a moment to work out what her idiot husband was going on about and then gave him a withering look.

"Czech."

"Check what?"

"She was Czech, and her name was Katya." Jess almost snorted trying to stifle a laugh.

"Yeah, well. Whatever," said Dave. "We had to let her go, didn't we?"

"She walked out, if you remember." Trish tried to correct him but it was futile.

"Yeah – before she got the order of the boot." She raised her eyebrows and shook her head then turned to Jess and put a friendly hand on her shoulder.

"Well done, Alice. I think you made an impression today."

"I think I need a lie down after that," said Jess, face beaming with pleasure at the compliment but also at Dave's twisted expression, and with that they parted, leaving Dave huffing and puffing at the bar.

***

It was 11.45 p.m. The evening shift was over and all the staff had either gone home or upstairs to sleep, apart from Jess who was wiping down the saloon bar. She would only have to do it in the morning if she didn't do it now. Dave strolled in from the empty restaurant as she was trying to stifle a yawn with one hand.

"All right, Alice?" he said as she quickly took her hand away.

"Yes, just tired. It's been a busy day."

"Welcome to 24/7 hospitality – no rest for the wicked!"

"Oh, I'm enjoying it" she protested. The last thing she wanted him to think was that she was complaining or not up to the task.

Dave had hung back after his wife had gone up, saying he wanted to check on the cellar cooling and review the proposed new menu. He had really wanted to have a quiet word with Alice when no one was about, and this seemed to him like an ideal opportunity. He had made several attempts at ingratiating himself with her, but his jokes had always gone over her head and his little asides and quips had fallen on deaf ears.

She was just like the others, he thought. The foreigners had the excuse that they couldn't be expected to understand good English humour, but even that Aussie bird Jade had given him short shrift. Admittedly, he did put his arm around her waist once to give her a friendly squeeze and the girl had firmly removed it, suggesting that he "keep his fucking hands to himself", so he had got the message and stayed well away from that one, permanently filed in the "too difficult" category. There were easier mountains to climb.

But Alice was a difficult animal altogether. She was quiet, enigmatic and had an air of vulnerability which he thought was a turn on, just the sort he liked best. So far, she hadn't given any indication that she was motivated by money or in any way dissatisfied with her job or pay, but he wondered whether perhaps a few words of praise accompanied by a small reward might smooth the way. She would see that he not only valued her as a worker but was kind and generous too.

"Now look, like I said before. You've been brilliant." Her eyes lit up and he was instantly encouraged. She turned to face him and spread her arms across the width of the bar.

"Thanks, Dave." She looked pleased and a little embarrassed, and that especially gave him a thrill. He took a step forward and lowered his voice to just above a whisper.

"Now listen. Trish normally does the wages" – he looked from side to side to make sure they were alone – "but I think you deserve a bit of a bonus for all the work you've done." Jess looked surprised and delighted by the compliment.

"You don't need to do that, Dave. I'm just happy to be here."

"I do need to do that," insisted Dave. "I want to," he said emphatically, and to add gravitas, "I own the business, it's my money and I can do what I want with it. So I'm going to give you a bit extra." He watched with satisfaction as she appeared to wilt under his piercing stare and then give in.

"Well, if you really want to. Thanks, Dave." He took another step and his voice got lower still.

"Yeah, well. Just don't tell Trish. Don't want her thinking I got any favourites" – he slid his left hand on top of her right wrist, and she looked down, instantly alarmed – "even if I do." She swivelled her head to her other wrist as his right hand alighted there. She jerked her head up. Her smile had gone as quickly as his had arrived. It was only a second or two, but she tugged both hands free and he frowned at her as she stepped back.

"Goodnight, Dave," she said and backed out of the bar. Dave watched her go, annoyed she hadn't responded and a little worried he may have gone too far. But he had to be sanguine about it. There would be another chance. Soon.

"Goodnight, Alice" he whispered to himself, smirking. "Sleep tight."

***

Jess tried to stay out of his way for the next few days and made sure never to be caught in a situation alone with him again. She told herself she was overreacting. They had both said how much they valued her, and although she knew their words of praise were reward enough, she should not be surprised if at least one of them backed it up with something tangible.

Dave was a funny guy in many respects. She had always thought of him as a harmless, cack-handed buffoon and it was Trish who really ran the show. But she didn't feel he was genuinely affable; she felt there was an ulterior motive behind his actions, and he had said some things that made her and the others feel uncomfortable.

What had Trish said? *"Watch yourself, wandering hands."* She hadn't fully understood what she meant at the time. Maybe Dave was just a tactile person for whom it was natural to show friendship and affection by placing a hand on the shoulder or arm, or wrist. In which case Jess was worried that she may have gone down in his estimation, may have offended him such that he might tell Trish and they both might look at her in a less favourable light in future.

She didn't want to appear unfriendly or ungrateful but when he had touched her that night, she had felt fear, a fear she had not known for a long time and certainly never before at The Navigation. It'll be fine, she told herself. It was just an awkward situation and best forgotten about.

She confided in Jade one night when the pub was quiet. "Ah, we've all had that. Dave's just a prize arsehole," Jade had said, "thinks he's a babe magnet." They had both laughed at that. "He's easy to deal with, he backs off as soon as you let him know what's what." The trouble with that, Jess thought, was she was not one for asserting herself. But she had rebuffed his advances, if that's what they were, and he hadn't bothered her again since.

She was now in her fourth week at The Navigation and she had put the incident firmly behind her. She entertained no thoughts about leaving. She was comfortable in her work and wanted it to continue indefinitely but always knew that one day she would have to move on. All things come to an end.

141

One evening, at the end of her shift, she was climbing the stairs to her tiny room, undoing her apron as she walked, and met Trish coming down.

"You off now?" said Trish.

"Yes, if that's okay." It was after midnight so she didn't really need to ask, but she was perfectly willing and able to do another job for Trish if it needed doing.

"Yes, of course. Get some rest, lots of bookings tomorrow. Goodnight." They passed on the stairs with a smile.

Before Trish had taken another step, she stopped.

"Oh, by the way" – Jess turned to look down the stairway at her – "I put a bottle of perfume and some other bits in your room. Dave gave it me a while back and it really doesn't suit me. If you don't like it, just bin it, but I ain't going to use it."

"Thanks," said Jess. She was touched by that. Perfume? What else? She hadn't worn perfume or make-up … well … ever, and she wondered what else Trish had left. She went upstairs to bed. She would have something to look forward to in the morning.

Trish watched Jess go. She quite liked the perfume really, but as soon as he had told her it was what one of his old girlfriends used to wear, she went right off it. *Tosser!* But she wanted to be kind to Alice and the girl always looked a bit dowdy compared to the others. And sometimes she could detect a faint whiff of disinfectant or cleaning fluid, especially in the mornings. Probably from the chemicals, but it did her no favours. *Nice to do something for the staff.*

***

"No you ain't!" Joe is screaming at her in rage and he's grabbed her arm. "Not with no fucking Paki you ain't." Madge is behind him clinging on to his other arm which is raised and about to hit Jess and she's waiting for the blow, but he's big and he's strong and instead he whips his arm free, whirls around and punches Madge on the side of the head, "Geroff!" and she tries to grab the sideboard on the way down but hits her chin instead and lands on the floor in a heap. His eyes are bloodshot and wild and there's foam around his mouth and he stinks of sweat and booze. "No daughter of mine is going with no fuckin' Paki, you hear me? It ain't fuckin' happenin', all right? I'll beat seven bags of shit out of him and then ... oi! Bitch!" And then she's wrestled herself free and she's crashing out the room and he's behind her but he's drunk so he falls over the edge of the sofa and there's a banging on the wall from next door, "Shut up, Butlers!" and she's reached the front door, but the bolts are done up and she grabs them but they're stuck and she can't move them and she's panicking, terrified she can't get out before he gets up and grabs her and then the top bolt springs loose and then the bottom one and the door flies open and bangs the wall and she's out in the street, in the cold night air, running, running for her life ... running to Mo.

Jess woke and after a moment, realising where she was, wiped her brow and got out of bed. The window shutter had opened and was banging in the wind. She breathed in the night air and exhaled a cloud of condensing breath. *You'll be all right here.*

143

CHAPTER 20

Jess stood in front of the mirror in her room looking at her pallid skin. She had finished her cleaning just before nine but instead of going for her usual walk along the canal, she went straight back to her room to examine the items Trish had left her and was excited about trying them out.

There was a bottle of Ennui perfume, almost full, a scarlet red lipstick, mascara and some foundation. She sniffed the perfume bottle carefully, judged it perfectly pleasant and dabbed a spot or two behind each ear. Then she smoothed some of the foundation into her cheeks, which bronzed up nicely, and finished off with the lipstick. She decided to leave the mascara for today as she wasn't used to it and didn't want to make a mess. A good brush of her long brown hair and she was finished.

She examined herself in the mirror. Transformed. She felt good about herself in a way she had not felt for a long time. Self-esteem a new concept. She decided she would start her shift early today. There was always something to do setting up for the day's trading.

Still in her tee shirt and trousers she stood behind the restaurant bar facing the wall-mounted bottle racks and decided to slice some lemons to make things easier for the bar staff later on. Dave kept his distance at the other end of the bar, performing his morning ritual which involved drinking coffee and flicking through the *The Sun*. They had exchanged pleasantries but were otherwise quietly getting on with the task at hand. Trish strode in from the kitchen wearing a shoulder bag and broke the silence.

"Right, anything else we need?" Dave looked up from his paper.

"It's all on the list," he said with mild irritation, nodding to a piece of paper on the back bar near Jess. Trish ignored him and picked up the list.

"I'm just off to the bank and then the Cash & Carry to get a few things," she told Jess. "Ooh, you smell nice. Is it okay?"

"Yes, thanks," gushed Jess.

"And that colour really suits you." Jess couldn't help smiling broadly at the compliment. But Trish was on a mission and didn't have time to stop. "Make sure you take it off before service though, we don't want to give the punters the wrong idea," she said, walking the length of the bar and around the other side.

"Yes of course," said Jess.

Trish stopped briefly to kiss Dave on the cheek, and Jess was amused to see him look puzzled and vaguely disturbed.

"See you later." Trish threw her bag over her shoulder and strode out of the pub, pulling the door behind her.

Dave briefly returned his attention to his newspaper. It was only when the outside door clicked shut that he looked up and down the bar to where Jess stood, still slicing.

He closed his paper and sidled around the bar, nonchalantly adjusting bottles and spirit measures and feigning inspection of the bottle fridges until he was standing right behind her.

Jess was so absorbed in the task at hand, she hadn't paid much attention to him. Dave wrinkled his nose a little and smiled. He leant forward until his nose was as close to her hair as possible without touching and sniffed gently. She froze.

"You do smell nice," he whispered, moving his head closer until she could feel his nose against her hair. "Reminds me of one of my old girlfriends," he went on, putting his hands on her waist and pressing his body against hers, jamming her up against the back bar. The knife slipped

145

in her hand and the point stabbed the other, but although the blade was sharp, mercifully the point was blunt.

"Dave, careful, I almost cut my finger off." She tried to sound calm, but the fear was now gathering pace as she felt his hands moving on her hips. As their bodies made contact, she could feel that he was hard. "Dave, what are you doing?" His breathing had started to get heavier and he was moving his body around against hers. She tried again but she was beginning to panic. "Dave ... don't."

"Aw, c'mon Alice, I just want you to know how much you're appreciated." He was breathing steadily, deeply inhaling her fragrance as he buried his mouth in her neck. He moved his hands around to her belly and started to massage gently while continuing a slow gyration of his hips. She could feel the breath on her neck, the smell of stale coffee and her own palpitations combining to make her feel nauseous, while her own breath came in fits and starts that she couldn't control. She had to think of something to distract him, to make him stop, because she was pinned to the counter and soon the panic would overwhelm her. She blurted out the first thing that came into her head.

"Where's my bonus?" she gasped, and his grinding motion stopped. He sighed.

"Ah, I get it. Want your bonus, eh? Well, you wait there. And," he said with menace, "don't move." He released his hold, stepped back and marched off down the bar towards the office.

Jess heard the click of the door and realised she had been holding her breath. She let it out with a long sigh but then her breathing resumed its erratic pattern and she could feel her heart pounding. She tried to force her brain to think. She could scream and cry for help, but that would destroy everything. Everything she had worked for over the last few weeks. And all for what? Just because this bloke had the hots for her. She should be able to manage this without damaging her own situation. Jade had done it. Why couldn't she?

***

Dave punched the security code into the office door, threw it open and knelt down in front of the safe. Feverish and sweaty with anticipation, he fumbled with the digital lock, getting the number wrong twice before the dial turned, releasing the large door handle. The little minx, he thought to himself. She knows what she wants, all right, and he was pleased his strategy had seemed to work. Far easier to slip them a few quid than try to wear them down with his charm, wit and repartee. On the other hand, he had been enjoying the chase and he wasn't ready to catch his prey just yet. He would have preferred that she resist a bit more, but then time was not on his side, so best get on with it. And that coyness in the bar the other night. She'd been playing him for a fool, winding him up so she could get her hands on some more money. So be it. He swung the safe door open and grabbed five twenties. He'd have to think of something to cover the shortage because Trish was bound to check, but that could wait. He was in a hurry.

***

Trish sped her small Alfa along the dual carriageway towards town, tapping the wheel to the music playing on Radio 2. She had surplus cash to lodge with the bank and was then going to call into the Cash & Carry to get some dry goods and cleaning supplies they needed urgently in advance of the next scheduled delivery.

The sun was out and she was pleased to get away from the bloody pub for an hour or so. She could never imagine doing anything else for a living, but running a pub and restaurant was all-consuming. She and Dave had not had a holiday in five years, and although their relationship had soured a bit recently, she was still fond of him. If only he wasn't such a letch; but then that was what attracted her to him in the first place – although in those days, the word was "charm".

Letch was a word normally ascribed to older men, those who had no right to be attracted to or to lust over younger women. Good job he was basically a coward, and any girl could deal with him easily if they had the confidence. She knew about the incident with Jade and she was not the only one; she suspected that Katya's decision to walk was based on more than just "banter", as he had claimed. But hey-ho, she had got Alice instead. She was a much better worker and, so far, he had shown no interest in her, so that was fine.

The radio was playing a song about money and she joined in singing the lyrics and tapping the steering wheel. She trailed off. Money! She had forgotten to bring the bloody money. Left it in the safe. "Bollocks," she hissed, and scanned the road ahead. She would have to go back. There was a roundabout coming up. It would only take her ten minutes.

***

Jess had done as instructed and stayed where she was. She was paralysed in fear, her mind racing, trying to work out what to do. She had to get away from him. But how? Where? Her room? She could lock it from the inside and she would be safe until Trish got back or the others came down for work. Then she could pretend nothing had happened, and she would tell him in no uncertain terms that she was not interested. And if he persisted then she would have to tell Trish. *Let me know if he bothers you.* She thought it was a plan, of sorts. She took a deep breath and started making her escape.

Too late. She hadn't even reached the end of the bar when Dave reappeared. She turned away from him as he approached, a lascivious smile on his face, and she stood at the front of the bar by the sink. He smiled broadly and resumed his position behind her. She saw, in her peripheral vision, his right arm raised in the air and she looked up. He was dangling some twenty pound notes over her head, grinning. She looked up and went to grab the money, but he pulled it away and snorted.

"Have to be quicker than that!"

He dangled the wad again and chuckled with delight as this time, he let her take it.

Fear and anger and hurt were taking hold but she stuffed the money into her trouser pocket and stood there, waiting. He wrapped his arms around her again and pressed his body hard against her, jamming her against the sink so she couldn't move.

"Now, say 'Thank you, Dave'," he whispered in her ear as her face twisted with indignation and shame.

"Thank you, Dave," she mumbled. But his hands were still wandering, and he was pressing his hips rhythmically against her. He slid both hands under her tee shirt and his touch made her flesh creep as one hand started moving upwards, the other just as slowly in the opposite direction. His right reached her bra and he squeezed her breast while his left slipped under the waistband of her pants. But then, as she squirmed in his grip, he whispered and moaned in her ear. "You're a good girl, Alice."

The words hit her like a thunderbolt. *You're a good girl, Jess, a gooooood girl.* She went rigid and the adrenalin surged through her body, igniting the memories, the bad memories of years ago.

"Aaaagh!" she shrieked, and with all her strength, pushed back against him with a force that made him loosen his grip and sent him crashing into the back bar. She took three steps towards the door and then stopped, panting, head bowed, chest heaving, exhausted, and bewildered that her legs would not carry her away.

Jess stared at the exit door, the way out, upstairs, to safety, a sanctuary of sorts, but still she could not make her legs move. She was overcome by self-doubt, humiliated by her own stupidity and unable to rationalise what had happened, what was really at stake. And while her mind tried to understand the ramifications and the options open to her, her legs remained steadfastly glued to the floor. She realised he must have seen her hesitate and decided it was not over yet when she heard his words, laced with menace, the usually affable Dave reduced to a contemptuous sneering animal, high on infatuation and desire.

"Well, well, well," he snarled, "so the mysterious Alice has a little bit of personality in her after all," his voice heavy with sarcasm and fury, spoken to her back, her heaving shoulders. "You can't go leading a bloke on like that," he lambasted her.

Her breath stopped. She could not comprehend him, absorb or accept what he was saying. *Leading him on?* She managed to summon the energy to respond, her voice quivering as she spoke.

"I didn't … lead you on," she said, the words coming out hesitantly in shock and surprise. She kept her back to him, but she started shaking again.

"Oh, I think you did. What was that make-up and perfume all about, then?" he mocked her. "Who was that for?" Jess contorted her face in disbelief. *I was trying to seduce him?* She turned slowly to face him. He was sweating, his eyes twitching and quivering with rage.

"That was … for me," she said. *I did it for me. To make me feel better about myself. To make me look nicer and make me more confident. To do what normal young women do and make the best of themselves. Like wearing nice clothes, and nice shoes and wearing jewellery and having nice nails and styled hair. It's obvious, isn't it? Why is it not obvious?*

"For you? Leave it out. I know what you are, parading yourself down here like a little tart." Her eyes widened in outrage and her face convulsed at the slur, but she couldn't speak. "You're just a little tease, that's what you are. We don't want none of that around here!" One finger jabbing in her direction, chastising, attacking, threatening. She stood, mouth agape, ready to burst into tears, but she was too frightened and upset at his tirade to do anything.

"Now then, I'm going to give you a second chance, because that's the sort of bloke I am." She sensed a glimmer of hope and waited for him to continue, but she could see he was still angry from the sweat on his shirt and the look in his eyes. "You can either pack your bags and get off back down the towpath," he said, gesturing with his thumb to the world outside, "or you can stay here. And be nice. Which is it?" He spat out the last few words. She stood transfixed, trying to assimilate the proposition.

Why am I to blame? What did I do? How did it come to this? Everything was going fine until this morning, and now I've committed some cardinal sin which might see me back on the road to … nowhere. I just don't understand. But I can't go back. I have to move forwards. There has to be a way. I have to stay. But at what price? Maybe I just say sorry for upsetting him, that it was all a misunderstanding and I definitely won't touch the make-up again. A lesson learnt. Yes. That's it. Experience. I flew off the handle. I misunderstood. It's all my fault.

She looked at him and he was staring her down, waiting for her reply.

"I want to stay," she said finally, crushed.

"And be nice?" She felt he had seen through her and was taunting her.

"Yes," she conceded.

"Nice to me?"

Then it all dropped into place.

The perfume and make-up was just the start of it, she thought. It wound him up. *Maybe I did it deliberately? Who knows. Then I asked for money. What else is he supposed to think?*

A calm came over her. She was back where she belonged.

I provoked my father and when it got too much for me, I punished him and fell into bed with Mo and when it got too much for me, he disappeared. And now I've provoked Dave and it spiralled out of control and I spurned him. Men can't be treated like that. It's not fair and it's not what they are made of. They have needs. It's not their fault. It's mine. Anyway, it's only physical. As long as he doesn't hurt me, it doesn't mean anything. What's the big deal? I've been here before and I'll be here again. That's the way it is. It's normal. It's me that isn't normal.

Without saying another word, she turned and slowly walked to the door connecting the bar to the kitchen and staff quarters. She was calm now. Collected. Get it over with.

She turned back to look at him and he was staring open-mouthed at her, breathing heavily, nostrils flaring, bursting with anticipation. She lifted her chin up in defiance, fixed him with a steely stare, and he seemed to wither. Then she turned and slowly exited through the door.

Dave watched as the door closed behind her and he could see through the glass panel that she had turned left. Upstairs. He was feverish with lust and excitement. The bitch flirts with him, then pulls away, pretending to have no interest in money. Then she tarts herself up and flaunts it in front of him and demands money when he tries to move in. Then she changes her mind, takes his money and tries to get out of it. She knew exactly what she was doing and he was angry. But he was turned on and he would have satisfaction. He gulped loudly and checked his watch. Trish would be another forty-five minutes. Now or never.

***

Jess sat on the end of her bed, subdued, staring out of the window but not seeing. She was thinking about the lunchtime session. They were two waitresses down today, so she would be busier than usual. Lots of bookings tonight, too, so it'd be a long day. She'd stick with it and work hard and things would get better for her. She could do without this distraction, this annoying intrusion into her regime, but it was just part of the job, part of the routine. It had been part of the routine all her life. She knew her place. She accepted it. That was just the way it was for women: to do what men wanted.

The door creaked open and Dave stepped gingerly into her room. He closed the door and she slowly raised her head and looked up without expression as he moved towards her. His eyes were wide and manic and he was twitching and clenching his hands as if he didn't know what to do with them. Maybe, she thought, he imagined she would already be in bed waiting for him. But she didn't know exactly what he wanted.

He stepped forward briskly and pushed her onto the bed where she flopped flat on her back. He dropped to his knees and his hands fumbled with the button on her trousers.

Trish was one minute away from The Navigation when she encountered a problem. A bus and a large lorry were having a stand-off just before the canal bridge, causing a tailback of traffic on both sides, and she was a hundred yards behind in the queue, tapping the wheel impatiently, wondering how long it would take to clear. The frustrating thing was she could see the pub. She just couldn't get there. She considered abandoning the car and walking the rest of the way; it would be quicker, but then there was nowhere to leave it and she still had to get to the bank. She stabbed at her phone, mounted on the centre console. Dave could get the banking bag out of the safe and tell someone, Alice maybe, to bring it to her. Then if she could turn round, she could get on her way. The ringtone played out through the car speakers. Once, twice, three times, four and then she heard a familiar voice. Her own.

"Thanks for calling The Navigation—"

"What?" she shrieked, her frustration getting the better of her. "Where the hell is everyone?" She shouted at the pub pointlessly through the car windscreen. *I can't leave him alone for five minutes! What's he doing?*

But then the car in front of her moved and she cancelled the call, muttering angrily under her breath. "Just wait till I get in there." Within a minute, she was pulling into the car park, bringing the Alfa to an abrupt stop, its front wheels skidding briefly on the gravel. She leapt out of the car. She was now half an hour behind schedule and irritated at herself for being foolish and wasting time. She walked briskly up the ramp to the side door.

***

She knelt on the bed, naked from the waist down, face flat on the duvet which she gripped with both hands, and he was inside her, thrusting frantically, groaning and sweating with the exertion.

She was elsewhere. Serene, calm, disinterested, unmoved by this loveless, animalistic, physical act of no importance, this primordial human function bereft of humanity. She had been here before.

She's been alone for three days now and Mo has only called once to tell her to take a suit to the dry cleaners, and she's gone to bed but the flat is deathly quiet and all she can think of is cleaning the kitchen again tomorrow, because there is nothing else to do, but then there's a noise and she's frightened but before she knows what to do, the bedroom door opens and it's Mo and she tries to get up and hold him because he's back, but he ignores her and doesn't say anything and then she's flat on her back and he's half-naked on top of her and it's not pleasant like it used to be and she's calling his name, 'Mo! Mo! You're hurting me ...' but he carries on and then turns her over and he carries on and it hurts and she's crying but he grunts for a while and then he lets out a big breath and suddenly he's a dead weight crushing her, they lie still and then he gets off her and puts his clothes back on and leaves without a word and she turns over and goes back to sleep ... her job is done again.

It would be over soon and she could get back to work, and Dave would move on to someone else. They all did. She heard his breath convulsing as his gasps reached a crescendo and for a moment thought he might expire, but then, in the background, another sound, a cry, a call she recognised.

"Dave?" Trish shouted as she strode through the deserted bar. She was mad as hell to find the door unlocked, and no one about, so anyone could have wandered in and nicked a bottle or two. The first thing she was going to do was find her feckless husband and give him a good slap. "Dave?" she shouted again, and headed for the door at the end of the bar. The sound penetrated the ceiling and reached the rooms above.

"Uh?" Dave froze. Then realisation hit and he panicked, slamming into reverse gear. Within a second he was stumbling over his pants, trying to pull them up and run at the same time like a kid in a sack race, and crashing out of the door which swung open, hit the floor stop and bounced back to slam with a loud bang.

He raced along the corridor and down the stairs, desperate to make progress, and equally anxious to be as quiet as possible. Halfway down he stopped, trying to work out where Trish had gone, but when he heard someone punching in the digital code to the office door, he finished tiptoeing down the stairs.

To his left, he could hear the clunk of the safe door, so turned right and re-entered the bar, still re-buckling his belt and tucking in his shirt, to take up position at the far end of the bar on the floor in front of a bottle fridge. He dropped to his knees, ripped open the door and pulled out several bottles.

Jess had stifled a cry at his clumsy withdrawal, flopped forward and remained motionless on her front. She stayed there for a moment, wincing at the burning sensation, her mind replaying. Hearing Trish's voice had interrupted her thoughts, had triggered something inside her, and she was momentarily unsure where she was or what she was doing. *What just happened? Was that just a dream?* She took a moment to gather herself and then reality struck her like a slap on the face. *What were you thinking?* She suddenly felt alone again. Manipulated, subjugated, abused, terrorised, violated and ultimately discarded. By them both.

Trish had warned her what he was like … *Watch yourself* … but had given her the perfume … *You smell like one of my old girlfriends* … and then left them together, left her to her fate. *There's no such thing.* Had she not imagined for one moment what the consequences might be? Did Trish plan this to test her and catch him out?

She felt betrayed and lost and lonely. She dragged herself up to a sitting position on the end of the bed and swept back her long brown hair. It was over. There was no going back.

Her life here in this place was as pointless as it had been before she arrived, as futile and worthless as it had been back in Wellingford. Everything Jess had discarded and run away from had been here waiting for Alice, and Alice had failed just as Jess had failed. She felt totally drained, sapped of energy and will. She had made a terrible mistake and paid the price, again.

And then, as she contemplated the hopelessness of her situation, she heard from deep within her soul a calling, an exhortation, a demand to take responsibility and act. She crossed both arms and grabbed the bottom of her tee shirt, lifting it over her head, using it to dry between her legs, grimacing, repulsed, cleaning away the violation. She tossed the sticky crumpled tee shirt into the corner of the room. No more.

He was just in time. Trish marched back into the bar clutching the money, looking flustered.

"There you are!" she said. He stood up and did his best to look casual and nonchalant despite his heart beating twenty to the dozen.

"Hello, love. That was quick?" Trish slapped the wallet down on the bar top in frustration and put her hands on her hips.

"Only forgot the bloody money, didn't I?" Then, noticing that he looked a little discomposed, she said, "Are you all right?"

"Me? Yeah," he said offhandedly, but it came out as a squeak and lacked conviction.

He could feel sweat on his brow and under his arms and hoped she didn't notice. She was looking at him strangely, so he turned back to the bottle rack on the wall and aimlessly started to rearrange them. But from the corner of his eye, he saw Trish turn her attention to the space on the bar where Alice had been slicing lemons. She was frowning. The job had been abandoned; half a lemon and one or two slices on the chopping board next to the knife. She was looking puzzled.

"Alice gone out?" Dave had to think fast.

"Gone upstairs, I think." His insouciance was impressive, he thought.

"I wondered whether she'd like to come with me. I'll go ask her."

She had travelled only two steps before he turned and blurted out, with rather more urgency then he intended, "No!"

Trish stopped in her tracks and turned her head to look at him. He needed to justify his outburst, and without time to prepare a plausible explanation, embellished the lie with another.

"She said she wasn't feeling well, went for a lie down," he said cautiously, willing her to swallow it and walk away. He tried to remain composed, but the sweat tingled in his armpits and he felt it drip down his side. Trish may indeed have swallowed it, but it made no difference.

"Oh, I'd better go see if she's okay, then."

"NO!" He calmed himself, wiped a hand across his dry mouth, deciding she needed be reassured with another lie. "She's okay. Just a headache," he said, following it up with a shrug of indifference.

"Oh. Okay." Trish appeared concerned, looking like she was thinking through the options, and he waited nervously for her to reach a conclusion. Which she did. "Well, I'll be off then."

He was just about home and dry. When she'd gone, he would go up and see Alice, check she was okay and explain to her what she had to say when Trish got back. Who knows? He may even get second helpings. She hadn't really participated, and he had had to do all the work himself, but it had been worth it. Once she had acknowledged who was in charge, any resistance had crumbled, and that meant in future he could pretty much do with her whatever he wanted. *Result!*

He had had a lucky escape, but then the adrenalin rush from doing something illicit, and the fear of getting caught, was as stimulating and exciting as the chase, the capture and the subjugation of the prey; not to mention the final tasting.

Then he saw Trish coming towards him and he recoiled slightly, but all she did was peck his cheek and turn away. He breathed again and tried to control his heartbeat which had spiked momentarily. She was walking away. *Stay calm*.

But she had only taken four steps when she stopped. She looked up and into space, as if trying to focus her eyes on a patch of thin air above her head. Her nose twitched. She frowned and then her expression morphed gradually from confusion to speculation to realisation and, finally, conclusion. Dave's heartbeat had slowed for a second or two but as his wife stopped, stood still for a moment then slowly

159

turned around to face him, it skipped and began pounding again in his chest. *She's coming back!*

He watched with disbelief and mounting terror as she approached him, slowly, remorselessly closing the gap between them, and he stepped back involuntarily; but he was at the end of the bar and there was nowhere to go. Her unwavering eyes transfixed him as she approached and he couldn't tear his own away as she bore down relentlessly on him, like a slow-motion car crash.

She stopped when they were twelve inches apart and, without blinking, sniffed once, and then, looking down to his trousers, sniffed again, longer this time, drawing in the cocktail of scents. The only sound he could hear was the background drone of the bottle fridges and his heart thumping in his head, and he couldn't stand the silence any longer.

"Whaaat?" he complained. She stepped back, and he thought he had got away with it so he relaxed for an instant. But she had only made space.

Before he could react, her left arm swung in a wide arc with the speed of a cobra and her flattened hand struck his right cheek like a wrecking ball hitting a building.

"Bastard!" she screamed, as his head went sideways with the force of the blow, knocking him off balance. He struggled to right himself.

"What the f—!" he wailed, clutching his face as he came back up for more. But she had moved up close again. Her teeth were clenched and the fury burst out of her in a rage he had never been seen before.

"You. Lecherous. Fucking. Scumbag." Her words, measured, slow and deliberate, chilled him to the bone. He had never seen her like this, and he was very afraid. "You had her, didn't you?"

Survival mode. *Deny, deny, deny.*

"Had who?" he wailed again.

Tell her it's black even though we both know it's white. Deny, Deny. Deny.

Her words hissed through bared teeth, snarling, preparing to bite like a Doberman terrorising its victim.

"I can smell her, for Christ's sake!" she said, rigid with apoplexy.

Deny, deny, deny.

"Smell who?" This outrageous denial tipped her over the edge.

"Right, that's it!" she screamed, and swung at him again with her left hand. But this time he saw it coming and caught her wrist before she could land the blow, so she swung her right arm instead, but he caught that one too. Their hands and arms interlocked, they swung and swayed like a pair of drunken ballroom dancers.

"Get off, you crazy bitch!" he shouted as she tried to wrestle free, but unable to break his grip and with both arms disabled, she deployed the ultimate weapon, bringing her knee up to his groin with the power of a pile driver.

"Aargh!" screamed Dave as her knee crushed into his scrotum, instinctively releasing his hold on her arms before crumpling like a demolished building, pulling an ice bucket and tray of glasses on top of himself on his way to the floor.

But she was already away, running down the bar, through the door and up the stairs two at a time, the sound of breaking glass, crashing bottles and metal trays and wails of anguish and pain echoing around her.

She had not exerted so much energy for many years and it had all been fuelled by adrenalin, but having reached the top of the stairs, she was puffing and out of breath. She raced along the corridor to Alice's room, and without knocking or stopping for a moment to consider what she might find, burst through the door.

161

"Alice! What happened?" she said without waiting to assess the situation in front of her.

Jess stood at the side of her bed, calmly packing her rucksack, dressed in the same clothes in which she had arrived, but clean this time. She was still wearing the lipstick, and the fragrance Trish had given her lingered in the air. Jess said nothing, just kept stuffing her white tee shirts and few possessions into her bag.

Trish was disorientated for a moment and didn't understand what she was seeing. The girl should be traumatised, weeping on the bed, battered and bruised, or perhaps even half clothed; but there she was, cool as ice, packing her bags. She thought for moment she had made a terrible mistake.

No, it's not possible.

There was no doubt. The perfume, the unmistakeable … smell. She looked at the girl for a sign of distress, a flicker of emotion. There was none.

"Did he" – she hesitated, she couldn't bring herself to utter the word she was thinking – "force you—?" She left the rest unspoken as Jess looked up quickly and interrupted her.

"No. I let him," she said, and then simply resumed her task, which confused Trish even more. It was inconceivable she would not resist. Maybe she had wanted to. Maybe she liked it. Maybe … She had to know.

"But why?" she demanded stepping forward, her anger returning.

"Why what?" said Jess. Trish raised her voice higher.

"Why didn't you just say no?" She needed to understand, understand what it all meant and why she wasn't getting an answer. Jess stopped packing her things and looked at her as if she had gone mad. She gave Trish a patronising look as if explaining two plus two to a child, and said, with a casual conviction,

"It's what men do."

Trish looked at her, stunned and bewildered, unable to process the meaning, astonished at the girl's statement, simply said and so casually delivered with such certitude. Then the anger took hold again.

"Stay there!" she demanded, pointing to the spot on the floor where Jess stood, and then whirled around and charged back out the door along the corridor, careering down the stairs, her shouts of "Dave! Dave! Dave!" gradually receding.

Jess stared at the open door and stood for moment, dismayed and overwhelmed, consumed with self-doubt and distrust of her own beliefs. As she spoke her last words to Trish, and before they had even finished coming out of her mouth, she began to doubt herself. There was something wrong in what she had said, something illogical, something vaguely unsound, and when she saw in Trish's look of horror, her inability to comprehend her meaning, she knew what it was. She needed to get away from here. From this madness. She sat down on the edge of the bed.

There was no way the damage could be repaired. Trish was incandescent with rage and looked like she was about to murder her husband. She seemed mad at her, too. How could she explain what had happened when the woman did not even begin to understand the way of things?

A fear came over her and from deep down she remembered running away from her father, and then running away from her home and her life; and here she was, running away again. Where was she running to now? She had thought The Navigation was a sanctuary, a place of sanity where normal things happened and people were nice to each other and everyone got on okay and men didn't see women as chattels and objects to be used and discarded. But it was just the same and it would be the same anywhere she went. *Wouldn't it?*

But she had made her decision. The bridges were already burning. The mistake she had made half an hour ago was to delay, to hesitate. Time to act. Now. She jumped up, closed her rucksack, tied the self-inflating mattress on top and threw on her red jacket.

Then she remembered the money Dave had given her and fished in her trouser pocket to pull it out: a £100 bonus. Money for sex. She knew what that made her and she felt a wave of disgust. She threw it on the bed, the notes separating and fluttering down onto the still crumpled duvet.

She ran out of the door but remembered halfway down the corridor that her tent was under the bed. She dumped her rucksack and raced back to her room, got down on her knees and felt around under the bed until she located the orange disc. She dragged it out and into the corridor to see Jade appearing from the room at the other end, wearing tee shirt and pyjama bottoms, tousle-haired and bleary-eyed.

"Alice, what's going on?" Jess ignored her, retrieved her rucksack and bundled herself down the stairs. "Alice?" cried Jade to her back, but she was gone.

She reached the bottom of the stairs and bumped into a frightened KP, an escapee from the kitchen where Trish and Dave were shouting and screaming at each in a fierce argument.

"Do you realise what you've done to that girl?"

"I didn't do nothing."

"You shagged her!"

"It was nothing!"

"Nothing?"

"Yeah, nothing. She was gagging for it."

"Don't give me that, you bastard."

"Look, she came on to me."

She slipped into the bar area and mercifully it was empty, but she knew any minute Jade and the others would appear, wondering what the commotion was all about.

164

"You're a sad, filthy letch who can't keep his hands to himself or his dick in his pants."

"Yeah, well you're a sad old crone."

"What?"

"You heard."

"Just because I don't fancy you anymore."

"If I got a bit more off you, I wouldn't be tempted."

"Don't you dare blame me!"

Jess sprinted for the side door but as she passed the centre of the long bar something caught her eye and she stopped. There was a transparent envelope on the bar and she could see it contained a wad of cash.

"Yeah, well a man has needs and you don't deliver."

"What's that supposed to mean?"

"It means it ain't my fault."

"It ain't your fault you raped a young girl?"

"Now wait a minute, it weren't rape."

"And what would you call it, then?"

"Well, she didn't struggle."

"I can't believe you said that! She didn't bloody struggle!?"

And then there was a crash and the sound of breaking crockery.

"Ow – watch out! Ow – for Christ's sake!"

The pots and pans were flying now.

Jess hesitated, then on impulse, leant over and grabbed the envelope, stuffing it into her jacket pocket. She raced for the door that led out onto the canal, the same door she had arrived through a month ago. She ran the twenty yards to the towpath and looked frantically up and down the canal. Which way? She had come from the left, which was north, and wanted to go south, but south was the obvious way to go and they would know.

She was confused but had to make a decision. To the north boats were coming down the locks and there were people on the towpath. Another backpacker in a red jacket was a hundred yards away and walking steadily north. That way. No! The sounds were muffled now but still audible.

"She's a tart, she'll do anything for money."

"Right, that's enough. Pack up and get out."

"I ain't going nowhere."

"I'll call the police."

"And tell 'em what?"

"Tell 'em what you did to that poor girl."

"Tell 'em what you like, I ain't bothered.

Crash.

"Ow – bitch. Oi – that cost money!"

Crash.

Jess was on the verge of panic, caught in a crisis of indecision, when she heard the sound of a large diesel engine starting up in the car park. She caught a glimpse of a white truck reversing away from the kitchen door and instinctively ran towards it, crossing the patio filled with wooden tables and benches, darting in and out of the gaps between them. It was the laundry truck, finishing its weekly delivery of clean restaurant linen and taking away the dirty stuff. She ran to the driver's side and banged on the door, startling the driver who rolled down his window.

"Can you give me a lift?" she asked desperately, chest heaving.

"Er, yeah, all right," said the driver, so she ran around the other side of the truck and clambered in, dragging her stuff behind her. The truck rolled off out of the car park and turned onto the main road, circling around the pub towards the canal bridge fifty yards away.

By the time the truck had mounted the bridge, Dave had appeared from the same exit in hot pursuit, frantically looking for her, blood trickling from a gash above his eyebrow and dripping onto his shirt. He wore a crazed expression as he scanned the towpath for signs of the bitch who'd taken his money. Then he saw her in the distance, heading north on the towpath, red jacket, backpack, long hair, walking steadily. He set off in pursuit.

"Oi!" he shouted as he ran towards her, "Come back with my money, you bitch!"

The backpacker turned and was astonished to see a bloodied angry man shouting, waving and running towards her. She took fright and broke into a run, hotly pursued by Dave.

Through the passenger window, Jess watched the chase with horror as the truck crossed over the canal bridge, taking her and everything she owned out of the village, heading west.

CHAPTER 21

The church clock was striking twelve noon as the truck pulled into Newhampton market square and, with a hiss of brakes, drew to a halt.

Jess thanked the driver, John, climbed down from the cab and shut the door. She hadn't been here before and didn't have a plan as to where she was going next. It hadn't mattered to her which way the truck was going as long as it was far away from The Navigation, but she had had the wit to establish early on that neither was John heading in the direction of Wellingford. Taking her back to where she had started would have been a cruel irony, but thankfully she was now fifty miles further away than ever.

She was still coming to terms with the morning's events and hadn't spoken much on the way, preferring to doze with her head against the window, but no sooner had her feet touched the pavement than something loomed large in her mind.

She felt in her inside pocket and pulled out the banking wallet. There was a paying-in slip attached to the bundle of cash on which was printed "JD & TP Morley T/A The Navigation", together with bank account details and the address of a NatWest branch. The sum of £1,220 was handwritten in the amount box.

She couldn't rationalise her behaviour in picking it up. It had just been in the heat of the moment. She hadn't been thinking. She had never stolen anything in her life and felt a sickening guilt about it. No matter what they had done to her, and she was still not quite sure what that was, she hadn't yet processed the bizarre sequence of events that led up to it, she felt ashamed, and despite having a desperate need for it, the money did not belong to her and she couldn't keep it. She had to give it back.

She looked around at the people and the cars and the buses and the general bustle of life at midday in an English market town and surmised there would be a bank nearby. Within five minutes, she found three, all within fifty yards of each other, and one of them was a small NatWest.

There was only one other customer inside and he had just finished his business at the glass-fronted counter when Jess wandered in. The woman cashier greeted her with a smile. "I'm so sorry, will you excuse me for a moment? I'll be right back," she said, before disappearing behind a partition.

Jess was suddenly nervous. Nervous that maybe word had got out that she had taken the money and that the woman would soon return with the manager or the police and she would be arrested and … She stopped herself and her racing mind. If they thought she had stolen it, they wouldn't expect her to turn up at a bank fifty miles away. Unless they had tracked down the driver of the truck.

She slid the wallet under the counter and quickly retreated onto the High Street. Best no questions are asked, she thought. The cashier would find the cash in the wallet to be £20 short of the amount written on the payslip, and Jess had no idea what would happen about that but decided they would work it out. She had calculated she was owed at least £50 for the last few days' work so convinced herself that taking £20 was more than fair and less than she deserved. Anyway, she would be hungry later and needed to buy some water too.

The High Street led onto London Road and Jess soon found herself standing on a road bridge spanning a wide river, looking downstream, just as she had on the day she left Wellingford. She watched the current drift slowly and it drew her in again, beckoning her to join it on its journey. Another new start, she thought.

Both sides of the riverbank featured grassy areas with cultivated flowerbeds and pathways with a succession of park benches, and there were many people out on a summer's day, young mothers pushing prams and older people simply enjoying the fresh air.

She opted for the far side and followed the path from the bridge down to the riverbank. The water was home to a large number of ducks, geese and swans who milled around, endlessly searching for sustenance, although she thought they all looked pretty well fed despite various signs urging people not to feed them.

She made her way to an empty bench facing the river and decided she might eat something before starting on her journey. She had bought a sandwich and a bottle of water from a shop in the High Street, so placed the brown paper bag on the bench, laid down her tent bag and threw off the straps of her rucksack, placing it on the grass next to the tent.

She sat down wearily on a bench that bore a black plaque, she noticed, as many of them did:

> In Loving Memory, Able Seaman William Jarvis
> b. 12 September 1910 d. 26 June 1982.

She wondered who he might have been.

A woman stood by the water's edge and, despite the instructions to the contrary, threw crusts of bread amongst an assemblage of assorted waterfowl who snapped and gobbled hungrily at the food. She appeared elderly and dishevelled and poorly dressed in a woolly hat, heavy ill-fitting overcoat, black socks and most incongruously of all, dirty old trainers.

Jess suddenly felt overcome with a profound weariness, and then, from nowhere, a surge of despair took hold and she felt her body sag and tip forward until she had to support her head with her hands. She wanted to shut out the world, shut out the sound of the ducks and geese clacking and the ripples and splashes and plops of the water and the cries of the little

170

children playing in the park and the cars and sirens and wind. She wanted to go to a dark silent place where no one could harm her, where she would be safe. She knew where that was, and it seemed strangely alluring. *The only option?*

She closed her eyes and as the ambient sounds blended into a muddled roar, she felt calmness, a serenity and composure that was somehow empowering. She started to drift off into a bubble of subconsciousness, but something burst it. Someone was speaking.

"Are you all right, dear?" Jess sat up with a start. The old woman who had been feeding the ducks was sitting on the bench next to her. She hadn't heard her walk the twenty feet from the riverbank or felt her sit down, so lost had she been in her own thoughts. The woman was very old, thought Jess, easily over seventy or maybe even a hundred, she couldn't tell. But she had a kindly face which radiated genuine concern, and Jess, ever polite, felt compelled to respond.

"Oh … er, yes." She sat up and pushed back her hair. The old woman went on, still obviously concerned.

"It's just that you looked a bit, you know, tired."

Tired was one way of putting it, thought Jess, and although she was touched by the woman's apparent concern for her wellbeing, especially one who herself looked like life had dealt a poor hand, she was not minded to explain how she felt or why. She decided to change the subject and nodded at the birds still quacking and honking on the river.

"They're a hungry lot."

The woman turned her head to the river to follow her gaze.

"Oh yes," came the brief affirmation and Jess thought that might be the end of the exchange. "Mind you," the old woman continued after a moment, "they ain't got much else to worry about, have they? Just finding something to eat and looking after the little 'uns."

Jess nodded but couldn't think of much else to say.

171

"That's the girls, of course," the old woman went on, "it's them boys that cause all the bother. Always fighting with each other, all trying to be top dog," she declared with satisfaction at the euphemism. "Some things never change," she added, a resigned weariness in her voice.

They sat quietly for a moment watching a swan family, mother, father and seven cygnets, glide gracefully up the river. Jess decided she might as well have her sandwich so opened the brown paper bag, pulled out a triangular carton and tore off the perforated seal. She pulled out one half of the sandwich but then felt a wave of discomfort about taking the first bite. The old woman wasn't showing any interest, but Jess had already judged her to be poor and therefore probably hungry too, so she thought it only polite to offer. She leant over, proffering the open sandwich carton.

"Would you like a sandwich?" The old woman turned in surprise and her eyes lit up with delight.

"Ooh, thank you, dear. I was feeling a bit peckish." She reached into the carton and pulled out the other half, which she waved in the direction of her avian audience who quacked and clacked and hooted in unison. "I gave my last crust to that lot!"

She took a large bite out of the corner and sat back chewing contentedly. Jess watched her for a moment with mild amusement, but then decided she wasn't hungry after all and put her half back. She would have it later, for supper.

Apart from the occasional "mmm" as the old woman chewed and swallowed, they sat in silence until she had finished, signalled by a brisk brushing away of dropped crumbs from the front of her overcoat.

"Would you like some water?" asked Jess, offering an unopened plastic bottle.

"Naah," she replied, "I'll just want to wee." Jess smirked at the thought and put the bottle back in the bag. The old woman sighed and sat back, her tongue working to extract the last morsels of sandwich from the back of her teeth, and then smacked her lips.

"You know. I was your age once," she said, looking at Jess. "Seems like a long time ago. But it feels like yesterday. I don't know where the time goes!" She left the question hanging before declaring, "I think it goes faster and faster the older you get." Jess thought there was probably a scientific explanation to prove this could not be true, but the woman had evidence of her own. "You get on with your life and then before you know it, whoosh! It's all gone." Jess didn't know how to respond to this but needn't have worried, as it seemed the old woman was content to talk out loud.

"We didn't have much when we was young," she went on. "Father was away for months at a time, workin' on ships and that, and I had to look after me little brothers after mum died. But we was happy." She smiled at the reminiscence. "We managed, we made do, you couldn't do anything else." Jess wondered where this was going.

"And don't fret about stuff you can do nothing about, me Dad always said," she said proudly. "And don't give up." Her tone had suddenly become authoritative and thoughtful and Jess recognised the change. The old woman had stopped babbling and had become incongruously erudite. "That's what he said when he went away: 'Never give up'." She remained silent for a moment as the thought sank into Jess's head.

"And when he came home, ooh ... he'd bring us sweets from India and tea from China and beads from Africa! Then he was off again." Jess smiled, charmed by the image of a loving father bringing home presents from his travels to exotic places, seeing his young sons and his daughter acting out the part of surrogate mother, and wondered what age this old lady had been. Sixteen? Seventeen, maybe? She could only guess.

173

"But one day" – the old woman had turned serious and Jess sensed a foreboding – "he never came back." Jess looked at her uneasily, expecting the worst. "They said his ship was missing and I thought, well, that's it, might as well jump in the river!" Jess's heart sank and she tried to imagine what it could have been like for her, a teenage girl, both parents gone and little mouths to feed. She was not the only one to have suffered hardship, had to battle adversity, when everything seemed stacked against you and you had lost all hope.

"But he never gave up," she said defiantly, pride welling up inside her, and then with some elation, "and we never gave up neither! And, ooh … it must have been two years, he came walking up the backyard with his duffle bag over his shoulder as if nothing had happened!" Jess's eyes widened and now she couldn't tear them away from the old woman, whose voice was gradually rising in a crescendo.

"And I ran, and I flung meself into his arms and he lifted me up high and I hugged him, and it was as if I was on top of the world!" she trumpeted, raising her eyes to the heavens, visibly moved at the memory.

Jess closed her eyes as the image of the young woman and her heroic father embracing loomed large in her mind and she battled to hold back the tears as they welled up inside her. The old woman's euphoria subsided as quickly as it came, as reality brought her back to earth.

"They're all gone now," she said quietly, "there's no one left. Just me." But there was pathos in her words as she put one hand on her coat where her heart might be and patted it. "But they're still in 'ere, I talk to them every day. It's what keeps you going."

Jess looked at her again, unsure of what she meant. The old woman sensed it and looked into her eyes.

"Love," she declared. "That's what keeps you going. You don't need nothing else." Her smile washed over Jess like a warm, comfy blanket and something stirred inside

174

her. She wasn't sure she knew what love was. She wasn't sure she had ever experienced it before. She always thought she had loved her mum and had cried when she heard the beatings her mum had endured at the hands of her husband, the man she loved, but who Jess hated. *So what did it mean?* Then she thought of Leila and the meaning was clear.

"I bet you got a lotta love in you." Jess looked up and saw the old woman was addressing her personally. "You'll be all right." The old woman was smiling at her, reassuring, determined. "Love will keep you strong and keep you going. And in the end, you and yours will all be all right. You'll see," her words delivered with such certitude that despite the absence of any justification, Jess was compelled to believe her.

Jess fought back her emotions. She wasn't used to showing them and they rarely rose to the surface, but she had been profoundly moved by this old woman and her simple story and she wondered what it might mean to her. For her. She decided it was time to go. Time to move on. She still had a long way to go. She rose to her feet and picked up her rucksack.

"Are you off home now, dear?" the old woman said. Jess smiled at the unintended irony and wondered where the old woman lived, where "home" might be. She noticed again the plaque fixed to the back of the park bench: Able Seaman William Jarvis, and the inevitable thought crossed her mind. She shook it off.

Er, no. I'm just going for a walk." Well that was certainly the truth.

"Oh, then have a nice walk, wherever it is you're going to."

"Well, must be off. Nice to meet you. Bye," she said awkwardly and headed downstream as the old woman called after her.

"Bye, dear. Take care. Don't go talking to no strangers!" and then she sat back on the bench, smiling. Happy and contented.

Jess had only gone twenty yards when something made her stop, and instinctively she turned around. The bench was empty. The old woman was nowhere to be seen.

CHAPTER 22

Jess followed the river as far as the footpath allowed, but like the rivers before and unlike the canals, it gradually petered out as it left the town. So she was forced to go across country again, taking the first footpath that appeared to go in the direction she wanted: south.

It was late afternoon, she judged around 4 p.m., and the path took her across wheat fields to the edge of a copse, which then spread out and upwards over a hillock that stretched far into the distance. She spotted a nature trail sign that directed her into the trees and took her uphill on a winding path, higher and higher through an ever-thickening wood. The afternoon sun streamed through the trees from the south-west like spotlights on a stage, and when each shaft of light reached the ground, it was dappled by the leaves of the trees above.

Upwards and upwards she climbed, until after thirty minutes the trees opened out onto a narrow plateau, a ridge from which she could see open countryside for miles on either side. The path followed the ridge as far as she could see, and with the sun at three o'clock, she calculated that it was taking her due south, which was what she wanted.

Two hundred yards along the ridge she stopped for a rest, unloading her rucksack and tent from her tired shoulders and laying it on the thick, coarse grass. She sat herself down and took a mouthful of water from the bottle she had bought at lunchtime. It would only just last the night, she thought, so she had to be careful. One of tomorrow's tasks would be to find some more, but she had enough to wash down the half a sandwich she had kept from earlier in the day.

She gazed out to the west and in the clear air saw rolling fields and hedgerows, isolated farm buildings and in the far distance, a conurbation she couldn't identify. The whole world seemed to stretch out before her and she felt insignificant in her tiny space. She wondered what lay ahead for her and where in the world she might find peace, if she found it at all. She reached into her inside jacket pocket and pulled out the crumpled picture of Leila, and the three-year-old's cheeky face beamed at her and she smiled tears of joy and heartache.

She would be four now, her birthday would have been last weekend. One thing of which she was sure, whatever Mo had been he would not have hurt their daughter and she clung onto that hope. It was all she had.

Clouds were forming from the south-west and the temperature had dropped. But a gap in the cloud caused a sparkle of light to shine on the ground far in the distance below her and she judged it was light reflecting off water, a river perhaps, probably the same river she had left this morning. It was too early to set up camp and the top of the ridge was too exposed, so she elected to make her way down towards the river and once the light had gone, find a sheltered spot to set up her tent. She stuffed Leila's picture back into her pocket and got to her feet.

**

Peter had been cruising for a couple of hours since lunchtime and had originally planned to cruise on to Lower Croxley where there were decent moorings and a pub where he could have a nice dinner. But the weather was taking a turn for the worse and he could see dark clouds gathering ahead. He judged he was a good two to three hours from civilisation and would not get there before the rain came down, and the weather forecast had suggested it would be heavy.

He knew this part of the river well, and around the next bend he remembered the land on his right would open out onto a wide field where the bank was vertical and clear of shrubs and trees, where he could safely moor for the night. He would have time to affix the cockpit cover before the weather broke and keep the old girl as waterproof as possible. Batten down the hatches, so to speak. He would then hunker down for the night and carry on tomorrow.

Within thirty minutes he had arrived at his destination, and as the river appeared otherwise deserted, he had his pick of the bank. The great advantage of this section was that the bank was more or less on a level with the deck, so he did not have to leap off the boat with a rope and risk a poor landing. They had taught him how to roll in parachute training, but that was over forty years ago; and at seventy, he decided it was asking for trouble to try that technique here, especially when there was no one around to help if he got into trouble. No, he would bring *Carician* in dead slow, parallel to the bank and make sure she was at a complete stop before stepping off.

The field came into view and he slowed the boat until she came to a halt, reverse drive engaged and engine revs at tickover, just enough to counter the current which would otherwise pull him downstream. *Carician* sidled naturally into the bank and he waited for a few moments with his hands off the controls to make sure she would not drift. If the bow drifted outwards once he had stepped off then he still had a chance to get back on and try again, but the thing he feared most was losing control of the stern and being stuck on the bank. He chose his moment, threw a hammer and two spikes onto the bank and then carefully stepped off, rope in hand. He checked for movement and there was none, so as quickly as he could, hammered in one spike and wound the rope around to partially secure the stern.

Then, because running was out of the question, he walked briskly to the front with hammer and second spike in

179

hand, hammered it into the ground, and was able to reach over and grab the rope he had left hanging over the forward deck rail. He did a quick wrap around the spike, walked back to the stern and reboarded. He took the engines out of drive and waited until he was satisfied the boat held. Then he got off again, hammered both spikes in further, tied secure knots around each and took them back on board to wrap around the deck cleats.

There was a distinct chill in the air but he felt warm after his exertions and there was still more to do. Back on board, he opened up the storage locker on the rear deck and dragged out a heavy blue canvas cover. He manhandled it over the cockpit windscreen, stretching it out over the entire rear deck, huffing and puffing at the effort involved in first lifting it up, then unfolding and positioning it so all the clips and ties lined up with the small chrome cleats on the superstructure.

He stopped for a moment to catch his breath. *You're getting too old for this malarkey*. He then resumed his task, the final elastic strap hooking on twenty minutes after he had started. Access to the rear hatch now cut off, he sidestepped his way along the landside decking and re-entered the boat through the forward hatch. Mercifully, the rain had held off, but it would come soon, he thought. But he was exhausted, and he looked at his watch: 6 p.m. *Get the kettle on. No, bollocks, get the wine open. You deserve something after all that work.* He pulled the forward hatch shut. He and *Carician* were secure.

***

Jess had left the ridge, and as the skies darkened, she found herself again in the woods but this time descending gradually. She had left the designated footpath in favour of

180

an unsigned track that she judged might take her closer to the river. She would need to find food tomorrow, and although logic dictated the marked footpath might lead her to a road and then perhaps to a village, she was instinctively drawn to the water and was sure she would stumble across civilisation at some point.

Her priority, though, was to find somewhere to pitch her tent. She thought she was in for some rain and she wanted to get set up for the night before it came down rather than spend a very uncomfortable night in damp clothes. But the woods were too dense and she needed to keep going until she found somewhere suitable.

Eventually, she entered a clearing where the land opened out into a field of wheat on her right, the woods continuing on to her left. She skirted the perimeter of the field and after half an hour came to a hedgerow that divided it from a field of open grass, and she decided this was a suitable spot.

The tent flew out of its bag and landed upright as if by magic. She had last used it four weeks ago and was relieved to find it was still in one piece, although it still bore some of the muddy stains it had picked up on its last outing. She pressed the guide pins into the ground with her walking boots, pulling the ropes taut – she hadn't lost the knack – and crawled in, pulling her rucksack behind her.

She unrolled her self-inflating mattress, spread her sleeping bag out on top and flopped over on her back. She dozed for another half hour, before deciding it was time for dinner. *Dinner!* She suddenly craved a bowl of pasta or egg and chips or a slice of pizza or bangers and mash, simple food that the chefs at The Navigation knocked up for the staff and which to her had been total luxury.

She thought about her time there and wondered whether Trish and Dave had called the police to report the theft of money. If they had called the police, then they may well trace the driver of the truck and he would explain where he had taken her. But that would all take several days, by which time they would find out that the money had ended up in their bank account, so no crime had been committed, not by her anyway, and surely no sane person would pursue her for the missing £20.

She remembered Trish and Dave arguing, no, screaming at each other, and she shuddered at the memory. Trish had accused him of rape and Jess remained deeply disturbed by it. The more she thought about it, the more she realised that that was about the sum of it. No, she hadn't struggled, nor tried to fight him off. And no, despite her token resistance at the beginning she hadn't said no to him. Her acquiescence had been a contributory factor, had maybe even spurred him on; although she couldn't imagine what might have happened if she had not given in.

Trish's face, aghast that Jess should be so casual about it, was etched on her mind. The fact remained she had endured such treatment before, at the hands of both her father and her husband, and had seen it perpetrated by her husband's friends on young women who seemed to accept it and knew no better. She was just the same, she thought.

Over time she had come to consider such behaviour to be normal. It had been second nature to her and although she took no pleasure in it, she had become inured to its effects. Maybe it was a survival mechanism. The least bad option. But maybe she could do something about it. Maybe she had more power than she imagined and maybe in future she could assert herself and protect herself and maybe it was not that difficult. Maybe.

She lay on her back listening to the breeze rustling through the hedgerow outside and the evening birdsong. She was hungry. She sat up and moved to the front of the tent and pulled out the plastic carton containing half a sandwich, now a little squashed and dried up around the edges. She took a bite and it tasted okay.

She wondered where the old woman was. *Where had she gone? Had it been a dream?* No, she was real all right and her words kept coming back to her: *"Never give up. You'll be all right. Love will keep you strong."* She only had one love. Leila. But how could that keep her strong? She was powerless to do anything. *"And don't fret about stuff you can do nothing about."*

But she did fret, and it was something she could do nothing about. It caused her anguish and pain and it would not go away; it would never go away. She felt herself welling up again and then shouted out loud, "Stop it! It happened. Move on!" Angrily, she wiped away a tear that had formed in the corner of one eye. She took a mouthful of water from the bottle. One mouthful left, for breakfast. Then what? It had been an eventful day. Tomorrow was another day. Another fresh start.

CHAPTER 23

She heard the first drops of rainfall after it got dark, the sound magnified as each drop hit the nylon roof of her tent. The tent was not meant for extended use outdoors in inclement conditions; it was more designed for occasional day use, at festivals and suchlike, and although she had been out in the rain with it before, she knew it was only a matter of time before it succumbed to the elements and started to leak. Not tonight. Please. But she remained protected and the sound of the rain had a soothing effect on her so that she soon drifted off.

***

There's noise in the hallway. Shouting and crashing. Leila's running towards her screaming and she picks her up and hugs her. Shouting in that strange language. Unintelligible but unmistakeable. A smattering of English, "You pay me now, you bloody bastard," Mo's voice pleading, "I will, will, you just have to give me a bit more time. Inshallah," and then the sound of impact, flesh against flesh, foot against body, slap, screams and she's terrified and Leila's terrified and wailing and she has to peer around the kitchen door to see, and Mo's on the floor and men, his friends, are kicking him and she cries, "No!" and they look at her and they stop and she's shaking with fear for herself and her baby. They turn and go, one last kick to Mo's face and they are out, door left wide open and she's quivering and shaking and she puts Leila down and runs to him and she's calling his name, "Mo!" and trying to help him but there's blood everywhere and she doesn't know what to do. And then he

184

gets up and she tries to support him but he pushes her away. "Mo? Mo? What's happening? Mo?" and then he crawls his way up the stairs into the bathroom and she is left, crying with Leila, "Mummy, Mummy," the sound echoes in her head and Leila is drifting away from her, the calls quieter and quieter and then disappearing.

Jess woke up, eyes wide and startled, sweating, whimpering, her mouth dry, lips cracked, breathless. She remembered where she was. Alone in a flimsy pop-up tent in a field in the middle of nowhere in the middle of the night in the rain. An owl screeched and she was afraid. Let the morning come. Please.

***

The rain had stopped during the night but the skies were grey and heavy rainclouds continued to threaten. She had no food and no water. She managed to get some of the rainwater that had collected in a fold in the tent into her bottle, and although it was only an inch, it was something. She ran her tongue over the wet fabric of the tent and despite the odd taste, she felt better for it because she was thirsty. No doubt there would be a stream nearby and she could boil up some water on her ministove, provided there was enough gas still left in the canister.

But food? That was trickier. Unless she stumbled across a field of broad beans she would have to find a shop, and that meant a town or a village. She still had about £15 in her pocket, easily enough to keep her going for a day or two, but there was no escaping the fact that, sooner rather than later, she had to find a new place to stay and a new job to do.

185

On that score, she wondered where and what that might be. Another pub with accommodation was an option, but she would never be able to put her experience of The Navigation out of her mind, however rare that may have been. She couldn't risk repeating the same mistakes and, as she reminded herself, she was as much to blame for the disaster by failing to spot the warning signs, failing to protect herself. No one was going to do it for her.

She collapsed her tent, trying to direct the stream of raindrops into her bottle but instead getting most of it over herself. She zipped it up in its bag. Time to go.

***

Peter stuck his head out of the forward hatch and climbed out onto the side decking. The boat was soaked but no damage had been done and, apart from a minor leak from the hatch seal, it had remained dry and cosy inside. But the weather was still looking grim and BBC radio had forecast even heavier rain today. He thought about trying to reach Lower Croxley but decided he was in no hurry, and the boat was difficult enough for him to handle by himself without having to cope with thunderstorms. There was no one at home waiting for him, and anyway, he rather enjoyed the isolation.

He had promised to meet up with Michael but he was in no rush and, frankly, he was content to postpone the dreaded day indefinitely if he could. He had plenty of stocks. Eggs, baked beans, bread, tea, milk and most important of all, wine, so he would certainly not starve. He decided to stay on board, listen to the radio and catch up on some reading.

***

By 3 p.m. Jess had been walking for six hours with only two short stops to rest her legs. As expected, she had found a stream, running down the side of a field and overflowing after the rainfall, from which she could draw water and boil up on her stove. She had nothing to put in it, but it quenched her thirst and allowed her to fill up her bottle.

She followed the stream, and it eventually brought her to the river. Part of her felt heartened by that, as it had been an objective achieved, but it did not mean she was any closer to finding something to eat.

There was a path, however, and she was grateful for that as fighting her way along an overgrown riverbank was not a practical proposition. But she felt drops of misty rain and the sounds of distant thunder so put up her hood and decided there was worse to come.

And she was right. She trudged on regardless and her rucksack seemed to get heavier, the tent bag, flapping in the increasingly bothersome wind, hampering her progress. By the time the footpath had opened out onto a large expanse of flat land, a field with no distinguishing features adjoining the river, the rain began in earnest. She put her head down and leant into the storm but it was getting worse, and a flash of lightning followed almost instantaneously by a crash of thunder made her jump and told her it was time to seek shelter. But where?

There was nothing in the field but distant hedgerows and they would be no use anyway. Neither were there any trees visible, nor bridges in sight. She determined that the best thing she could do was throw up the tent and crawl inside until the storm had passed. But she was tired and she was hungry and she wasn't thinking straight.

She threw off her rucksack, which landed with a squelch in the sodden grass, and hastily pulled the tent bag off her shoulder. She was only a few feet from the water's edge and the rain lashed down on the rapidly flowing river, turning it into a bubbling cauldron.

Another flash of lightning made her squeal, and with her hood flapping over her eyes, she fumbled blindly for the zip on the tent bag, willing it to open; but it was stuck, a piece of the tent fabric jamming the cheap mechanism. She pulled and pulled and jerked at the zip while she felt water penetrating her jacket through her hood, dripping down her neck and onto her back, sending a chill which pervaded her entire body and exacerbated her panic.

"Come on! Come on!" she screamed irrationally at the inanimate object in her hands as the rain and wind increased in force, battering her like a water cannon. And then the zip broke, the flap came down and she tugged at the frame of the tent, ripping it out of its sack.

A brief moment of triumph turned immediately to disaster. The tent exploded into shape and at that precise moment, a gust of wind filled it like a sail, ripping it from her grasp and propelling it in a lazy arc into the fast-flowing river.

Jess screamed in shock and flung herself towards the edge in a vain attempt to catch hold of one of the trailing guide ropes, but she was too late. Her tent, her only shelter, her home, sagged forlornly on the surface for a moment then drifted away on the swollen current and headed serenely downstream. Lost.

She sat back on her knees staring at the river, her hood blown back exposing her hair, now drenched by the torrents of rain which continued to pummel her from above. She couldn't think. She was cold, shivering, hungry, exhausted, soaked to the skin; and now her tent had gone and there was nowhere for her to go. She was completely alone and completely lost.

She sat back on her folded legs, threw her head back and let out a primeval scream of rage that made her throat burn, temporarily drowning out the sound of the storm. Her head tipped forward and she stared down at the water, and the infernal sounds of the thunder and the flashes of lightning began to subside. In reality, they were louder than ever, but in her mind the water offered her peace and sanctuary and beckoned her forwards. This is where it ends, she realised.

She longed for release from the torment she had had to endure, it seemed, forever. She lifted herself up on her knees and looked out across the swollen river. One tip forward and it would be over. *This is my fate.*

"Mummy, Mummy! Mummy! MUMMY!" Leila's cries came from a long way off, starting quietly but then increasing in intensity until they broke through the din around her and shook her to her core. She swivelled her head frantically in an effort to see where they came from, expecting to see her daughter standing there in the rain, as soaked as she was, crying for help. But she could see nothing.

The cries persisted and got even louder. *"Mummy! MUMMY!"* Leila was screaming at her, not for help, but in warning, desperately urging her not to go, willing her to pull back, and as if in harmony, the old lady nagged her mercilessly, *"Never give up, never give up, never give up,"* again and again, in an interminable, infernal loop that only made her head spin even more.

She clasped her hands to her ears to try and block out the noise but it just got louder. She shook her head and rocked and whimpered and wailed at the onslaught, willing it to stop, willing whatever spirits were at work to cease the torment.

She twisted her head to her right and then, in a flash of lightning which lasted only a fraction of a second, saw something in the distance, something beside the riverbank about two hundred yards away. She squinted, trying to focus through the torrential rain that poured into her eyes, her hair whipping into her face through the force of the wind. She swept her hair away with one hand and looked again, trying

189

to focus. Another flash. A boat! There was a boat, a large boat, and it was moored downriver. *There's no such thing as fate.* Jess knew what to do.

She scrambled drunkenly to her feet, slipping and sliding in the mud, and wrenched her sodden rucksack over her shoulder. She ran.

The rucksack was several kilos heavier now but it didn't matter. Adrenalin surged through her body, fuelling the strength in legs that propelled her across the waterlogged field as if she were floating on air, her head and body bent forward, cutting through the bombardment of rain and wind that desperately tried to hold her back. But she was not going to give up. Never would she give up.

Her lungs burned and her eyes stung and still she sprinted towards her goal; and then she was there, alongside the vessel, which sat serenely at its moorings, seemingly oblivious to the water that bounced off her and cascaded down her sides.

The boat was dark, no light showing from the side windows. Unoccupied but not abandoned; it was too good for that. The entire stern was covered by a heavy blue tarpaulin or canvas, the boat made ready for inclement weather. She gauged the distance from the bank to the deck at only three feet but now fatigue grabbed hold of her and she felt suddenly weak. She would have to leap across the gap with her insanely heavy rucksack and then find a way to get under the tarpaulin. She looked down at the river swirling rapidly between the bank and the hull and contemplated for a second the consequences of slipping and falling between them. But there was no time for that.

Her chest was heaving from the exertion of the run, but with what remained of her strength she hurled the rucksack across the gap and over the guardrail onto the side decking, and then launched herself across, frantically grabbing the rail with one, then two hands and hauling herself on board. She made it. The rain, seemingly further enraged, pummelled her head and shoulders as she dragged herself and her rucksack to the stern, and the thunder increased in ferocity, deafening her and making her cry out involuntarily in fear.

She swept her hair back again so she could see what she was doing, examining the heavy blue canvas for an opening, any way she could get inside, but there was no door or zip. Eventually she noticed the tarpaulin was held down by six elasticated straps stretched over hooks built into the boat, and off centre, a tiny set of wooden steps that led from the stern deck where she crouched, up under the canvas.

She fumbled with one of the straps and it came loose easily so she worked briskly on either side until she had loosened as many as she needed to be able to lift up the tarpaulin and slide her head underneath. Satisfied the gap was big enough, she dragged her body up and over the tiny staircase, under the tarpaulin and into the dry cockpit, turning herself round immediately to reach back out and drag the sodden rucksack after her.

She flopped on her back, gasping and wheezing, chest thumping like a sledgehammer, water dripping off her body onto the dry caulked decking, forming a rapidly expanding puddle around her. She lay between two heavy leather-upholstered armchairs mounted on thick chrome pillars screwed to the cockpit deck, one of them set in front of an array of dials and levers. She closed her eyes and tried to stabilise her breathing.

Peter sensed the commotion because it was different. Something had thudded onto the deck, perhaps a wayward branch, he thought, broken off and flung around in the wind, but his mind was still only in a state of semi-awareness and he brushed it off as nothing to be concerned about. His drowsiness pulled him back under, and despite the thunder cracks, he drifted away again. Immediately, a second unfamiliar, incongruous noise pierced his senses and it

191

sounded much closer to home, something on the other side of the hatch.

He raised himself up off the banquette seat and instinctively lifted the blinds on the riverside. *Good Lord! There's a bloody tent floating down the river!* He had no time to assimilate this information before he heard a ruckus followed by a thump and a cry coming from the stern cockpit on the other side of the hatch.

Without considering the potential for danger, he flicked the lights on, got to his feet and climbed up the few steps to the rear hatch, reaching up to release the bolts keeping it in place.

Jess felt the movement before she heard a sound. The boat had rocked slightly as if its weight had shifted and she could only guess what it meant. Before she could react, she heard the distinct clatter of bolts: one, two, three, and then the rattle of wooden doors thrown open, light flooding into the cockpit, and with mounting horror, realised she was not alone.

Peter took two more steps on the wooden ladder, bringing his head up to the level of the cockpit, and peered into the gloom, intrigued but unperturbed.

"Are you all right?" he said with an insouciance that suggested incidents like this were a regular occurrence on his boat. The person lying flat on their back with their head towards him and arms and legs outstretched like a crucifix was clearly not a threat. Jess was still struggling to come to terms with what she imagined might turn out to be the biggest misjudgement of her life.

"I'm sorry. I'm sorry," was all she could manage, and then, "I didn't know there was anyone here." She gabbled incoherently. "I'll go."

Peter realised instantly that he was dealing with a young female so made every attempt not to react to the crass nonsense she was babbling and tried to keep the impatience out of his voice.

"Wait! You can't go back out there! Here, give me that," and before she could do anything he reached over, grabbed her sodden rucksack and dragged it down the steps into the saloon below. She twisted onto her front and made a vain attempt to reach out and catch hold of it before it disappeared, but she was too late and saw him striding off down the boat, rucksack in hand.

"You'll need something warm," he shouted from the galley as he reached for the kettle and started filling it. She could see the man was old and grey-haired but bulky and fearsome, and all she could think was how she was going to extricate herself from this mess; not least because he had taken all her belongings.

"Come on. Come on!" he bellowed from the galley, further aggravating her fear. She crawled further towards the hatch opening so she could see a little better.

"I'm sorry, I don't want to bother you," she said limply, thinking the first step perhaps was to placate the old boy. He was having none of it.

"Look. You'll catch your death out there. Come down at once!" Realising resistance was futile, she swung her body around and climbed backwards down the steps into the saloon, where she stood shivering, arms around her body, head down in submission, lank wet hair dangling over her face.

She heard him approach and was momentarily afraid he might attack her, but to her surprise, he moderated his aggression, sounding suddenly concerned as he took in the image before him. He thrust a towel under her nose and she took it, burying her face in it and then using it to rub the back of her head.

"Goodness me, you're soaking! Have you got anything to change into?" Head still down, she sniffed, and not daring to look at him, mumbled through her dangling hair.

193

"In the rucksack, but I expect it's all wet. Don't worry, I'll soon dry off," she said without conviction.

"Hmm," he snorted at this latest piece of nonsense and marched off, huffing and puffing. After a moment or two, during which it sounded as if cupboards and drawers were being ransacked, he returned clutching two items of clothing in one hand.

He thrust them at her. "These are the best I can do, I'm afraid. Go up for'ard, take that wet stuff off and put these on," he said, poking a grey tee shirt and green woollen pullover in her direction.

She hesitated but then thought it best not to argue. She swept her wet hair back to see what she was doing and turned to face him for the first time, holding out one hand to take the clothes. He froze.

They stood for a moment staring at each other and she thought her worst fears were about to be realised. *What's the matter? Why is he looking at me like that?* She felt the panic rise again and her heart begin to thump. He remained immobile, transfixed, eyes cold and dark and disturbed, as if he were in a trance. They stood, gripping the clothes like protagonists in a tug of war: she, terror-stricken by his numb expression; he, rooted to the spot, frozen by her hypnotic spell. She decided not to make any sudden movements, simply draw back slowly. She gulped and broke the awkward silence.

"No. It's okay. I'm fine, thanks," she said guardedly, lowering her hand. The trance ended and he exploded.

"Now look here!" he bellowed, shoulders back, standing rigidly to attention. "I'm captain of this ship and whilst on board, you will do as you're told. I will not tolerate insubordination on my vessel!"

She stepped back, jaw dropping open, eyes wide in fear, but in the same instant, the rant was over. He relaxed, collected himself and grinned sheepishly. "Sorry. Habit of a lifetime, giving orders." He smiled at her and the fear subsided, if only a little. He went on, and this time his words were gentle but firm. "But you know I'm right."

She nodded unconvincingly and carefully took the clothes from him. "Go on," he said, directing her with a nod of the head. She slid past him gently and went to the for'ard cabin, closing the door behind her.

***

Still shaking from her bizarre and terrifying encounter with the old man, Jess stepped into the cabin and pulled the sliding door shut behind her. It was compact to say the least, if not claustrophobic, but she could stand up, which was more than could be said of her tent. The walls curved inwards following the shape of the bow and on each side was a single banquette bed, curving in to meet at one end in the middle.

There were several varnished wood drawers and lockers fixed under the bed and similarly finished shelves, cubbyholes and pockets above. A small window was set into the hull on each side, and she leant over to open one as she needed some air; and anyway, if her clothes were to dry, they would need a flow of air to help.

The rain continued to fall steadily outside but it had relented a little and the thunderstorm had passed. Her sodden rucksack lay on one of the beds and dripped water on a floor covered in coarse matting. She shivered despite the relative warmth of the boat and decided there was no option but to strip everything off and put on the dry clothes he had given her.

Naked, she rubbed herself down with a towel, but hearing him clattering around in the galley on the other side of the door again made her feel vulnerable and nervous. "Milk and sugar?" The sound startled her and she instinctively clutched the towel to her chest.

"Oh, er, just milk, thanks." She tried to hang her wet things on anything she could find: hooks, window catches, cupboard knobs, but knew they would take time to dry. She gave her hair a brisk rub with the towel and soon felt better. She was still nervous about the old man. He had shown he had a fierce temper when provoked but then he had calmed down instantly when she had acquiesced. She wondered what his attitude might be to someone invading his space without asking and, cautious as ever, what his motives were. He was entitled to be upset, but then she could not understand the look he gave her when she tried to take the clothes.

There was a small mirror on the back of the door and she examined her face to see if she had a black eye or a scar or something which might have explained his shock at seeing her. All she saw was Jess. Plain Jess, drawn, weary, pale with soggy dangling hair. Maybe that had been enough. Although maybe he sensed an opportunity?

She began to think the worst. It was possible he was just another man whose "needs" were for her to satisfy. She felt dismayed at the thought but, as always, was philosophical about it. She had no choice at the moment. As long as he didn't hurt her.

She decided she wouldn't stay any longer than necessary. She needed an escape plan, but what was there to plan? If she had learnt anything about her life on the road it was that plans were pointless, as what lay around the next bend was always unexpected. One step at a time, she told herself. Everything will drop into place.

She examined the tee shirt he had given her. It was huge. The label said 5XL and she thought that might well be his size. She pulled it over her head and it stretched all the way to her knees, the arms reaching below her elbows like a

196

baggy nightdress, but she was relieved to find it covered her modesty.

The heavy woollen sweater was dark green, with green leather patches on the elbows and khaki cotton epaulettes fastened by faux brass buttons. It was the same size as the tee shirt though not quite as stretched and shapeless, but the sleeves were a good nine inches too long for her and she rolled them up so she could at least use her hands. The sweater, too, fell way beyond her thighs but stopped above the level of the tee shirt.

She felt swamped but relieved to be out of her wet clothes. She did her best to arrange her hair in the mirror, and took a deep breath. Time to re-emerge.

Peter sat in the saloon, contemplating his encounter with the young woman and the profound effect it had had on him. He was a little ashamed of his outburst, especially as it had frightened her so much and that was the last thing he had wanted to do. He had just been taken by surprise, that was all. Still, he cursed himself for his lack of self-control – *wouldn't have happened back in the army* – and like most things, put it down to age. No, he told himself. This had nothing to do with age, nothing at all.

He heard the for'ard cabin door slide open and he could feel his heartbeat rising again. Maybe it had been a trick of the light or maybe he had just been tired and mildly hallucinating. Perhaps when he saw her again in the full glare of the cabin lights, he might realise it was simply his imagination running riot. Michael's well-meaning intervention the other day had ensured the issue remained at the forefront of his mind.

He heard the wooden floorboards creak as she moved towards him but avoided turning his head until the girl had come through the galley and climbed the two steps up into the saloon. She appeared nervous and embarrassed in her ridiculous outfit so he gave her a welcoming smile to try to put her at ease. "Sit down there," he said, gesturing to the banquette seat opposite, "and get warm." Two mugs of tea sat steaming on a low-slung coffee table separating them and she leant forward to pick one up, cupping the mug in both hands, clearly savouring the warmth. She took a mouthful and closed her eyes.

He watched her intently as she drank, and a wave of emotion washed over him. She was exactly as he had remembered; not surprising since she had only been away for fifteen minutes. No trick of the light. No hallucination. He considered for a moment that he was in fact still asleep and this was a cruel dream, a wicked punishment; but then if this was punishment, he didn't want to wake up, ever. He would happily sit there, locked in this dream, and look at her for all eternity. But it was no dream, it was all real. Time to act real.

"I must say you picked a poor day to be out walking," he admonished her gently "Where on earth were you trying to get to? There's nothing around here for miles." She swallowed another mouthful of the nectar and shrugged.

"I was just seeing where the path took me," she said. He thrust a hand across the table.

"Peter Jeffries, colonel, retired." She cautiously held out her hand. His huge hand enveloped hers completely, warm and soft and comforting. He held on for a second. She was real, all right.

"Alice," she said shyly.

"Pleased to make your acquaintance, Alice." Reluctantly, he let go of her hand, aware that he might be squeezing it a bit too hard. "Don't get many visitors on board."

"The lights were off," she pleaded in self-defence, "I thought there was no one here."

"Afternoon snooze," he explained. "It's an age thing. Recharges the batteries, though, and there's not much else you can do in weather like this." He looked up at the ceiling to indicate the sound of the rain that continued to pound the top of the boat.

"Now, you'll need some food, too. When did you last eat? I'm not much of a cook, but I'm an expert when it comes to beans on toast. Years of practice," he announced with pride and a wide grin, slapping both thighs and getting out of his seat.

"Please don't go to any trouble," she said anxiously as he stepped towards the galley. "I'll have to be making a move soon anyway." He turned to face her and put both his hands on his hips. She appeared to wilt under his gaze, but he was smiling in his gentle reproach.

"Now that is preposterous. No one is going out there in this weather. You can bunk down in the for'ard cabin tonight and see what it's doing in the morning."

"Oh ...no, it's okay. I've got my tent, you see!" she blurted out without thinking. He looked at her and stifled a laugh.

"You mean the one floating down the river?" He said it with a heavy irony but she looked embarrassed and, sensing her disquiet, did his best to put her mind at ease. He adopted a soft but authoritative tone.

"Now look, Alice. It's raining, it's getting late and your things are wet. I assure you, you will be much better off here in the warm than out there in that." He thought she still looked worried, and reading her mind, said, "You can lock the door to your cabin. You've nothing to fear from a silly old fool like me." She looked up sheepishly and he smiled broadly, gently.

"Are you a gentleman as well as an officer?" she asked, at which he snapped to attention and saluted.

"Colonel Jeffries at your service, Ma'am!" He stomped one foot on the deck, whirled around and marched down to the galley.

Jess had felt uneasy, not being in control of events and the colonel was clearly a force to be reckoned with, despite his effusive character. She was nervous about arguing with him again, afraid that he may react the same way as he had earlier and fly into a rage, but she was desperately hungry and it made sense to take him up on his offer of food while trying to keep her options open. But when he had mentioned staying the night, her alarm bells had started ringing. This was going too far. She wasn't ready to trust him. She might never be ready to trust him, and she needed to stay in control. Yet, for the moment at least, she had to trust him. She had no choice.

***

The rain had stopped, just a few stray drops sporadically dripping from the superstructure and hitting the roof over their heads.

Jess forked the last few baked beans into her mouth and smacked her lips. She carefully put the cutlery down on her plate and noticed he had been watching her with a broad smile as she ate, grinning foolishly in delight.

"Thank you so much," she said. "That was delicious."

"Good Lord!" he exclaimed in mock surprise. "Never heard my beans on toast described as delicious!" And then, as if bolstered by this testament to his culinary skills, winked at her. "Told you I was good."

"I mean, you've been very kind," she said quietly, and she meant it. It had been a long time since she had thought of saying that to anyone, had reason to say that to anyone. She was feeling much better than she had an hour ago. She had been clothed, fed and watered, and she was warm and dry. He had been the perfect host, generous and welcoming; nothing like the bombastic tyrant he had appeared on first impression. He picked up both plates and headed for the galley. Jess was feeling a little guilty that he was doing all the work and called after him.

"Can I help you wash up?"

"No, I can manage. There's not much room down here. Just make yourself comfortable." He set about filling the sink with hot water and a splash of washing-up liquid.

Jess sat back on the banquette, pulling her legs up beneath her as he went on. "You know, I do love messing about on the river, even in terrible weather. I often thought I should have been Navy, not Army," he mused. "It does get a bit lonely at times and it's always tricky managing the locks when you're by yourself, but I just love it. It's like another world when you're on the water. All your cares seem to drift away when you're on the water." He dunked the plates into the bowl and swirled soapy water around them with a brush. "And a bit of solitude is good for the soul. Switch your mobile phone off and no one can find you. It's almost as if you don't exist." He chuckled at the notion. "Still it's very nice to have visitors whatever the circumstances. Now ... you haven't told me where you're from, or indeed where you're going?"

He placed a washed plate down on the rack, expecting her to respond, but she didn't. He pulled a tea towel from a hook and wiped his hands, leaning back so he could see up into the saloon. He smiled.

The girl had keeled over on the banquette with her legs curled up and was fast asleep. Poor kid, he thought, she must be exhausted. No sense waking her now just to tell her to go to bed. Best leave her to rest.

He retrieved a soft blanket from the aft cabin and, careful not to disturb her, arranged it over her legs and body, pulling it up to her neck. He got himself a glass of red wine, picked up his book and glasses from the shelf and stretched out on the opposite banquette with his back to the aft bulkhead. It was 9.15 p.m. by the small clock that sat on the ledge behind him. He opened the book but within fifteen minutes his eyes

201

grew heavy and his head fell forward onto his chest until he too was asleep.

At 10.10 p.m. he woke up, confused but pleasantly dopey from his nap. He removed his glasses to rub his eyes and glanced across the coffee table. She had gone. He felt a rush of panic and was suddenly alarmed at the prospect that she might have taken off into the night, despite everything he had said, and although it was inconceivable that she could have been so irresponsible, he cursed himself for not taking extra care to make sure she remained safe.

There was no sound except for the faint lapping of water on the hull, so he got to his feet and tiptoed down the saloon, through the galley to the for'ard cabin. The door was closed. He put his ear to it and rubbed his chin, uncertain for a moment. If she was in there, he didn't want to frighten her, but he needed to know. Needed to know whether to put his boots on and go out in search. He reached for the door handle, careful not to make any noise. He applied some pressure to the door to see if it would slide open. It didn't. It was locked. He sighed with relief and went quietly back to the saloon.

He finished his wine in one gulp and reflected on the strangest of days, trying to rationalise what had happened, how this girl had appeared from nowhere in the eye of a fierce thunderstorm. She had not said anything about herself that gave him any clue as to where she came from, only that she was "seeing where the path took me". He was acutely aware that despite a distinguished career in the Intelligence Corps, he had refrained from applying his formidable interrogation techniques to find out more. There would be plenty of time for that. He would make sure of it.

He decided it was simply serendipitous that their paths had crossed, and he had been entranced the moment he laid eyes on her. Her hair, her eyes, her build, her age, were all too familiar to him, as if he had always known her; and then he remembered with a deep sadness that he didn't know her at all. Anyway, he was astute enough to know that whoever she was, she needed help, his help, and she was going to get all the help she needed, whether she wanted it or not.

He turned out the lights and retired to bed in the aft cabin, but he couldn't sleep. His mind was still buzzing, full of confused thoughts and emotions, planning a strategy for tomorrow to ensure he remained in total control of this extraordinary situation.

He left his door open so that he would know if she moved from the for'ard cabin. He was terrified she might take flight during the night or maybe early in the morning whilst he was asleep, and he couldn't let that happen. *"Jeffries, you're on the midnight-to-dawn watch!"* Ah, those were the days.

CHAPTER 24

The sun streamed through the window and into the galley, where Peter was up and making preparations for breakfast. He had decided not to wake Alice, considering that letting her sleep for as long as possible was the best thing for her, so he held off making her a mug of tea but had everything ready to respond as soon as she stirred.

Despite hardly sleeping a wink, he was bright and alert and felt better than he had for a long while. Most importantly, he knew he had work to do, even though he still had no idea how hard it would be. His objectives were clear, but there were still too many unknown factors to take into account and he would have to modify his tactics along the way. He heard a latch flick behind him and the sound of the for'ard cabin door sliding open.

He turned slowly so as not to alarm her. He didn't want her to think he had been listening the door, but when he saw her his heart lifted. Alice was standing there, one bleary eye visible, the other concealed behind dangling hair which hung over one side of her face. She smiled at him and she glowed.

"Good morning!" he barked, unable to conceal the joy he felt at seeing her again. "Did you sleep well?"

"Yes, thanks," said Jess. "Sorry I dropped off. Couldn't help it." She had abandoned the army sweater and wore only the grey tee shirt, but it was more than adequate to cover her slight frame. He leant back, hands behind him on the sink, as non-threatening a pose as his bulk would allow in the confined space.

"Don't be sorry, my dear, I expect you needed the rest. Now, the water's piping hot if you want a shower. It's back there by the aft cabin, and you'll find a large towel and shampoo and all the bits and pieces in there."

"Thanks," she said without hesitation. The thought of a hot shower evidently filled her with delight.

"Breakfast is at oh nine hundred hours, then we tidy up, cast off at ten thirty hours and set course for a midday rendezvous with the Duke of Wellington," he announced. She frowned, not understanding at all what he meant, but he was just playing with her. "Pub at Lower Croxley." He smiled at her, and she smiled back.

***

The shower was heavenly. The water was hot, as he had said, and there was plenty of soap and shampoo and even conditioner, which made it the most luxurious she had had for as long as she could remember. The shower in the communal bathroom at The Navigation had been adequate, but nothing compared to this, even though by any normal standard it was rudimentary. The flow of water may have been weak, but to her it felt like a cascade and she let it flow over her soapy body until all traces of the awful last two days had been washed away. She felt cleansed and refreshed. Another new beginning.

She dried herself off as best she could in the confined space, wrapped the huge towel around her and slid open the door. She poked her head out and looked around where she could see down the saloon and into the galley. The colonel was nowhere to be seen. Perhaps he had been gentlemanly enough to vacate the premises whilst the lady was carrying out her ablutions, giving her maximum privacy. It was a delicious thought and she hoped she was right. It couldn't have been a normal state of affairs for someone as old as him to share his boat with a young woman, so she was content to regard this as an act of chivalry rather than a simple necessity, which was probably more likely.

Jess scuttled through the saloon and the galley clutching her towel around her tightly and made it to the forward cabin without incident. Miraculously, a white tee shirt and a pair of black trousers, clean when she had left The Navigation, had dried overnight, hanging in a cupboard which housed the water heater, as had a set of underwear; and although all of it was crumpled, it was serviceable. Her boots, however, would take much longer to dry, and she decided they would best be left outside in the sun for a while.

She brushed her wet hair roughly with a hairbrush she found in one of the drawers and ventured out of her cabin to find he had come back and was busy in the galley frying eggs and making toast. *What a gentleman!*

"I forgot to mention, eggs on toast is my other signature dish; in fact, just about anything on toast would define my repertoire," he chuckled.

"Lovely. Can I do anything?" she asked, eager to help.

"Yes, of course. I've set up a table on the rear deck, thought we would have our breakfast *alfresco*. You can take the cutlery and all the bits and pieces and lay the table. I'll bring the food in just a minute."

***

They had eaten simply but well, and she had done the washing up while he went about some daily checks to prepare the boat for departure. She poured herself another mug of tea and returned to the rear deck where she sat on a canvas chair immediately behind the cockpit.

It seemed like a lifetime ago that she had dragged herself under the tarpaulin like a drowned rat, not least because of the change in weather. The sun was out, the birds were singing and the trees were bright and vibrant. She heard Peter coming up the cockpit stairs, tea mug in hand. He stopped at the top and made a great show of sniffing loudly at the fresh air.

"Glorious!" he bellowed to no one in particular and then took a seat opposite. "The rain has certainly freshened things up."

"Yes," she agreed, "I didn't realise how beautiful it is," and she meant it. But she had to be realistic. This was not her world and her primary objective remained to find some form of civilisation, get a job and a roof over head and restart her life as Alice. She would not make the same mistake as she had at The Navigation. She was much wiser now.

The colonel had been very kind and generous, and although he had frightened her initially, he had quickly mellowed, and she felt at ease in his company. But a lingering doubt remained. There was nothing she could do for him, and while she hated to think he might have sinister designs on her, she could not rule out the possibility. In any event, even if she was wrong, and she was almost certain she was, she couldn't impose upon his hospitality a moment longer. She looked at him.

"Look, I really must get going," she said reluctantly. But if she had been thinking about it, then so had he, and he was ready for her.

"In case you'd forgotten, my dear, your home floated down the river last night," he said in mild admonishment, and she immediately felt embarrassed at having indeed forgotten this crucial detail. "Even if we were to chase after it, it will have gone over the weir by now." Jess let her shoulders sag a bit but she had to admit this was a problem; and anyway, she also had to admit she was willing to be persuaded.

"Look," he said, encouraging her to see some common sense. "We're going the same way, why don't you cadge a lift? I live just a couple of days' cruising from here and it's always tricky managing the locks by yourself, so you will be doing me a favour and paying for your passage at the same time. And then, when we get there, you can go on your way. How does that sound?"

He had had it all planned and he had executed it perfectly. She couldn't think of any reason to object, and she smiled shyly at him.

"Sounds ... good."

"Excellent! That's settled." And they clinked their tea mugs as if in celebration.

***

Jess lay back in the sunshine, supported by her elbows, and stretched out on the front deck as *Carician* glided almost silently along the river at a stately and serene three knots. She could hear the water caressing the bows and sense the distant vibration of the engines, but otherwise she was lost in the tranquillity and the warmth and she was thankful for this escape from the world, her world, whatever that was.

Periodically she saw moorhens, ducks, swans, coots and geese gliding gracefully across the path of the boat or else scurrying for cover in the reeds that lined the banks. Occasionally they passed fields of inquisitive cows, chewing remorselessly, regarding the vessel with disdain, and she briefly saw an iridescent flash of blue on the branch of an overhanging tree. A kingfisher, maybe? She didn't know for certain, just used her imagination.

They had stopped at The Duke of Wellington as the colonel had decreed, and she had been treated to a hearty lunch of bangers and mash, which she quickly realised was one of his favourites. She had struggled to finish it, but as he insisted on paying, had made the supreme effort. She still had £15 in her pocket, which thanks to the invention of plastic banknotes would otherwise not have survived the rainstorm, but he would have none of it.

She could still feel the weight of the food in her belly, alien but nevertheless comforting, and it raised her spirits. She had studiously avoided alcohol, preferring sparkling water, which to her was just as exotic. The only "drink" she'd had in the last few years had been the bottle of cheap sparkling wine the day before she left home, so she wasn't used to it. Something told her that she should remain in control of her senses and not take the colonel's generosity for granted. Her instinct remained to go her own way. That was what brought her here, and that was what would take her away.

She turned to look back down the boat and the colonel stood tall in the cockpit, wheel in hand, soft, wide-brimmed hat flapping in the breeze, smiling broadly. He waved at her like a schoolchild and she could do nothing other than smile and wave back. The moment would end, of course. She knew that. But for now, it couldn't get much better.

On the rear deck, Peter's exhilaration was complete. Bangers and mash and two pints of Old Hooky, the sunshine, piloting his beloved *Carician* along the river he loved and, above all, this extraordinary creature as a passenger, accompanying him on a voyage to … who knows where?

He considered the limited conversation they'd had so far. He had done most of the talking, which Michael would have declared normal practice had he been there. But she had said little about herself and he had not probed further because he wanted her to feel comfortable; and anyway, there was plenty of time, provided he could manage the situation properly.

He was minded of his time in the Intelligence Corps when he had always believed the best way to draw information out of a target was to allow them the space to talk openly. Put them at their ease, remove the threat and, in time, they were far more likely to open up. Meanwhile, observe, respond, manoeuvre and steer the target to the conclusion. He was a past master at the "good cop" routine. Regrettably, he could play the "bad cop" even better if necessary, but it would never be necessary in Alice's case. She was neither a suspected terrorist nor a member of a factional militia, but he was intrigued, and his professional training demanded he think through and assess the facts as he knew them.

He had introduced himself, full name, rank and status, to which she had replied, "Alice." Nothing controversial there, but the absence of a surname could be significant. An alias, perhaps? He had asked her where she thought she was going and she had replied, "wherever the path took me." She was wandering aimlessly. She had no food and apparently little money. She had no phone, which was notable in itself, had not wanted to call anyone or expressed any desire to go anywhere other than to get away, be by herself.

She hadn't offered an opinion on anything, was just taking it one moment at a time. Nor had she asked anything about him, presumably because she had already decided her stay was temporary and she didn't need to know. But questions provoke questions which demand answers, and she showed no inclination to talk about herself.

And she looked haunted. Haunted by something or someone or some place. She had reacted quickly and apparently without logical thought to the slightest threat to her independence, the merest suspicion of danger, and he had done his utmost to tread carefully, keep a wide berth. He would get to the bottom of it in time, but it was not a priority. His priority was to make sure she did not disappear and that she was safe.

But at the same time, he wrestled with his own emotions and continuously challenged his motivation. What was he trying to do? And the answer was clear and simple. He was going to put things right.

**

Jess was sitting in the same canvas chair on the rear deck, taking in the evening sun, reflecting on the best of days and wondering at what point she would take her leave. Her tent was gone and she had £15 to her name, so that was a logistical problem to which, at the moment, she had no answer.

In truth, if she could spend the rest of her life here, on this boat, on this river, with the colonel, then she would have no complaints. But she knew enough about life to know it was not like that. All things come to end. Good things as well as bad. She would be forever grateful for the colonel's help, for his consideration, generosity and kindness, but he had his own life to lead and she had hers and they could not be more different.

While she had been alone that afternoon, basking in the warmth of a perfect English summer's day, floating along and watching the countryside go by, she had wondered who the colonel really was. He mentioned living "a couple of days downriver", but where? He had talked a lot about current things, the stuff of the moment, but there was no mention of family. What was he doing out in his boat, doing this all alone, if it was so difficult? And he must be well off, she thought, having a boat as grand as this; but then she didn't think you got rich being an army officer.

Anyway, she didn't dare ask in case that might prompt him to ask her questions she didn't want to answer. Alice's life had begun only six weeks ago, so there was literally not much to tell apart from her unfortunate experience at The

Navigation, and that was not a story she wanted to relate or relive.

The colonel appeared up the steps from the saloon carrying two glasses of white wine. They had had a simple dinner of cold meat and cheese, all they needed after their big lunch, and she had stuck to tea.

"I thought you may like a glass of wine?" he said, offering her one of the glasses. She decided it could do no harm and she didn't want to offend him now he had poured it out, but resolved to go slowly and remain on her guard.

"Thank you," she said unconvincingly, and he took the seat opposite. They clinked glasses and she took a sip. It was cold, fresh and fruity, and when she swallowed it tingled her throat and filled her head with a warm glow that was both delicious and instantly soporific. They would get to his house sometime tomorrow afternoon, he had said, so she had less than twenty-four hours to enjoy the experience. It would be memorable for many reasons.

"Now, you haven't told me where home is?" he said casually. The wine had caught her off guard and she wondered whether it had been deliberate ploy on his part. But it was a perfectly reasonable question, reasonably put, without any sense of impertinence or intrusion, and it was inevitable that he would ask her something about herself in normal conversation.

But it was a question to which she did not have an acceptable answer. In fact, any question about herself or her background was impossible to answer without risking a flurry of further questions. It was just too difficult. She opted for one version of the truth.

"Nowhere I can call home, really." She shrugged and made it sound as casual and ambiguous as she could. It didn't mean she didn't have a home; just not one she considered as such.

"Then how do you know you're going the right way?" he persisted gently.

"I'll know when I get there."

"By yourself?" he said with some concern, but she spotted the leading question, concealed in innocent curiosity.

"I'm perfectly happy with my own company," she said, skilfully evading the point, and then, conscious she may have sounded ungrateful, "which doesn't mean it hasn't been a pleasure meeting you, Colonel."

"Peter," he corrected her.

"Peter," she smiled, and they clinked glasses again.

***

After the girl had retired to her cabin, Peter thought again about their latest exchange, and to his analytical mind, something had become instantly clear. She had no home. She was running away from something, maybe even towards something, but she didn't know what that was. Everything she owned was in that rucksack, on this boat, he was sure. She didn't even have a real name. He hadn't blinked when she had originally introduced herself as "Alice" but he was sure that was not her real name, and he wanted to understand if there was anyone else in her life: family, friends, perhaps, but she had dodged the question and left the impression she was totally alone.

He decided he would tread carefully and not risk pushing her into a corner by asking too many questions. He did not want to distress her and, for the moment at least, she appeared relaxed in his presence and, at times, even happy.

And he was happy too, because when she had smiled at him, his heart had lifted and filled with a joy he thought had gone forever.

CHAPTER 25

It was late afternoon when Jess, lying in her usual position on the front deck, sensed the engine note change. Peter slid the throttles into reverse and slowed *Carician* to a virtual halt mid-river and parallel to some moorings on the port side. He nudged the controls backwards and forwards until slowly the boat drifted towards the bank.

In the short time she had been afloat, Jess had become adept at handling the ropes and managing the lock gates, especially as they were all electrically operated, so that had not been a major challenge. Consequently, she was ready to leap off the bow and stood for'ard, rope in hand, until the gap had narrowed and *Carician's* large white fenders were within touching distance of the Armco barriers.

But she was distracted by something else. Beyond the moorings was a huge field bordered by trees, a large expanse of grass that sloped upwards for almost two hundred yards to a grand country house that stood proudly in the distance at the top of the hill. She had seen many luxurious riverside residences in the last couple of days, but none had come close to this in size and stature, and she wondered why they were stopping here. But as the fenders made contact she returned to the job in hand and jumped ashore, rope at the ready.

Peter manoeuvred the stern and when he was close enough, stepped ashore. He wrapped the stern rope around an iron bollard, before striding towards Jess to do the same.

"There. That'll do it," he declared. She looked around again at the imposing house at the top of the hill, still confused.

"Is this where you live?" she asked. He followed her gaze and put his hands on his hips.

"Not quite as grand as it once was and a bit decrepit, just like me really." He snorted at the joke and climbed back on board.

He set about securing the boat for the night, planning to come back tomorrow morning and prepare her for a lengthier layoff. Jess gathered her belongings and offloaded them onto the concrete standing. Eventually, Peter stepped off carrying a leather holdall and a blue cool box.

"Come on, let's go see if the place is still in one piece," he barked, and set off at a pace up the grassy bank towards the house with Jess trotting behind him, trying to keep up.

***

Peter turned the key in the lock and pushed at the large wooden door with his body, with Jess following behind hesitantly. The house had looked big from a distance but it had loomed over them as they had approached, and she felt some trepidation as she stepped over the threshold. The front door was half glazed with stained glass and sported a huge knocker on the front in the shape of a lion's head. As she closed it behind her, Peter disappeared down the hallway with a cry of "Come on in," but she stood there for moment, taking in the magnitude of her surroundings.

Her first impression was that her entire house would have fitted into the hallway. The floor was stone and mosaic-tiled, the ceiling at least twenty feet above her head and there was a large spiral staircase at the other end. There were large open doors to her left and right: one led into what she thought looked like an exotic drawing room, the other presumably a formal dining room, given the row of partially visible dining chairs.

The hallway itself boasted three standard lamps and several pieces of antique furniture adorned with a variety of porcelain figurines, vases and a large clock. In the corner by the door stood an ancient grandfather clock with French inscriptions she couldn't understand, but she could tell it functioned because the pendulum swung as it emitted a languorous tick-tock sound. On the walls hung several oil paintings in gilt frames illustrating ancient scenes, the type you might see in a museum. She had once been taken to Hampton Court as a child, and Peter's house, although nowhere near as grand and opulent, reminded her of that.

She slowly set off in the direction he had gone, following the sound of his booming voice saying, "Let's have a brew, shall we?" and found him at the sink in the kitchen, filling the kettle. The kitchen was equally gargantuan by her standards, with a long ten-seater table in the centre, a row of powder blue units down one side, the other taken up by a conventional electric cooker and a huge cast-iron range from which rose a tall chimney. That must be one of those Agas she had read about but had never seen for real.

She stood awkwardly, rucksack still strapped to her back, not knowing what to do, but looking like she was ready to depart. Peter flicked the kettle switch and turned around to face her. He looked earnest and serious about something and he put his hands behind his back as if about to deliver a speech.

"Now, Alice," he said by way of introduction. "It's getting late, soon be dark, and you are without a roof over your head. It makes eminent sense for you to stay here tonight, and then tomorrow I can run you into town and you can buy yourself a new tent or get on the bus to wherever." Jess listened intently as his words flowed, and she mused that only two days ago, she would have been determined to get away as soon as possible.

But try as she might, she had not identified any sinister intent and had always felt comfortable and safe in his company. He came across as a doddery old fool, but she was sure that was just bluster; and although a tiny part of her remained wary, she liked him. She had absolutely no desire to take to the road immediately, with or without a tent. One day at a time. So she simply said, "Okay."

But for some reason the word did not register and he carried on regardless.

"I mean, correct me if I'm wrong, but it's not as if you have any pressing engagements to attend, so another day won't make any difference."

"Okay," she said again, smiling, rather enjoying his earnest delivery.

"Now I won't take no for an answer, there could be rain at anytime ..." She saw his brain finally catch up with her response and he beamed in delight. "Excellent! We'll rustle up a nice dinner and then have an early night."

"Will it be beans on toast?" she mocked him gently with a smile, and he looked delighted at her little dig. She was getting to know him.

"No, no, no, I have fresh vegetables from the garden and there must be something in the freezer to go with them," he announced confidently but then looked uncertain. "Mind you, I can't promise a gourmet supper. Not my strongest point, cheffery." He looked at her and asked speculatively, "Are you a cook?"

She shrugged. Her mother had taught her to cook from an early age and she was a natural. She had never had much chance to practise in her own house but still knew intuitively what to do in most circumstances.

"I get by," she said coyly.

"You know, I was hoping you'd say that." She seized the moment, surprising herself with a new-found confidence that sprang from who knows where.

"Let me cook something for you. It's the least I can do."

"Excellent," gushed Peter, rubbing his hands together like a glutton before an imaginary feast. "Come on, I'll show you your room," he said, striding past her and out of the kitchen without waiting for any further comment.

She followed him up the spiral staircase and noticed more oil paintings on the walls, portraits of lords and ladies, ancestors perhaps, all staring at her as if she had no place to be there. She didn't, she thought. She looked up and could see the stairs spiralling upwards three floors to a bright, domed skylight in the roof; but he turned right on the first landing and marched down the long corridor, arms swinging as if he were on the parade ground. He waited in front of a large white door at the end while she caught him up, and then swung it open for her, standing back to allow her to enter.

The room was huge, at least thirty feet square, and the walls were decorated in pastel shades of pink, topped with a white ceiling at least fifteen feet above her head. Two walls featured giant sash windows with Georgian panes dressed with floral curtains swagged together at each side with a matching pelmet above, and there were two ornate handwoven rugs on top of a pale blue carpet she could feel was lush and deep.

A king-size bed with a velvet padded headboard and quilted cover, flanked by two marble-topped bedside tables with capiz shell-shaded lamps, dominated one wall. Against another, a large mahogany chest of drawers stood below a gilt wall- mounted mirror. Next to a matching wardrobe was a walnut dressing table with stool, the dressing table sporting a jewellery stand and two velvet-covered boxes and backed by a triptych mirror. And, most extraordinary of all, a chaise longue languished in one corner opposite the bed, covered with a hand-knitted blanket and soft cushions.

"En suite over there," said Peter, following her in and pointing to a white door in the corner. "And you'll find plenty of clothes in the cupboards and drawers that you are welcome to. You should find something to fit."

Jess's alarms bells had started ringing the moment she walked into the room. This was not the spare room she had imagined. Not the basic, utilitarian, hardly ever used, poor man's room, which to her would have been perfectly adequate, if not luxurious in its own right. This magnificent, opulent, frankly gorgeous boudoir belonged to someone. A girl. And Peter had just confirmed it with the mention of the clothes. She turned to him with a look that fell somewhere between confusion and unease.

"Whose room is this?"

"My daughter Lisa's," he said casually and without hesitation. But deliberately or otherwise, he had appeared to miss the point of her question, which in her view needed further explanation.

"Won't she mind?" asked Jess, getting more disturbed by the second.

"No. She's away at the moment," said Peter, skirting the issue. But something in him had changed and she sensed it immediately. The ebullience was gone and his smile seemed laboured, and the fingers of both hands twitched and clenched. Something was wrong and she tried to steady her nerves, pinched by mounting anxiety.

"But what if she comes back and finds me wearing her things?" spluttered Jess, her consternation turning rapidly into a mild panic. *Why can't he see this is a problem?*

"No, she won't," he said with a reassuring shrug that did little to calm her, and she noticed that although the smile remained, the happiness was gone. "She hasn't been home for a while." And before she could complain again, he said, "Please, settle in, make yourself at home. I'll go and dig up some spuds. I'll see you downstairs when you're ready." With that, he turned for the door.

"But ..." Jess protested, but she was too late. He was gone, the door shutting behind him with a loud click. Her shoulders sagged and she sighed heavily. *So, he has a daughter. That much I now know. But she's not here and not expected here at any time soon or else he would never let someone use her room, never mind wear her clothes.* She felt decidedly uncomfortable about the whole arrangement and was beginning to regret not following her original instinct.

Things had been going so well between them and she thought she had gauged his character correctly as a kindly old gentleman, on his own, generous, self-deprecating and amusing but with an authoritarian streak borne out of his time in the army.

But a window had opened into another side of the colonel. He had seemed evasive and a little awkward when talking about his daughter, Lisa, and Jess wondered why that might be, and, more importantly, where she might be. It was a mystery and she would have to get to the bottom of it.

She unhooked her rucksack and laid it on the bed and then, worried that it might dirty the cover, hastily dropped it on the rug which would not so easily show any stains. She kicked off her boots and socks and sank her toes into the deep carpet. It felt good. She strolled over to the en suite and nervously opened the door. A pull cord revealed itself and she tugged on it, bathing the enormous bathroom in a luminescent glow from a dozen LED lights set into the ceiling.

Lisa's bathroom was even more opulent than her bedroom, featuring a walk-in shower cubicle sparkling with chrome and glass, and a large free-standing white ceramic bath set in the middle of the floor complete with ornate Victorian-style taps. A large vanity unit below a glass shelf and mirror with overhead lights was on one wall, another taken up by a row of white built-in wardrobes.

She wandered around, running her hand over the surfaces, marvelling at how clean and fresh it was. It had clearly not been used for some time and she took some comfort from the fact that this was consistent with what Peter had said. And she was warming to the notion that, at least for a short while, she could enjoy the trappings of luxury Lisa might take for granted.

She opened the built-in wardrobes one by one. Rows and rows of dresses, skirts, blouses and trousers in every conceivable colour hung from rails below shelves which supported dozens of shoeboxes. A hundred or more! She scratched her head and the doubts returned. If Lisa was away and had been away for a while, had she not taken any clothes? There were no obvious gaps and not much room to spare on the rails. It didn't ring true, but she shook her head and tried to banish the difficult and conflicting thoughts from her mind. She would simply ask Peter and he would explain, and everything would be clear.

She turned her attention to the bath and sat on the edge. On a ledge behind it set into the wall sat bottles of shampoo, conditioner and bubble bath. All the things a young woman needed and more. She couldn't remember when she had last had a bath. It was all too tempting. She twisted a large chrome knob to drop the plug and turned on the hot tap, pouring bubble bath into the flow of water that foamed up instantly and began to fill the tub with froth.

While the bath filled, she examined her face in the mirror above the vanity unit and noticed that despite the relative comfort and plentiful food she had had in the last two days, she still appeared pale, drawn and featureless. A variety of cosmetics were arranged on the glass shelf and she found more in the drawers. There was enough there to effect some repairs, she thought.

***

Peter sat on the sofa in the drawing room, an open bottle of New Zealand Sauvignon Blanc and two wine glasses, one half full, arranged before him on a lacquered mosaic table. He had showered and changed quickly and had been waiting patiently for three quarters of an hour for Alice to reappear.

But he didn't mind the wait and it had given him time to think carefully about how she had reacted to his admission about Lisa. She was clearly more astute than he had realised, and he had simply got carried away with enthusiasm. But it was also clear Alice had been discomfited by his answers, and he cursed himself that he had not anticipated her questions, rash in his assumption that she would be so impressed by her room, there would be no questions asked.

He had never set out to mislead her but he knew he had sounded disingenuous, that this had upset her, and it had upset him in return. He was not prepared to explain everything to Alice just yet. It was far too soon and far too difficult for him. The right time would come for that, and he fervently hoped no lasting damage had been done to their relationship.

But she had been gone a long while and he desperately hoped it was not related to her nervousness about Lisa, or his behaviour. He looked at his watch. Over an hour. How long do young ladies need to have a quick wash and brush up? he thought, and then berated himself for being daft. 'Twas ever thus. *Have you forgotten already?* But he had to admit he was a little worried and considered whether he dare venture upstairs to enquire. He needn't have worried.

Footsteps on the stone floor outside in the hallway and then on the oak floorboards of the drawing room caused him to look up in the direction of the open door. She was standing in the doorway, hands clasped behind her back, nervously waiting her turn to be announced at the ball or, at least, invited in. Nervous. Self-conscious in someone else's clothes, someone else's shoes and someone else's make-up.

She wore a simple pale blue cashmere sweater over blue skinny jeans and flat black shoes. Lisa's. He looked at her for a moment and his mouth dropped open. His heart

222

skipped and a lump formed in his throat, such that he thought he would not be able to speak.

"Gosh," he said finally, and he could feel his eyes watering. He fought back the instinct and bit the inside of his mouth to distract himself from the thoughts whirling around his head. "Aren't you a sight for sore eyes?" he said, his voice beginning to break.

If he had meant to calm her nerves, he would have failed, but at that moment he was capable only of saying what was on his mind. Jess looked away, embarrassed, uncomfortable, and he saw it.

"Please, come in," he said softly, but then remembered his manners and stood up briskly.

"Please, sit." He gestured to the sofa opposite and she automatically obeyed, just as she had done that first night on the boat. The moment was over for now and the colonel was back in control. "Would you like a glass of wine?"

"Yes, thank you." He poured a glass and handed it to her, topped up his own and sat back down on the sofa opposite.

He sat back, and watching her sip the wine filled him with joy. He had not planned to interrogate her just yet, if ever, but he was on his second glass and he couldn't resist. Anyway, he just wanted to hear her speak.

"Now, Alice, I don't know where you came from and I don't know where you're going, but I'm very pleased I found you huddled under my canopy the other day." She smiled a thank you. "You know, I know nothing about you, you've been very" – he paused to find the right word – "reserved."

"I'm sorry," she jumped in quickly, clearly wrestling with a suitable reply, but he came to her rescue, again.

"No, stop there. I am not being nosey, just concerned. If there's something on your mind you want to chat about, then feel free to do so in your own time. I can assure you I am a good listener. On the other hand, I have no problem with those who prefer to keep themselves to themselves." He leant forward conspiratorially. "I'll have you know, I am a founder member of the M.Y.O.B.S." He announced gravely. She looked at him, puzzled, before he bellowed, "The Mind Your Own ... Business Society." She helped him finish the sentence as the penny dropped, and they both enjoyed the joke; but then he became more serious.

"I used to interrogate people, you know, ghastly business." He made a face expressing his distaste. "But they had things I needed to know. So, I don't speak lightly. Everyone has a right to a private existence without others poking their noses into their affairs. Anyway, it's not what people say, it's what they do that matters," he declared, taking another swig of his wine.

She nodded in understanding. In fact, he had little interest in her background, deciding that, despite his career in intelligence gathering, the need to know a fundamental part of his professional life, the less he knew about Alice the better. If she was unable or unwilling to open up to him, then so be it.

The one thing they had in common, did they each but know it, was that life had begun again two days ago when they first met. Day one of the rest of their lives. There was no past, no future, just the present; and, like her, he was content to take things one day at a time. She smiled at him, embarrassed at the silence. He rescued her again.

"Now," he went into command mode, "where's this dinner I've been promised?" She brightened immediately and glanced at the clock on the mantelpiece.

"Dinner coming up, Colonel, at nineteen thirty hours," she announced with aplomb.

"Ha! Marvellous!" he hooted with delight at the military reference. "Don't hesitate to shout if you need some help." He leant forward conspiratorially. "But I'm best kept out of it if I'm honest."

"I'm sure I'll manage," she said and jumped to her feet.

He watched her go, and as she did, his smile faded and, not for the first time, he was overwhelmed by sadness. He sat back and rubbed his forehead. From time to time she looked like the proverbial rabbit in the headlights and he desperately wanted to comfort her, to hold her and prove to her that she was safe. Whatever her background was, whoever she was, Alice, he was sure, was not her real name. Whenever he used it, there was a fractional delay in her response, a disconnect, a sliver of doubt which revealed an inconsistency she was trying to resolve. He had seen this many times before in his career, the innocent or not so innocent lie; that was the distinction that had to be struck.

But worse, if she was living a lie, then he was too, and the self-loathing he had endured for the last year or so hung like a cloud over his head. He could not, would not let this girl come to any harm, but that relied on her staying within his sphere of influence, and that was the challenge that faced him now. *It's all for her own good. Or is it for mine?*

***

Jess scurried around the huge kitchen, opening cupboards and drawers at random until she found the right implements. She had all the ingredients and after a slow start, things began to come together. She had set herself a deadline and was determined not to miss it. What would the colonel think if she did?

She thought back to that moment when she had presented herself in the drawing room, when she had expected to see the garrulous, voluble, energetic Colonel Jeffries she thought she had come to know. Instead, she saw an elderly gentleman named Peter, frail and vulnerable, his piercing blue eyes curiously vacant and lost. She was already uncomfortable wearing Lisa's things and, seeing his reaction, had thought for a split second it had been a mistake, but he had seemed to recover his composure just as quickly. She had resolved to stay totally sober, but after her arrival at the house and the extraordinary experience upstairs in Lisa's room and then again in the drawing room, she had decided she needed it. The wine had tasted cool and fruity but then warming and pleasantly relaxing.

She had been thrown off balance by his observation on her reticence and her apology had been genuine, but she had no desire to rake up the past just yet, if ever. And the same could be said about him, she thought. She knew nothing about him either, other than he owned a huge house, a classy motorboat and had a daughter, Lisa, who was away somewhere and not expected to return in the near future. But then that was quite a lot, she had to admit, a lot more than he knew about her. She had stayed quiet, relieved he had not pressed her, at least for the moment. But she had noted that given his statement about personal privacy, he too was likely to be less forthcoming than she wanted.

Her biggest problem was that she could not bring herself to trust anyone, not even Peter, and she could only satisfy herself that Peter was not a danger to her by knowing more about him. But trust had to be earned and that took time, and as she still harboured the belief that her stay there would be short-lived, there might not be enough.

By seven thirty she was ready to serve. She strode out into the hallway and banged the dinner gong, surprising herself with her sudden display of bravado and self-confidence.

Within seconds Peter marched into the kitchen clutching his wine glass and the remains of the bottle of Sauvignon Blanc.

"By Jove, that smells marvellous!" She put two plates down on the table and he sniffed the one in front of him loudly.

"Chicken casserole, with fresh vegetables from the estate," she announced. He refilled their glasses and they clinked.

"Bon appetit," he said.

"Bon appetit," she said back, and they laughed together.

***

Jess lay in the huge bed, gazing at the full moon as it drifted past the tall window. The bed was supremely comfortable and the goose down pillows, soft and luxurious. She had everything she could possibly need at her fingertips, the polar opposite of her circumstances a mere forty-eight hours ago. And yet she could not accept it nor take it for granted. She felt like a fraud. This was Lisa's bed, Lisa's nightdress, Lisa's bedroom, and she, Jess, an intruder for whom time would inevitably run out.

And then it would all come to an end, *everything comes to an end*, and who knows where she would be. She was, however increasingly relaxed in Peter's company and had no immediate desire to rush off into the night. She would not abuse his generosity any longer than necessary, but he seemed to enjoy having her there and, she guessed, would be very upset if she disappeared unexpectedly.

But she was unnerved by Lisa's absence and if she needed to know anything, it was where Lisa was and when she was likely to return. Until she knew that, she was merely an interloper. She was tired but her mind continued to race, and it was a long time before sleep eventually came.

***

She's up and it's early and Mo is just leaving and he's in a rush, always in a rush, never has time to talk, always working, always on his phone speaking in his strange language, and she's feeling sick again and she's been to the doctor and he's confirmed it. She's excited and frightened and nauseous at the same time and she wants to share it with him and he puts his phone down and she's telling him and he ignores her and dials someone else and holds his palm up to her and he jabbers on and on, "Two thousand to win, inshallah," and she is pacing around and then he finishes his call and he tells her to stop working and they are moving house and getting out of this shithole and make sure it's a boy and then he calls someone else, "Thirty k a kilo, twelve for a quarter, aap khoye hue hain*," but then she's in the hospital and Leila is crying and her mum's there with a purple eye and blood streaming down her face and says, "Your Dad's poorly, sends his best," and she look down at her new baby daughter but the cot is empty and she knows and Mo's nowhere to be seen and she gets the bus home but there's no one there and she knows and she calls him, "Mo, where are you? Mo, where are you? Mo, please, where are you?" – but she knows.*

She sat up, wide awake, and her face was wet. She turned her head to the window and the moon was gone, replaced by an orange glow on the horizon. Jess wiped her eyes and looked east, hoping, no, certain that Leila would be having her lunch by now and that soon she would be resuming her lessons. One day at a time. Sleep comes again, and this time, it's gentle and kind to her.

***

The silence of the morning woke her. The house was very quiet. But, she thought, that's understandable because it's so big and no one lives here.

She looked at the bedside clock and noticed with mild horror it was 9.35. She had never slept in, never in her life, but she realised she had been in bed for almost twelve hours. Maybe her body needed it – but what would he think of her?

She threw back the covers and dived into the shower with every intention of rushing downstairs as quickly as possible to apologise to him for her outrageously rude behaviour. But the water was too warm, the pressure too exhilarating, the shower gel too fragrant and foamy and she didn't want to get out. He had obviously not tried to wake her, but then he was a gentleman and wouldn't come into her room unannounced. *I hope he hasn't been waiting for breakfast.*

The grandfather clock in the hallway was chiming ten when she descended the spiral staircase, still straining to hear signs of life. She was wearing another of Lisa's cashmere sweaters because she loved the feel of cashmere on her skin. It was a peach colour this time, paired with black jeans and soft shoes, and she had tied her hair back with clips.

She sauntered into the kitchen but it was deserted. There was a handwritten note on the table: "Gone into town for a few supplies. Back in a couple of hours. Have fun!"

She made herself tea and had a piece of toast and then decided to go for a wander.

She had not had time to appreciate the drawing room the previous night. All four walls were adorned with bright yellow wallpaper featuring exotic birds and plants; three sofas sat in the centre of the room around a lacquered table in front of a large marble fireplace. Mahogany tables stood in each corner, on which sat ornate Chinese lamps, and daylight flooded in from two huge sash windows with internal wooden shutters, just like in her ... in Lisa's bedroom.

But the place was a mess, she thought, in her professional cleaner's opinion. Books were strewn everywhere on every horizontal surface, as were old newspapers. The odd dirty mug with dried-up tea and coffee stains lurked on a mantelpiece covered in dust, as were most other surfaces.

The dining room was equally unkempt, the centre taken up by a large mahogany table littered with more books and newspapers, surrounded rather haphazardly by twelve chairs upholstered in dark green velvet. A huge gilt mirror sat above a jet-black fireplace, either side of which were glass-shelved alcoves featuring a range of exquisite porcelain, all of them, she couldn't help noticing, sitting under a uniform coating of dust and grime.

She ventured outside to the back garden and found his vegetable patch, with runner beans, tomatoes, carrots and onions all growing in raised beds, and a greenhouse containing cucumbers, aubergines and chillies. There were also numerous flowerbeds burgeoning with species she could not possibly identify and a lawn the size of a football field looking out onto open countryside. She walked around the perimeter of the house to the front and could see *Carician* still and serene at her moorings two hundred metres away at the bottom of the lawn. She did a full circle and re-entered through the back door. She hoped Peter would be home soon.

She made another pot of tea and was reading a two-week-old *Times* on the kitchen table when she heard the front door latch and the unmistakeable sound of Peter's voice calling her name. She leapt to her feet.

"Alice!?" bellowed Peter as he barged into the hallway, shopping bag in hand, barely stopping to fling the door shut behind him. "Alice!" She met him halfway and he froze.

"Morning, Colonel!" she said, hands pressed into the front pockets of her jeans and happy to see him, although he looked surprisingly flustered.

"Oh!" he sighed, "Thank goodness for that!" putting one hand on his chest and affecting a huge sigh of relief.

"Thank goodness for what?" she said, confused.

"Well," he said, looking a bit sheepish, "while I was out, I got this horrible feeling that by the time I got back, you might be gone."

"Gone?"

"Well, you know … you seemed very anxious to be on your way. I'm so glad you decided to stay," he said, clearly relieved. But Jess's inner alarm system sounded again. He was going too fast for her. She hadn't made any decisions about anything, and her instinct as always was to resist any and all pressure to make her do anything not of her own choosing; even though, truth be told, leaving here was the last thing on her mind. She made a half-hearted attempt to assert some control.

"Well, I—"

"I got us some nice fish in town," he interrupted her, lifting his shopping bag as evidence. "Thought I might impose upon your culinary excellence again?" he asked tentatively, and she was sure he had winked at her. She caved in easily.

"Okay, that will be nice."

"And a nice bottle of Prosecco for aperitif," he went on.

"Lovely," was all she could say in response, but she was charmed already and he wasn't even finished.

"And Chablis for the Dover sole." He beamed with satisfaction and she pulled her hands free from her pockets and raised them in surrender.

"Okay – I give in!"

"Anyway, you'll have to stay till the weekend now," and without waiting for a reaction he strode past her, the wine bottles clinking in the bag. The alarm sounded again, louder than ever.

"What's happening at the weekend?" she anxiously tried to ask as he brushed past her, apparently oblivious to her concerned expression, and she turned to watch him disappear in the direction of the kitchen. She set off in pursuit, to find him unloading his purchases onto the kitchen table. She marched to the opposite side of the table to confront him, for the first time feeling uneasy at his manner, his presumption.

"What's happening at the weekend?" she asked clearly and deliberately with a hint of seriousness which he ignored completely.

"Oh?" he said, as if he had just remembered something entirely trivial. "I bumped into my lawyer, Michael, and his wife, Emma. Haven't seen them for a while so I invited them over for Sunday lunch. Told him what a brilliant cook you were!" he said proudly, delighted to issue the accolade. Jess's eyes widened with horror and she slumped onto one of the kitchen chairs.

"Oh God! Peter?"

"What?" he said, feigning concern that may he have said or done something out of turn.

"I ... I" she stuttered, thoughts whirling around her head.

"You'll be fine," he said, but if he was trying to reassure her, it wasn't working. "They're lovely people, and they're dying to meet you. Now, any tea in that pot?"

Exasperated, she put her head in her hands.

***

She forgave him after a couple of hours. She couldn't help it. She had been mortified, not only fearful at the thought of being introduced to two of his friends but also terrified that she had to cook something too. Peter was no gourmet, that was plain, and if she had slopped out Welsh rarebit he would have found it exotic and exciting; but for all she knew, Emma and Michael had more sophisticated tastes.

What could he have told them? What expectations might they have? She was just a cook, an okay one, but she had never cooked for strangers, never mind well-heeled ones. It was all too much for her to think about, but she had to admit to herself there was an element of flattery involved in his actions which she enjoyed, even though it was tinged with fear.

She took pleasure in berating him for his apparent thoughtlessness and only relented when he put on a hangdog look of contrition, until she realised he was only play-acting, which made her madder still. Peter knew exactly what he was doing, and it was only his charm and his impish smile that won her over.

***

He had taken a risk, he knew, but a calculated one. He had barged into Michael's office without an appointment, and fortunately Michael did not have any client meetings that day. He knew it was impetuous, but he had lain awake most of the night thinking about it and come to the conclusion that he had to get it off his chest; and who better to confide in than his best friend and confidant?

In any event, he had promised to arrange a meeting with Michael to review his affairs and he wanted to tell him that for the time being, that was on hold – and the reason why. Michael, of course, had tried to talk him out of it, but Peter had been insistent and suggested he and Emma come over for Sunday lunch to see for themselves, and then all would become clear.

He then had to dash into the supermarket and get the ingredients for dinner and hurry home in his battered old Land Rover before Alice had any thoughts about disappearing, however unlikely he judged that to be. But before he had left home early that morning, Peter had carried out a quick risk assessment and taken action to mitigate the risk.

Alice had left her boots in the utility room along with all the other footwear and outdoor gear, and he had taken the precaution of hiding them in the garage so that even if she had wanted to escape, the only choice of footwear she had was from a wide range of size twelves. He needn't have worried.

He had wondered how she might react to his announcement that he had invited his friends over for lunch. When for a moment, she looked genuinely horrified, he thought it might have been a step too far. But he allowed her to vent her rage on him and, if he were honest, he actually enjoyed being told off. He didn't know her at all, of course. But then he had known her all her life.

***

She lay in bed that night, replete with Dover sole and far too much wine, contemplating the forthcoming weekend and the pressure she was now under to cater for his friends. Her initial reaction had been one of fear and foreboding, that perhaps Emma and Michael may be more inquisitive about this stranger in their midst; certainly more inquisitive than Peter had been so far. Even if they were not suspicious of her, common courtesy would demand they ask general questions about home, family, work et cetera, none of which she was prepared to answer. To that extent they posed a risk that she would have to manage carefully, and she decided this might be achieved by cooking and serving the lunch and staying out of the way.

On the other hand, she thought, meeting two of Peter's friends might show him in a different light, put a fresh perspective on his character and perhaps reveal something about his past. They were bound to talk of things of common interest and that might include family, which in turn might lead to her finding out more about Lisa. And if there was a daughter, there must be a mother too, a wife probably, and he had made no mention of her.

As she dozed, another thought occupied her mind. When Peter had been out this morning and she had been looking around the house, she was left with a feeling that there was something missing, something strange she couldn't put her finger on. Then it struck her.

The house had no shortage of contents: paintings, vases, pots, mirrors, lamps and furniture, but she had not seen a single photograph anywhere. There were no pictures in Lisa's room, and although she had not seen inside his, she thought it was highly unusual to live in such a large house bereft of family photos. It was true, there were many old paintings of the Jeffries dynasty, but none that could be regarded as modern. Before she could reach any conclusion, she drifted away.

"Help me, please help me, I don't know what to do."

"I am very sorry, madam, the ambassador is very busy."

"Please, just for a moment, please," and there's a man in a dark suit and he has a big black moustache, and it's Mo's uncle and he says, "Madam, you must respect your husband, your duty is to stay home and keep house, cook and clean and give him boys and respect and inshallah he will return, you must know your place," and she is wailing and her legs are weak and they are carrying her outside and her father is

there on the pavement, bottle in hand, "Paki waster!" he shouts at the man with the moustache.

"Unless you make the minimum payment," says a passer-by, "we are going to have to let you go."

"Don't want her thinking I got any favourites," says another.

"Yes, Mrs Khalid, you have an appointment with the Home Office, just make the minimum payment and we won't cut you off."

"Discount? Negotiate a discount ..."

She heard the remnants of her own cry as it receded, the cry that woke her, and she sat up, shaking and sweating, looking around the room, Lisa's room. The house was deathly quiet. All she could hear was the faint rustle of leaves on the trees outside, the sound seeping through the open windows. She glanced at the bedside clock, squinting to read it through wet eyes: 2.35 a.m. She lay back and wiped her forehead, afraid to go back to sleep, afraid to go back. Afraid.

***

There was work to do tidying up Peter's detritus of books and newspapers, cups and saucers, and vacuuming and dusting the drawing room and dining room, and cleaning the downstairs loo. Then she had to think of something to cook, so in between cleaning sessions, she looked through the cookbooks in the kitchen and found a recipe for salmon en croute, which she had never made before but was sure she could manage.

Then she and Peter had to go to town in his rattly old Land Rover and buy the ingredients, and then she had to get out and wash the best crockery and glassware and ... it was a full-time job. Peter stayed out of her way for the most part, pottering around outside in the garden and in his greenhouse, making no demands, letting her get on with her arrangements.

But Sunday came, and when it did, she was ready.

CHAPTER 26

The doorbell rang shortly after noon and Peter, casually smart in check shirt, brown corduroys and brown brogues, marched down the hallway to greet his guests.

"Welcome, welcome," he said effusively as he opened the door wide.

"Peter, how lovely to see you," drawled Emma Goodman, expensively elegant as always in sleeveless summer frock and pearls. She stopped inside the doorway to present each cheek in turn.

"Emma, you're looking radiant as ever," gushed Peter, a hand on each shoulder.

"Thank you," she purred. "How was your trip up the river?"

"Marvellous, thanks. Michael!" he said thrusting out a hand to his lawyer and friend.

"Hello, old man," said Michael stuffily, taking his hand and thrusting a Bordeaux Superieur at him with the other. "Bottle of plonk for you there." There was nothing precious or affected about Michael.

"Ah, thank you. Was there much traffic?" he asked Michael, noting Emma was visually conducting a circular tour of inspection of the hallway as if she had never been there before.

"No, not much for a Sunday," said Michael, lugubrious as ever. Pleasantries over, Peter got to business.

"Right, come on into the drawing room and I'll get us all a drink." His guests turned dutifully on the spot and meandered into the drawing room, followed closely by their host. "Now, what'll it be? Prosecco?"

"Oh, I love Prosecco," cooed Emma, still examining her environment.

"Me, too," said Peter. "Michael?"

"Tonic and lime, old boy, I'd better be good."

"Well, sit yourselves down. I'll be back in a sec."

In the kitchen he found Jess hard at it, rushing around, clattering pots and pans, lifting lids, stirring frantically, poking, staring through the glass oven door and generally panicking.

"Anything I can do?" he ventured as he assembled the drinks on a tray.

"Yes, you can let me get on!" she snapped at him but then made the mistake of turning around to see his infuriating grin. He was clearly enjoying himself too much. Her anger evaporated and she smiled back.

"Come on in when you get a moment, and I'll introduce you," he said and disappeared, tray balanced carefully in both hands. Jess had abandoned her plan to stay out of the way, considering it unworkable, and decided instead she would just have to play it by ear.

She had chosen an elegant floral dress from Lisa's wardrobe, one that fitted her perfectly and which appeared to be brand new and unworn. She also found virtually new black suede court shoes in one of the myriad boxes, and although she was not used to wearing four-inch heels, had so far managed to move around the house in them without incident.

She had also taken time to plait her hair and modestly apply eye shadow and lipstick from Lisa's cosmetic collection. She wanted to make a good impression. She didn't want to let him down, but he had made no comment when she presented herself for inspection. He had been speechless. She would give them another five minutes, she thought.

***

"Here we are," said Peter, back in the drawing room, carefully placing the tray on the Japanese lacquered table then proceeding to remove the foil and cage from around the top of the Prosecco bottle.

"Peter, have you had a tidy?" said Emma from her position on the sofa, casting her eyes around the room. "Last time we were here, the place looked like a bomb site, like some old man lived here by himself," she mocked him gently, and he knew the question was mildly rhetorical.

"Well, there'll be a good reason for that," he replied as he popped the cork and poured two glasses.

"Ah, yes," gushed Emma, "we're dying to meet her." He passed her a glass and Michael a tumbler.

"Cheers!"

***

Jess could put the moment off no longer. The salmon had another five minutes to go, after which it could sit out for another half hour, the potatoes were just warming up and the salad was already prepared. She could put in a brief appearance and then plead kitchen duties as a means of escape.

She pulled off her apron and nervously brushed down her dress at the front to remove imaginary wrinkles. She took a deep breath and made her way briskly to the drawing room but stopped in the hallway before she got there. She could hear animated conversation and laughter. What were they talking about? Her? *Stop it! They are just talking. Happy. Friends together.* She carried on, slowing her pace, trying not to disturb the revelry, trying to slide in without anyone noticing.

She stepped cautiously into the room. The woman she assumed to be Emma seemed to sense her presence immediately and twisted her head towards her. She sported a wide grin, presumably from something one of the others had said. It vanished the instant their eyes met. It was shock or surprise, or both, and Jess felt a wave of panic and confusion. In a flash Emma swung her head to the left and Jess followed her line of sight. Michael was looking at her, equally disturbed. Jess sensed the temperature had dropped dramatically and gave serious thought to flight, when Peter intervened.

"Alice! Come, come!" Reluctantly, she took a few tentative steps into the room as Peter and Michael both stood. "Alice, this is Emma and Michael," he announced, beaming from ear to ear. Emma got to her feet too as Jess shuffled up to her and held out a limp hand.

"Pleased to meet you," said Jess, wondering whether a curtsey was appropriate. Emma had quickly recovered her composure, her steely eyes examining Jess closely as she proffered her hand, palm down, like the Queen at an investiture.

"How do you do, Alice? My, what a pretty frock. Suits you very well," she gushed provocatively, and Jess immediately felt awkward. This had not started well, she thought. Her self-confidence had dissolved under Emma's withering stare and pointed comment. She was rescued by Michael, who stepped forward, holding out his hand.

"Very pleased to meet you too, Alice," he said, but his wife was in full flight, her tone imperious and condescending.

"Oh, my dear, I do hope Peter hasn't imposed us upon you. When you've known him for as long as we have, you'll find its par for the course." She smirked at Jess, who shuffled back a step and looked at her feet.

"Here, have a glass of fizz," said Peter, holding out a glass to Jess which she took, relieved at the distraction.

"Shouldn't really," she said, attempting a joke, "drunk in charge of an Aga!" regretting it straight away from the look on Emma's face, although Peter was still beaming with pride.

"I hope you haven't gone to too much trouble for us," said Michael, and his non-threatening tone put her at ease.

"No!" she blurted out, then thought that sounded wrong. "I mean yes!" But that didn't sound right either. "I mean, I'm just not sure what it will taste like."

"It will be excellent as usual," declared Peter, and Jess decided it was time to withdraw as gracefully as she could.

"Well, I must get back, in case something boils over," she said, turning to go, but Emma wasn't finished, and as she sat back down on the sofa, called out disingenuously.

"Can I help?" she said, having not the slightest intention of helping at all.

"No, I can manage," said Jess, and strode off, glass in hand. Emma watched her go and they resumed their seats on the sofas. Emma couldn't help herself and turned to Peter, her voice low but urgent.

"My God, Peter! I was quite dumbstruck for a moment."

"First time for everything," mumbled Michael under his breath, which drew a withering look from his wife. Emma pressed on regardless as the men exchanged glances, enjoying the joke at her expense.

"Where on earth did you find her?" Peter took a sip of Prosecco.

"She rather found me, Emma. It's a strange tale and I don't want to go into it now, but I would ask you both a favour, if I may? She may be sensitive to questions about her background, so I shall be grateful if you did not, er, put her under any pressure, shall we say."

Emma put on one of her faces as Peter continued. "And I haven't explained my situation either, so I would appreciate it if you could, you know, not mention it."

Unlike her husband, for whom discretion was stock in trade and who no doubt understood Peter perfectly, she wondered how she might cope with these constraints.

Peter concluded. "But I would appreciate your views."

***

Lunch had gone well. Jess was very pleased with her first ever attempt at salmon en croute, and the simply boiled Jersey Royals and green salad had been the perfect accompaniments. The fresh fruit salad and ice cream was equally delicious and had taken little effort to prepare.

Peter and Michael had dominated the conversation, laughing boisterously at each other's jokes, while Emma frequently raised her eyebrows and issued the occasional put-down, which of course made them even merrier.

Jess kept her head down, picking at the tiny portion of food on her plate and totally ignoring the wine in her glass. It seemed that whenever she looked up, Emma was staring at her with a knowing expression, making her feel increasingly uncomfortable. Emma could not resist probing the girl of whom, it was self-evident, she was very suspicious, and ignored both Peter's grunts and groans and Michael's kicks under the table.

For her part, Jess was able to deflect Emma's attention by offering more wine, affecting to "check on things" in the kitchen and, where possible, diverting the question to Peter; but while she successfully navigated the treacherous waters of lunch, she failed to discover anything substantive about Peter's family or his past.

"Alice, that was delicious," decreed Michael at the end of the meal, and Peter looked like he would burst with pride at the efforts of his young protégée. Jess could not help feeling satisfied with what she had served and was mildly embarrassed at the compliment, but more importantly, relieved the worst was over.

"You're welcome." she replied. "If you'd all like to take a seat in the drawing room, I'll bring some coffee."

"Excellent!" said Peter, still intoxicated with pride.

Jess gathered up the dessert plates as the others decamped to the drawing room, but no sooner had she reached the kitchen than she heard footsteps behind her.

"I'll come and help," said Emma, empty wine glasses in both hands. Jess cast a glance over her shoulder and to her dismay saw Emma taking up position on the other side of the kitchen table.

"No, it's okay, I can manage," she said, trying to put her off; but it was futile, she knew. She kept her back to Emma, busying herself aimlessly as the hunter considered her prey.

"That was a wonderful lunch, Alice, thank you," said Emma, oozing gratitude yet spoken in a way that sounded false and disingenuous. "Lunch at Peter's is such a rare event these days. It's about time he got himself a new housekeeper."

At this latest provocation, Jess swung round. Her face betrayed the fear that decisions had been made, her future presumed, control being taken from her.

"I'm not his housekeeper!" she said, trying but failing to keep the anxiety from her voice, and Emma must have known she had hit a nerve.

"Oh! I must have misunderstood," she said, heavy with sarcasm. In her rush to correct the error, Jess then entangled herself further in the spider's web.

"No. I just bumped into Peter and he was kind enough to help me out." It sounded lame and implausible, even though it was true.

Emma studied her for a moment and Jess's head dropped. The woman had seen through the facade and was not going to be placated by irrelevancies such as the truth.

"You know, Alice, despite all that conversation over lunch, I still feel I know nothing about you," she said, probing, looking for a chink in the armour.

"There's nothing to tell," said Jess.

"And whenever one made a simple enquiry into your background, you seemed adept at steering the conversation towards another subject."

"Did I?" said Jess innocently, although she knew it was true. She had. Emma paused for a second.

"Peter knows nothing about you, either."

"He hasn't asked," said Jess, subdued, desperately hoping someone or something would come and save her.

"That's not his way," said Emma casually, assuming full control and ramping up the tension. She paused again, waiting for the moment to strike.

"Who are you, Alice?"

But there was no answer, easy or otherwise, and Jess stood, head down, dismayed, oppressed as ever, wishing she were somewhere else and, not for the first time, wishing she had never been born.

Jess lowered her head. She felt fragile and vulnerable, rather than confident and resilient. She was well dressed and beautiful and polite and she had cooked an exquisite lunch for people she had never met, and still they were lining up to challenge her, attack her, question her motives and demean her.

In the ensuing silence, Emma seemed to relax a little, and to Jess's surprise she began to sound conciliatory.

"You'll forgive me if I appear overprotective, but we're all the family Peter has. He's been through a lot of pain. We don't want to see him hurt again." The instruction was clear and unequivocal and the threat implicit. Jess's head flicked up at the slight and the injustice.

"I'm not here to hurt Peter!" she protested, riled by the impertinence of the woman.

"Then why are you here?" shot back Emma, clearly taken aback by the girl's sudden renaissance of spirit.

"I don't know," countered Jess, taking a step forward, and for a moment she thought Emma looked unnerved. "I'd be gone by now if he hadn't invited you and Michael for lunch." Her frustration bubbled to the service.

"He wanted us to meet you," drawled Emma.

"What for?" Jess realised she was raising her voice in exasperation but couldn't stop herself. "A second opinion?"

"Oh no, his mind is quite made up," said Emma with conviction, but now it seemed it was she who was on the defensive.

"What do you mean?" said Jess, her eyes focused now on her opponent.

"Best Peter tell you that in his own good time," said Emma imperiously, but her demeanour had changed.

They remained silent for a moment or two, each contemplating their next move, but it was Jess who took the initiative. She had resented the intrusion, the unjustified attack on her motives from someone who knew nothing at all about her, and was minded to walk away from them all and slam the door behind her. But she had grown in the past few weeks, more so than in all her preceding years; learnt lessons the hard way, learnt that sometimes you needed to fight your corner. She had nothing to lose. She looked Emma directly in the eyes.

"Emma ... what happened to Lisa?" She had put her adversary on the spot, and Emma stared back at her, lifting her chin up almost in acknowledgement.

"I can't explain that to you, Alice," she said wearily, "only Peter can." It was as close to a white flag as she would get. Emma walked off leaving Jess hurt and confused and none the wiser, yet more determined than ever to find out the truth.

They stood outside together, waving, as Emma and Michael's car pulled slowly away from the house, its tyres crunching on the gravel driveway; Peter sporting a large grin, as he had done all day, Jess, solemn and pensive.

Her encounter with Emma had brought home to her the fragile nature of her situation. It had been naïve to assume she could maintain the pretence, perpetuate the myth of Alice, and Emma had seen straight through it. Women's intuition. There would be a reckoning, she knew; she just had to decide when that might be. In her own time, or Emma's?

As they exchanged polite embraces at the door, Emma had said, "We must have coffee together, then we can have a good chat, just us girls," and she had shuddered at the thought. The woman was not going to give up easily.

Jess reflected on the last few days she had spent with Peter. They had been the best she had known for a long time. But it wasn't sustainable. Their relationship was artificial and she was a fraud, a fact made only too clear today when exposed to the light of the real world, put under the spotlight by others.

The car reached the end of the long drive and turned onto the main road. Peter went back indoors, leaving Jess alone for a moment, contemplating, considering. She could hear them talking about her.

"Extraordinary!" said Emma the moment they reached the main road.

"I know," Michael sighed. His wife was on a mission and it was not over yet.

"Especially in that dress." Emma was still frustrated she hadn't been able to get to the truth. "Well, I for one am not taken in. I can spot a gold-digger when I see one," she huffed.

"I think that's a bit harsh, dear. The girl is perfectly charming and unassuming, and you really don't have any evidence." As a lawyer, Michael only ever dealt in facts. Admittedly he was skilled at presenting them in any number of ways in order to make them more useful, but speculation of the type frequently employed by his darling wife was, to him, futile and dangerous. But Emma wasn't finished.

"He has no references, you know," she said. "He doesn't know anything about her. It's all very worrying."

"Peter's a big boy, I'm sure he knows what he's doing."

Michael sighed again, hoping that would be the end of it, but he knew better than that. His wife could talk for England, and they were another twenty minutes from home.

CHAPTER 27

The grandfather clock in the hallway chimed a muffled ten, and Jess glanced at the clock over the drawing room fireplace to confirm the time. She had let her hair down and changed out of Lisa's floral dress into another of Lisa's cashmere sweaters, a dark red one which she wore over skinny black jeans. She sat on the sofa opposite Peter, the silence total apart from the periodic rustle of the Sunday paper in which he was engrossed, and the occasional snort he gave when something in it piqued his interest.

She sat quietly, legs tucked under her, still, but inwardly agitated, mind whirling with possibilities, risks, threats, decisions. She would have gone to bed sooner but something held her back. Maybe she wanted to postpone the bad dreams that plagued her each night, dreams that had seemed somehow worse, more intense, since she had arrived at Chalton Manor. The facade she had put up at The Navigation was of no consequence, but here, in the company of this generous, well-meaning old soldier, it was despicable and cruel, and she felt ashamed. Maybe that was why, she guessed, the demons came back to haunt her each night, punishing her for her dishonesty.

But maybe she had stayed up to talk to him, and was just waiting for the right moment? Part of her desperately wanted things to stay the same, but she knew they couldn't, not while she persisted with the lie.

She felt like she was standing close to a cliff edge and was being drawn inexorably closer by some uncontrollable and invisible force. It was something that terrified her, but something she could not resist. A rustle of newspaper startled her, breaking her train of thought. Peter folded the paper, pulled off his glasses and rubbed his eyes.

"I think I'll turn in," he said stifling a yawn. "You must be tired after all that hard work?" *Considerate as ever.*

"I'm fine," she smiled, and then, unwittingly, took a step closer to the edge. "I got used to long hours." Too late, she had alluded to a different time and place, one of the many she wanted to forget or at least bury in the past, and she feared he would be prompted to enquire further. He didn't.

"Well, it was an excellent day. Thank you." The simplicity, the courtesy, heartfelt and warm. He went on, "I hope Emma and Michael didn't frighten you too much?"

"No, not at all." She stopped herself, thinking she had jumped in a little too quickly. "They're nice people." She meant it, despite the contretemps with Emma, who she knew had only wanted to protect Peter. Who wouldn't?

"Emma thinks I'm your new housekeeper."

She couldn't stop herself. It was another step. She meant it to sound like an ironic aside but there was more to it than that. She would make a good housekeeper, she thought. She had all the skills and the temperament and the commitment. Was it possible? *No, it isn't.*

"Yes, I'm sorry about that," said Peter, looking contrite. She didn't want him to feel guilty about mentioning it or giving that impression to his friends, knowingly or otherwise. She didn't find it presumptuous or demeaning. She was proud of it. It was something she wanted, but at the same time knew she couldn't have. He went on.

"Thing is, I did have a housekeeper. Latvian girl. Very pretty. Good English. But she moved on. Got a bit bored, I expect." Again, he said it with regret. A self-deprecation, a sense of failure that she found moving but surely misplaced?

"And you didn't try to replace her?" Another step.

"Well, I thought I could manage, and the thing is, Iveta was recommended to me and it's always a risk taking on someone you don't know."

It sounded perfectly plausible, but she sensed something else in what he said. It was as if he could see her approaching, had been monitoring her step by step and could tell where she was going, even if she couldn't do so herself. He had opened the door. Just a fraction. He was inviting her in. *Wasn't he?* She wrestled with the conflict raging in her head. She wanted to move forward, but that would mean opening up the past, and the consequences could be catastrophic for them both. She could not conceive how he might react, nor how she might survive the ordeal of reliving it and although she desperately wanted to pull back, she couldn't stop. She was so close to the edge now, she could see beyond it and there was nothing but darkness and terror. Yet she moved closer still.

When she spoke, it sounded dismissive, almost reproachful of him for not forcing her, not making the decision for her, not making clear what should be blindingly obvious to them both.

"You don't know me."

Peter put the newspaper to one side and leant forward, arms on his knees, hands together as if in supplication, glasses dangling aimlessly from the fingers of one hand. He saw a young woman, curled up on the sofa, legs folded beneath her, arms crossed, head down. Defensive, the posture designed for self-protection. And he sensed the change in tone from conversational to something bordering on provocation. He recognised the characteristics and behavioural patterns of someone on the edge. In his past life, he would have had to work hard and patiently over time to steer his opponent towards just such a state of mind so that whatever came next would seem like a relief to them both. He hadn't done anything to entice, direct or manipulate Alice to this point, but for whatever reason, here she was. He had to be very careful now. He was in danger of losing her, and she, in danger of being lost.

"Maybe I know all that I want to know," he said gently. His words were meant to calm her. He did not need to visit her past, or revisit his. He knew he was deluding himself, but he thought he already knew. The past he had lived for twenty-three years was crystal clear to him, and now, it was hers for the taking. If only she would grasp it, take it as her own. Maybe then, they would be able to move on together. She needed encouragement but she needed to do this for herself, and it had to be her decision.

"Look," he said, putting his glasses down on the table and spreading his hands, urging her to take his course for the good of them both. "I need some help." The words never sounded truer to him and, he thought, she could not possibly know the degree to which they so clearly defined his situation. "I don't know what your plans are, but I should be very grateful if you would stay a while. See how it goes. I'll pay you a salary, you've got your own space, all you have to do is keep the place tidy and do a bit of cooking. Well, what do you say?"

The clocked chimed once: 10.15 p.m. It was a signal. The clock was ticking, requiring her to speak, but she didn't know what to say. He was asking her to stay with him, for an indefinite period, without any question as to who she was, where she was from, where she was going, or what she may have already planned for her future. She looked up and saw him watching her, unintimidating, kindly, patient. And then, as she watched him watching her, she began to understand. It was Peter who was drawing her in, drawing her close to that terrible edge, and despite all her instincts telling her to resist, to back away, she couldn't stop. She could feel the rocks at her feet beginning to crumble. *How do I know I can trust you?*

"But how do you know you can trust me?" Another step. But somehow the words had been jumbled and come out backwards. She had no idea what she was afraid of more: the truth about Peter, or the truth about herself. Her voice trembled and she knew he sensed it. He smiled. He was probably trying to steady her, reassure her, but she didn't even know whether she wanted it or not.

"I can trust you, Alice." He sounded calm and confident. Certain but with no basis for certainty. Convinced without the evidence. Trusting, through faith. She was being welcomed and accepted by someone who knew nothing about her, beckoning her forward, his eyes urging her to trust that he would not let anything happen to her. But she had reached the edge and beyond; there was nothing but darkness.

They sat quietly for what seemed like an eternity while she wrestled with the fear and the doubt and the intolerable but irresistible pressure. There was no way back. Only forward. She closed her eyes, and with her voice reduced to a whisper, stepped over.

"My name's not Alice."

She thought for a moment he had not heard her. She waited for the scream, the explosion, the eruption of fire and rage that would inevitably accompany her fall into infinity, into oblivion, her helpless plunge to disaster. But there was none. Just two words.

"I know."

Just two words, softly spoken, without emotion or drama. He had caught her before she could fall.

She blinked, and in the silence, slowly regained her composure. She had stepped over the edge and survived. And not only had she survived; she thought she could see something faint before her. A bridge. She took another step.

"It's Jess."

"I see." Gentle, calming, reassuring. "So. Why Alice?" he said, encouraging her, coaxing her gently forward. She shrugged.

"I wanted to be someone else." He remained still and quiet, and she knew she had to do the rest by herself.

"My full name ... is Jessica. Anne. Khalid." The last three words came slowly, deliberately so he could not mishear.

"Khalid?" She could tell he was surprised. He could not have expected that. Not expected that at all. But she sensed nothing in his voice to indicate distaste, disdain or anything that might bar her way. She was on the bridge and it felt steady, and she felt confident enough to continue.

"I was seventeen when I married Mo. He was very handsome and charming, and ... different." She seemed to smile at the recollection but it quickly faded to a frown. "And I had to get away from home. I loved my mum. But my dad drank a lot and then he would hit my mum. She just took it," she said, with the same feeling of incomprehension she had back then, "and used make-up to cover the marks."

She did not want to despise her mother – she loved her – but she had never understood how her mother could have been so feeble that fighting back against such cruelty was beyond her. But now, confronting the facts and relating the events for the first time, with the benefits, or rather, the curse, of experience, maybe now she did. She hesitated and took a deep breath.

"Then. When I got a bit older" – her face twisted in pain and disgust at the memory and she didn't know how to say the words, but to her surprise they came easily – "he used to come up to my room" – she stopped and swallowed – "at night."

Peter had been listening intently, letting her find her own way, but at this, he felt the hairs on the back of his neck prickle, the blood surging to his hands, and he clenched his fists in suppressed rage. *What kind of monster?* He rubbed a temple, trying his best not to react and interrupt her flow. But she was talking again, gaining in confidence.

"He was always gentle, he never hurt me, but I knew it wasn't right. He said I was a good girl, and that it was usual for dads and daughters to … to be like that, but it was just between him and me and I shouldn't tell anyone about it."

"He said Mum knew and she was okay with it, but when I saw the sadness in her eyes, I knew it wasn't true. I got more and more frightened every time he came, and I knew how mad he could get, especially when he was drunk, so I just let him." *There, just like Mum.*

"So I used to stay out late just to avoid him. That's when I met Mo." She smiled again, remembering the good moments. "He was very kind and generous and gave me presents and wine, which made me feel better; and when he asked me to move in with him, I just said yes."

How could I refuse? What choice did I have?

"Dad was not happy. He shouted and screamed" – she shook her head – "and he called me a Paki's whore, and threw things and smashed up the house. I had to get out of there. So we married straight away, I got a cleaning job and we rented a house." And then she stopped and she saw Peter, clearly reeling from the horror, looking at her with dread. She didn't know whether he was horrified for her or at her. She just tried to focus on the bridge.

"I had Leila six months later." Her voice broke for a second as her daughter's face came into her consciousness and she swore she could hear her cries in the distance: "Mummy! Mummy! Mummy!" She looked up to the ceiling and beyond.

"My baby," she gasped, the words barely audible.

After a moment, she realised the sound of her daughter's voice was just a trick of her mind and she pushed it away.

She nervously tucked a strand of hair that had fallen across her cheek around her ear and went on.

"Mo was earning lots of money driving cabs, so we bought a house. He said I didn't need to work. But he was always out, working nights and weekends. I hardly ever saw him. I never saw his family either. I don't think they approved of me and a mixed-race child. And although Mo always wore a big fancy watch and gold bracelets and chains, Leila and I never had much to live on. He used to give us money for food, but that was it." She sighed deeply, remembering when she had found out the awful truth.

"Thing was, he was into drugs. And gambling" – she grimaced at the utter horror and depravity – "and young girls …

"Him and his mates. There was a gang of them. I know, because he brought them round once, told me to take Leila upstairs and not come down. But I heard them talking ... and laughing" – she looked into the distance, she could still hear it – "and I heard girls voices … crying … in my house." Her anguish was evident in her voice, as was the disbelief. *Did that really happen? How could that have been possible? Who was responsible?* She shook her head in a vain attempt to clear the debris of the past, wipe clean the memory.

"After a while he began to change. He got anxious and angry, and whenever I tried to ask him, he just pushed me away; and once, he raised his hand to me, and although he never hit me, I knew the signs and that … it was just a matter of time.

"One night his mates came round and there was a big argument and they beat him up in the hallway and his blood was everywhere and still he pushed me away, and then he disappeared for three days and I knew then that Mo was in serious trouble. I found a letter he'd got from the bank. We hadn't paid the mortgage in six months." Jess was talking faster now, agitatedly. She was back there, less than a year ago, frantically trying to hold together their lives as they crumbled around her.

"So I went back to cleaning because we needed the money but these horrible guys in black coats came round and he took most of it to pay them off. He wouldn't talk to me about anything, certainly not money. I tried, but ... he just ... got ... angry." She closed her eyes and her breathing deepened.

Peter's torment and rage had been growing steadily throughout. She had escaped one monster and married another. No wonder she had been afraid of him at first. But he feared the worst was yet to come and he forced himself to hold his nerve and let her do this in her own way.

He had watched aghast as the full horror of her life unfolded before him, and he marvelled at her composure. He desperately wanted to hold her, to comfort her and tell her it was all okay now. But he feared the bloodletting was not over and if he was right, it must continue. But she had stopped. There was something else. Something she couldn't face. She looked numb and distressed but there were no tears. She was strong, this girl. He waited and waited, and just when he thought he could wait no longer, she spoke.

"One day, I went to pick Leila up from pre-school. But she wasn't there." Her voice trembled again. "They said Mo had already collected her. But when I got home, they weren't there. I called him and left messages and then called his mum, who just said she hadn't seen him and then put the phone down. After a couple of hours I got panicky and called the police, but they said it was too soon to say anyone was missing." She sat, quivering, arms around herself, reliving twelve hours of hell, the terror of the unknown, knowing for certain that something terrible had unfolded, yet hoping that if she spoke of it again, perhaps it may turn out differently this time.

"I didn't sleep that night. The next morning I called his mum again ..." She paused to gather her strength. She was halfway across the bridge, but it was getting steeper and narrower and she was struggling.

"She said he'd gone. Back to Pakistan ..." Her voice rose in pitch and she gulped in breath to find the words because although she had lived with the pain for months, she had never spoken of it, hoping it had all been a bad dream. But it was real.

"... and he'd taken Leila."

She threw her head back to stop the tears but they flowed anyway, cascading down her face, the anguish visceral and unbearable, turning swiftly to rage.

"No one would do anything." She was angry now, angry at her own tears, angry at the world and the cruelty of indifference. "Police just fobbed me off, so I went to London to the Home Office and they said they'd make enquiries. But nothing happened. I went to their embassy but they wouldn't even see me."

The bitterness and frustration of injustice was written all over her face, but then was replaced quickly by acceptance, defeat. "I never saw them again."

Peter had willed her on silently, knowing something was coming, hoping upon hope he was wrong, but he had already worked it out. Filled in the blanks. He tried to analyse it.

Why would this monster, running away, trying to save himself, take his daughter with him? Did he love her or did he think she might have some value? His money was on the latter, and another wave of rage threatened to engulf him. But at the moment she broke, in that instant, her pain was his pain and his already broken heart broke once more for her. He could see she was already exhausted, drained, but she was more than halfway across. And he was waiting for her, patiently, agonisingly, willing her on.

Jess had never told this to anyone before and saying it out loud now, for her took on a new significance and a new perspective.

Years of trauma, endured, repressed, denied, now laid bare. She shocked herself by the scale and intensity of it, as if she were talking of someone else. She couldn't rationalise it, but the further she went and the more she unloaded, the more she left behind. As the flow eventually subsided, she wiped away the tears and pushed back her hair defiantly. She had never given up, and she never would.

"Mum suddenly got ill, but before she died, she made me promise to look after Dad. His drinking had caught up with him, and without Mum, he went downhill fast. Had to go into a home. But Mo had left all these debts and these horrible guys would come round every week and I had to pay them.

"So I couldn't pay my council tax or the electric or the mortgage, and then the bank started proceedings to take back the house and it just spiralled. I was doing a dawn shift cleaning and then working in an office during the day, but all my money went on paying debts and they still got bigger and bigger. Then, just before the house was repossessed, they found out at work the trouble I was in. They fired me. And the very same night, Dad died.

"So ... no family ... no job ... no house ... nothing." She shrugged, the dam filling again. But she was almost there. One more step. "I destroyed everything with Jess's name on it and just left."

She looked straight at him and he looked straight back. Strong, solid, safe. He was waiting there for her after her long journey, waiting for her to come home.

"I didn't want to be Jess anymore."

She sat quietly. She had crossed the bridge and reached the other side. There was no looking back now. No going back. Everything that had happened was behind her and would soon be a distant faded memory of a forgotten life. Someone else's life. A girl she used to know called Jess.

Alice looked up at him, her face still etched with foreboding and fear. Fear of the unknown. Jess had taken a leap of faith and placed her trust in him. Absolutely, completely, unconditionally.

He could not imagine the position she had been in, alone and fighting for her life, through no fault of her own other than having placed trust in others; and he, privileged, comfortable and secure, oblivious to her suffering. He had remained silent and engrossed in her testimony. But now she was free and she was his and he looked back at her, overcome with admiration for her spirit and in awe of her bravery, and he loved her and he vowed never to let her go, again. He leant forward and spoke at last.

"And how is Alice now?" His voice warm, gentle, comforting, trusting.

"Afraid." Her voice, hoarse and broken, tore through him, and he wanted more than anything to wrap his strong arms around her and show her she would always be safe. But it was beyond him. As ever. Even now.

"Don't be afraid. Nothing here can harm you." It was a promise he would keep forever. "If Alice would like to start a new life here, looking out for an old fool, she'll find an old fool who'll be very grateful." He smiled at her and, miraculously, she smiled through her tears.

"Thank you," she said, "for being kind." His smile widened and he got back to business.

"Now, off to bed. You've got work in the morning," and she relaxed a little and smiled again.

"Goodnight," she said softly and got to her feet.

Peter kept staring at the place where she had been sitting, and only when he heard her footsteps in the hallway was he able to reply, "Goodnight, Alice."

He slumped backwards on the sofa and closed his eyes. He had never expected to hear something as terrible as he had tonight, but it was done. Alice would want for nothing. It would be his life's work, however short that might be.

But it was not yet over. He had his own demons to confront and destroy and if his love for her was to survive, it had to be done. And soon.

***

She lay awake in Lisa's bed, totally exhausted but unable to sleep. She had bared her soul to Peter, and he had listened to her without a word of comment or criticism or reproach. He had comforted her, welcomed her in and invited her to stay with him, unconditionally, indefinitely, which was everything she wanted. She felt exhilarated at the catharsis and, for the first time, in control of her own destiny, her new identity a symbol of her new life. Her new start.

She had failed to mention the episode at The Navigation, not because she was ashamed but because, truthfully, she had already put it behind her and decided it was of no consequence. But it fascinated her to think that had those unhappy events not taken place, she would not be here now, lying in Lisa's bed, wearing Lisa's nightdress and forming an intense relationship with Lisa's father. *Fate? Of course not.*

And something else troubled her. All those whom she had trusted before had let her down, brought her to the brink of destruction, and yet she had seen fit to place her trust in Peter without finding the answer to the one thing that troubled her the most.

Lisa's bed. Lisa's clothes. Lisa's father. Lisa's life.

CHAPTER 28

She threw herself into her work, the only way she knew how. She dusted, vacuumed and cleaned every room in the house, one by one, concentrating on the ones they used most and then moving on to those that were rarely, if ever used.

Chalton Manor boasted seven bedrooms on two floors, four of them with en suite, plus a separate large bathroom on the second floor and another on the ground, and although no one came to stay, it did not mean that they didn't need cleaning. The house was ridiculously large for just two people, never mind one, but it was Peter's home and he had no intention of moving elsewhere.

She cooked all the meals, honing her cooking skills along the way, and he jokingly complained that she was causing him to put on weight with the constant supply of pies, cakes and delicious dinners.

She did all the laundry and ironing and all the food shopping. Peter set up a new bank account in his own name, giving her a card to use and into which he transferred £500 per week from which she was to provide all the food, drink and cleaning materials she needed to run the house. Anything leftover was hers to spend as she liked.

He explained that it would not be possible to open an account using either her new or previous identity as it would not pass bank scrutiny, and they left it at that. She had never seen so much money before but had no use for it, as she already had everything she needed. When she helpfully suggested he reduce the size of the allowance, he simply smiled and changed the subject.

They went to see Emma and Michael for lunch, and Emma could not have been more pleasant and welcoming towards her. She didn't know that Peter had had a robust conversation with Emma, in which he agreed to brief her on

Alice's background on the strict condition she did not ask any questions or raise the matter unless Alice did so first. This was enough to satisfy Emma's curiosity, and she now looked at Alice in a new light.

For his part, Peter busied himself in his garden, tending his vegetable patch and greenhouse, deadheading the summer flowers and clipping and pruning whether it was necessary or not.

They saw few regular visitors other than postman, the window cleaner, and the men from the gardening company who mowed the acres of lawn and cut the voluminous hedges, all of whom were polite and deferential to the colonel's pretty new housekeeper. At other times, Peter was often to be found in his study, reading from his extensive library of novels and books on military history, or, more often than not, when she brought him tea, asleep in the chair.

They took *Carician* out on the odd weekend when the weather was fine and laughed about thunderstorms and beans on toast and obstreperous, bombastic army officers. Above all, they enjoyed life and were kind to each other.

She had been there six weeks when one morning he was out tending his roses and she found herself in his room, cleaning and tidying, a normal part of her self-imposed regime. A pullover had been abandoned, left lying on the bed, so she folded it neatly and pulled open a drawer in the large mahogany chest by the bed to put it away.

The drawer was stuffed full of sweaters and jumpers all in a jumble, so she decided to take them all out, refold and replace them. At the bottom of the drawer, buried under the pile of sweaters, she came across a picture frame, face down. She hesitated for a moment but couldn't resist lifting it up and turning it over.

It was a photograph. Two women, sisters maybe, but on closer inspection, one clearly older than the other. The older, taller one, possibly early forties, had long dark brown, almost black hair, high cheekbones, brown eyes and sparkling white teeth revealed by a broad, easy smile; her bronzed arms wrapped around the younger one in the foreground, her beauty classic and unassailable and her happiness complete.

The younger one was probably twenty, smaller, but in all respects other than age, just as lovely. Two stunningly beautiful women. Jess froze. She saw herself there in the picture. She may as well have been looking in a mirror.

Lisa.

She sat down on Peter's bed, unable to tear her eyes away, unable to move, unable to comprehend. She could feel the fear and panic building from deep within and she desperately fought the urge to scream, battled an irrepressible urge to get away, to escape.

She sat for a moment, heart pounding, trying to understand, fearful that Peter may appear and find her with his most private of possessions. She hastily put the picture back where she found it, quickly folded and replaced the sweaters and left, confused and bewildered.

***

Peter noticed the change in Alice immediately. She became quiet, withdrawn, perfunctory in speech; but although he was concerned, he was not unduly worried. Everyone was entitled to a bad day. But when it persisted, he began to fear something was wrong, something was upsetting her, destabilising their otherwise idyllic lifestyle. He worried most how best to broach the subject. He needn't have.

Alone in bed, she tried to rationalise what she had seen in that picture. Lisa and someone maybe twice her age, but at the same time, at least thirty years younger than Peter. Sisters? They could easily both be daughters, but the older of the two looked foreign. No, not sisters. Mother and daughter? More likely. Both beautiful, happy and vivacious, smiling for the camera. Smiling for Peter? She couldn't make it fit. But then she recalled that look on his face when he first saw her, wet and bedraggled on the boat, the same expression of shock as Emma and Michael, *that frock suits you very well*, his insistence she stay on the boat and then at the house. The attention, the kindness, the love he had shown her; and he had not touched her once, not since that first shake of her hand.

Lisa was away, he had said, hasn't been home for a while, he had said, and she believed him and trusted him and hated herself for doubting him.

But what of the older woman? No mention of this goddess, ever. The possibilities raged in her mind until one took hold, gained traction, and, no matter how hard she tried, would not leave her alone. Joe was a monster who terrorised and abused his family and ultimately lost them. Peter's family, if that's who they were, were nowhere to be seen. She tossed and turned, tormented by this recurring nightmare even though she knew in her heart it could not be true. She could not ignore it. She had to know.

CHAPTER 29

She did her best to put aside the dark thoughts that plagued her, and he did his best not to notice she was not her usual self. But there was a different atmosphere now and it had to change, for both their sakes. She had known Peter for over six weeks and, apart from his initial reference to Lisa on the day she arrived, she was no wiser about Lisa's absence, nor the likelihood of her returning; and now there was another woman to consider, as she had always suspected. The tall raven-haired beauty in the photo with Lisa, the resemblance and intimacy between them unmistakeable. She had to be Lisa's mother: Peter's wife.

She refused to believe that Lisa, like Jess, might have run away; at least not for the same reason. Peter was not like Joe, in any respect. It was a horrible thought and inconceivable, but she couldn't get it out of her mind. She needed him to tell her himself and couldn't understand why he could not simply explain. In any event, she had to be prepared for the day that Lisa, inevitably, would return. She could not carry on playing the surrogate daughter until such time as she was no longer required.

***

One evening after dinner, they took a stroll out into the garden, examining the late autumn blooms and soaking up their fragrance. They sat on the patio with a glass of wine, basking in the warmth of the evening sun and enjoying the scents of autumn. It was early September and the leaves were already beginning to turn, the flowers dying back in preparation for the new season. They sat quietly, absorbed in their own thoughts, awkward, in sharp contrast to the fun they had had before. Jess wrestled with hers. They swirled around her head, chipping away at her confidence, and also, without realising it, their relationship. A festering sore. She could bear the silence no longer.

"I love being out here." She meant it. "I never knew a proper garden like this."

Peter shifted in his chair, seemingly relieved to hear the most innocuous of comments.

"Well, I never did much gardening, not with the army," he said, "just picked it up when I retired. Rather enjoyed it. Still don't know what I'm doing half the time," he chuckled. "Emma taught me a lot. Great gardener, Emma," he declared.

She had never thought of Emma getting her hands dirty, but she smiled at the image of Emma in dungarees, wellies and straw hat, secateurs in hand, no doubt issuing endless instructions to Michael as he manhandled the lawnmower. But she saw an opening and took it. She tried to keep her voice as casual as possible.

"She said they were the only family you had." It was if he hadn't heard her, but she noticed him stiffen and she knew she had struck a nerve. She needed to know. She hunted around for the words, the right way to ask, without causing hurt or offence or intruding on the private affairs of a self-confessed founder member of M.Y.O.B.S. But there was no other way of saying it. She needed to know.

"Peter …" She tried to tread carefully, but he remained impassive, unresponsive, and she could wait no longer. "What happened to Lisa?"

Peter had always known this moment would eventually come and had thought through many times what he would say when she, inevitably, asked the question. She had a right to know, and it was not as if knowing the truth would harm her. Harming her was the last thing on his mind and he would do anything to avoid it. In fact, he was certain

268

knowing the truth would help her, make her life easier, and he had selfishly withheld it. *Why? For what reason?*

But he knew why. He dreaded talking about it. He dreaded reliving the torture, admitting the guilt he felt and the responsibility he bore for all that had happened.

She had come into his life through chance, and he had simply merged her with his own past to create the illusion that things could go back to normal. The way they were. But it was no illusion, he realised. It was delusion. There was no past. There was no future. There was only the present. She was here with him now and she was all he had, and she meant everything to him. She had given him a second chance. He could not make the same mistake again.

Jess saw the darkness engulf him, a fierce expression spreading across his face, and was reminded instantly of their initial exchanges on the boat, when he had exploded with rage. He frightened her then and he frightened her now. She had said something terrible to him. She had mentioned Lisa, and she regretted it immediately.

"I'm sorry," she blustered, "I shouldn't have asked." She took a sip of wine to steady her nerves. She needed to change the subject, but it was too late. There was no other subject of any relevance. She was incapable of painting over the cracks; they would reappear in an instant. Her mind was consumed by one thing alone, and only he had the power to release her from its hold.

Peter's fierce expression, such as it was, reflected neither anger nor irritation at what she had said, no offence at the apparent intrusion, nor reaction to any perceived impertinence. It was borne of no more than a profound sense of self-loathing, and it softened as he started to speak.

"This is my father's house," he said, gesturing to the decrepit old manor that had been his home for as long as he could remember. "When he died, I took early retirement and moved here with my second wife. My first wife couldn't cope with army life. All that moving around, never being able to settle, and all that time I spent away. We didn't have children, and once when I was away on tour, she had an affair with a young subaltern. She said it was just a fling, just a moment of madness. But I could no longer trust her. We divorced."

It was matter of fact, but he knew he sounded subdued, regretful that he had not done more to recognise the pressures and strains the army had placed on them both. But then, as he told himself, he would not be here now, and here was where he wanted to be, more than anything else. He looked up at her and she turned her head away, vaguely embarrassed that she may have made him relive that painful experience. But then he felt a glow of warmth and his face suddenly lit up.

"I met Janica in Yugoslavia, as was, when I was serving with the UN Protection force back in '92. She was a translator, some years younger than me. Montenegrin, very beautiful," he said, basking in the memory.

"What she saw in me, someone twice her age, God only knows, but I was besotted and we married. Then, within a year, we had Lisa." His eyes glowed. "She was a joy. Life could not have been better when she was growing up." And then, without warning, the darkness returned. "You would have thought army training would teach me to expect the unexpected," he said with a profound bitterness.

"Janica died, three years ago. Leukaemia." Jess sucked in her breath. She didn't know what to say. "She and Lisa were like sisters, went everywhere together. So Lisa took it very hard. Just couldn't come to terms with it. She once asked me, "Daddy, why did it happen?" And all I could say was, "Because it happened, get on with it.""

The regret was written all over his face. If only he could turn back the clock, rewind and relive the moment. Take it all back and do it all over again. "I didn't mean to sound heartless," he pleaded, craving understanding and forgiveness, "and it wasn't that I didn't feel anything. Quite the opposite; I was torn apart inside. I just thought I had to be the strong soldier for her. Lisa withdrew into her shell and I couldn't bring her back. We drifted apart." He had agonised over this time and time again. What could he have done? If he had a second chance, he would throw his arms around his daughter, hug and kiss her, never leave her side, battle through the pain together and she would still be with him.

But he thought back to those early years, just the three of them. Perhaps it had been the age difference, but he had always been in the shadows and it was somewhere he was content to be. The women in his life were a true partnership, full of love, utterly committed to one another, bonded as one, whilst he watched from the side-lines, always there to protect and serve, but somehow disengaged. And then there was his own personality. Garrulous and officious in his professional life, yet reticent, reserved and humble at home. A commanding presence in a uniform yet withdrawn and pliable within the family. But without question, the rock on which they all depended. Someone willing to lay down his life for them. For them all. That was the way he was.

"Then she announced she was taking a gap year to Nepal with a friend from university. Initially I was quite worried but then I thought it might be good for her, give her a different perspective on life. And death." Peter was more animated now. He had judged this a positive step and he had been pleased Lisa had taken the initiative, optimistic this might have been a turning point. Jess was studying him intently now, as absorbed as he was in the telling.

"She called me when she got there, and seemed like her old self: happy and full of life." He smiled, remembering the way Lisa had talked so enthusiastically about the Himalayas and how she had plans to travel the country and learn more about Nepalese culture.

"But after a while, contact dwindled, and although I worried about her constantly, I decided it was better that I leave her alone. Better she found her own way." The regret was evident in his voice.

"She didn't come home as planned and she didn't answer my calls. So I got in touch with her friend who said Lisa had decided to stay on a while longer."

Jess had been listening closely to him speak, articulate; concise and largely matter of fact. But she watched as the rock on which they had all depended, herself included, began to shake.

"Then ..." He was staring into the abyss, reliving the news reports, the footage of temples and apartment blocks shaking and collapsing, people screaming and running in all directions in a desperate attempt to save themselves and their families. "...Nepal was hit by the earthquake."

Jess vaguely recalled the incident, but the seriousness of it did not register with her at the time. She had other things on her mind: Mo's disappearance with Leila, her own little world collapsing around her, while out there in real world, disaster unfolded on a monumental scale for others. But it was now all dropping into place, and she shared the despair he must have felt not knowing where Lisa was and fearful that she may have been injured, or worse. She remembered the agony of losing Leila, not knowing where she was, not knowing why she had been taken and the desperate helplessness and impotence she felt. Jess had been there too.

Peter continued.

"I contacted the embassy, all the aid agencies, but there was no sign of her. I did all I could from here, and finally, in desperation, flew to Kathmandu. I asked around, following her last known movements and found a mountain guide who remembered her. He said she had gone to teach children in a village called" – and here he paused, seemingly unwilling or unable to say the name – "Langtang," he said at last, with solemnity and finality. She looked at him, expectant, fears growing, and saw he was trembling. She didn't know the significance so she hesitated, but he was stuck in the moment. She needed to know.

"And, did you go to .... Langtang?" she asked gently. He paused and the full horror unfolded.

"Langtang was buried in a landslide. Totally wiped off the face of the earth." She gasped, a hand clasped over her mouth to stifle the cry. "I have to assume she's dead, but I don't know for certain. I just hope, wherever she is, she's at peace."

Abruptly, he stood up. He had to be alone, had to deal with his grief privately. It would not do to show his emotions to anyone. He stepped away but only got two paces. Jess launched herself at him and threw her arms around his broad shoulders, clutching him tightly and pressing her body against his, burying her cheek into his back. They stood together as one, each afraid to let go.

"I'm so sorry," she said, distraught. Sorry for his loss and for his pain, and sorry for doubting him. He stood ramrod straight, gripping her hands in his, holding on to her for support. He would once have felt awkward at the physical contact, the tenderness and the unbridled display of emotion, but it seemed the most natural thing in the world, and in that moment the mists cleared.

"I loved her dearly. I can't bear to think she may not have known that." Jess, still holding on tightly, struggled to understand.

"How could she not?" she said, though her tears were flowing and it was difficult to speak.

"I don't think I ever told her." His confession was absolute and she clamped her eyes.

Peter had always known he was to blame. Lisa had gone to find a love he could not give her, was incapable of giving her because of who he was. She had needed him to hold her and comfort her, to cry with her and laugh with her and remember Janica with her. But instead he had shut away his

273

grief, buried his feelings in the mistaken belief that they would simply go away. And in doing so, he had driven Lisa away, to her death. The grief, the guilt, the lesson learnt. It was done. That was who he was.

He carefully unclasped her hands and turned to face her, a gentle, giant hand on each shoulder. Her eyes were wet and she prayed for the inspiration to help him, but he was back in control. Back in command. Protect and serve.

"Enough," he said, addressing them both. "It's just life. Everyone has a sorry tale to tell and everyone just needs to get on with it." He was smiling at her now. They were together now, and would stay together. He leant forward and gently kissed her forehead and she closed her eyes. He released his hold and the parade ground beckoned. "Onwards and Upwards!"

She watched him march up the garden path towards the house, arms swinging in military fashion, and she felt emotionally drained. Now she knew. They had trusted each other and the way ahead was finally clear. Alice was home at last.

***

She reflected on Peter's story as she lay in bed that night, and how, like her, the things he loved had been taken away from him, even though their circumstances could not have been more different.

She had always considered herself a victim, and although she had eschewed self-pity, she never sought help and had never given up despite all she had endured. Her troubles were a direct consequence of the actions of others. Joe's alcohol-fuelled depravity, Mo's perverted criminality, Derek's selfish inhumanity and Dave's twisted predilections. All men. All takers.

But Peter was a man, and he too was a victim. A victim, but not of anything done to him by his beautiful girls, Janica and Lisa. He was a victim of circumstance, and it was no more or less tragic for all that. And what they had in common was that they both had lost a daughter, a daughter they loved but were powerless to protect. Lisa was dead. Leila was lost. But it was a fine distinction. Neither would return.

She was also torn. Since she had arrived at Chalton Manor, she had been looking over her shoulder, living in Lisa's shadow, feeling guilty about using Lisa's possessions and dreading the day Lisa returned to reclaim them. The threat had gone, but she could feel neither relief nor satisfaction given the circumstances.

But the one thing she could not do was impersonate Lisa. She could not be Lisa. She was someone else. She would use the money Peter gave her to buy her own things, gradually replacing Lisa's, and eventually help him lay her to rest.

Finally, she was surprised by her rush to embrace him, to hold him and not let go, a precious feeling that had been lost, taken from her by the other men in her life. She had trusted him and he had not let her down. She loved him, like a daughter loved a father, should love a father. She vowed to redouble her efforts to help and support him, to repay the kindness he had shown her. She slept soundly.

***

Peter, too, lay awake in contemplation. He had finally been forced to confront his demons, and it had been Alice who had helped him come through it. He had been stricken by grief at the loss of his darling Janica, and then racked with guilt that he may have driven Lisa away by failing to show her the love she needed, when she needed it most. He had always meant to explain to Alice what had happened to his family. His beautiful wife and daughter.

But from the moment he had laid eyes on her and seen not only a vulnerable and desperate young woman in need of help, but one who also bore a striking resemblance to Lisa, he had become obsessed with making amends for his failings. He could not have known the extent to which Alice had suffered at the hands of the people she should have been able to trust, but when he discovered her awful truth it seemed to justify his actions.

Lisa was gone. He resolved to quash the delusion that Alice could replace her. To do otherwise would both undermine his precious new relationship with Alice and defile Lisa's memory. He loved her like a father loves a daughter, like he loved Lisa. He vowed to make sure she knew it, whatever it took.

CHAPTER 30

Alice woke early. She had been spared the regular torment of voices in the night, and she hoped it meant the ghosts of her past had finally been exorcised. But she felt queasy and sweaty and shivered when she dragged herself out of bed to go the bathroom. She got there just in time.

She lifted her head from the toilet bowl, flushed it and got off her knees. She rinsed her mouth at the basin, put on her dressing gown and stood in the doorway of the en suite, leaning against the door frame for support. She knew what it was. She had her suspicions when she missed her period and had convinced herself it was an aberration. But she had been here before. She knew what it was.

***

They sat silently at opposite ends of the kitchen table, the only sound coming from the hum of the fridge and the sporadic ignition of the gas boiler and its pump cutting in.

A shaft of autumn light streamed in through the kitchen window, creating a ghostly glow that separated them like a luminescent barrier. She had told him about The Navigation, about being violated, about not resisting, about believing she had no choice and that the alternative was probably worse. And then realising, too late, she had been wrong.

She had put it out of her mind, another painful lesson learnt, but not something to dwell on, or be relived. Of no consequence, she thought. She had never set out to deceive him; it was just that relative to all the other crimes committed against her, it seemed of little importance.

She sat, head supported by one arm, bowed in shame and regret. Her skin was grey and damp with sweat, her hair lank and greasy, and she smelled faintly of vomit.

"I'm sorry."

Peter had listened quietly to this latest appalling chapter in the life of this young woman, and when she finished speaking, he moved to the other end of the table, pulled up a chair and sat down next to her. Without saying anything, he lifted her head and pulled her into his arms. She clung on as if she might fall, but he held her tightly until she knew she was safe.

"Whatever you want to do is fine by me," he said softly as her body shook with the pain and she wept.

CHAPTER 31

Peter stood at the tall Georgian window looking down at the market square, watching the good folk of Hareton going about their daily business, his hands clasped firmly behind his back, a grim expression on his grey, increasingly lined face.

A rhythmic tapping noise was the only sound in the room where Michael, seated at his desk and leaning back in his leather-trimmed executive chair, twirled his expensive Mont Blanc fountain pen in one hand, tapping each end in turn on the pad in front of him.

Peter had explained his proposals to his friend who, it was fair to say, had had serious doubts about his sanity and had said as much. Peter had defended his views robustly and he believed Michael had some sympathy for them, telling him in his own calm and understated way that they were not totally without merit. Peter knew Michael had an obligation to play devil's advocate, the same obligation he owed to all his clients and especially this one, his friend. But he had pushed Peter too far, and cross words were exchanged: a highly unusual event, and it disturbed them both.

They both decided a moment or two's silence was required and each had been waiting for the other to resume their discussion, but it was Michael who spoke first, extending an olive branch whilst seeking to justify his actions.

"Peter, I'd be failing in my duty if I did not ask. Are you sure about this?"

"Yes, I'm sure," said Peter. He was still bristling from the implied criticism, not least because Michael's assessment was probably accurate and he was often right. But there would be no compromise, not this time. Michael tried one more time.

"And you've thought through all the implications?"

"I've thought of little else for the last few months," he said to the window, refusing to meet his friend's eyes. "Anyhow, I have to get a move on, according to Mr Edwards." He knew Michael was already well aware of his consultant's prognosis. Coronary heart problems, exacerbated by emphysema, a chronic obstructive pulmonary disease, a legacy of breathing in a toxic cocktail of fumes from a burning frigate, which, together with the fragment of Argentine shrapnel lodged in his spine, made his condition virtually inoperable. All of that, for Peter, brought matters into sharper focus, even though Michael might still think him misguided.

"Is that what's driving this?" he probed. Peter was aware of his lawyer friend's technique. Seeking to expose the fundamental flaw in the argument, or something that had unduly influenced his client's thought processes and judgement. He knew Michael had no inherent desire to talk him out it of it; he knew he just wanted him to be sure in his own mind. For his own sake.

"Partly. But it's time I put things right," said Peter with that familiar tone in his voice, that air of finality and determination that he hoped Michael would recognise. Instead, Michael sighed.

"You can't carry that cross forever, my friend," he said with sadness. A kindly admonishment. Peter swung around to face him, the flash of irritation in his eyes conveying to Michael an unmistakeable message. It worked.

"Okay. I'll prepare the papers and send them to you." Michael had done his best and could not be sorry he had failed.

"No," said Peter quickly in response. "Don't send them to the house." He walked over and resumed his seat opposite Michael. "I'll come back, next week."

"As you wish," said Michael wearily. But although the battle had been won, the war was not yet over.

280

"Now. About this other matter—"

"I know what you are going to say," interrupted Peter before Michael had a chance to express any views. He was not going to argue any more about this. He had made his mind up and all his lawyer had to do was carry out his wishes.

"You are going to say it's a waste of time and money." He could swear Michael had nodded his head in agreement and it irritated him further. "It's not going to be easy. You are going to need professional help. But I don't care how much it costs. I want to do it properly this time, before it's too late," he said with a weary resignation.

"But how do you know she's still alive—"

"I know she's out there, Michael," jumped in Peter, pleading for understanding, knowing he had no evidence for his last statement but still believing it to be true.

"And if she is, she wants to come back?" Michael had, of course, got to the crux of the matter. He was right, thought Peter. The last throw of the dice for a tired old man. *Immortality is temporary, young man.* But this time, the words fortified him, emboldened him. This was his shout, his instruction, and he would not be frustrated or persuaded otherwise.

"Just find her, and bring her home."

CHAPTER 32

It had been another glorious summer at Chalton Manor, three years after Peter had brought Alice there, persuaded her to stay and make it not only a new home for herself but also one for him too. After a while it seemed that they had always been together.

His precious garden had, over time, proven more and more difficult for him to maintain by himself, so a succession of garden labourers came and went, carrying out the more laborious tasks, which allowed Peter to preserve his dwindling energy and focus on his vegetable patch and greenhouse.

For her part, Alice kept the house immaculate. She had honed her cooking skills to gourmet level and had overseen redecoration of the drawing room, the hallway and spiral staircase, as well as both main bedrooms, his and hers, the latter undergoing significant and necessary modifications.

Alice had become aware of Peter's increasing fragility, and although he never talked about his condition in great detail, she knew enough to be careful about what she fed him and to monitor his activities lest he try and do anything too strenuous. But she had her hands full in more ways than one.

This Sunday afternoon, she was in the kitchen preparing a roast lunch, Peter's favourite, and he had gone out to pick some potatoes. She heard the grandfather clock in the hallway strike twelve noon and then, from afar, a familiar voice: "Mummy, Mummy, Mummy!" followed by the patter of tiny feet.

She listened and smiled, and knelt down as a little blonde girl ran up to her clutching a sweet pea.

"Mummy, Mummy!" she shouted.

"What's that, Lucy?" said Alice, crouching to the level of her three-year-old daughter and holding her by the waist.

"Grandad gave me a sweetpea!" she shrieked excitedly.

"Ooh – isn't that lovely," said Alice before she was interrupted by another small voice.

"Mummy, Mummy, Grandad gave me a sweet pea too!" Another little blonde girl, identical to the first, appeared and muscled in on the act.

"Ooh, Sophie, isn't that lovely too?" said Alice. The twins continued to shriek with delight and wave their flowers in the air, which began to wilt under their indelicate treatment. "Come on. Let's go and see if Grandad has found us some potatoes." Alice took her twin daughters, one in each hand, and led them out of the kitchen towards the garden.

***

Peter had reached the vegetable patch at the far end of the garden and decided to stop and catch his breath before wielding the fork. His left upper arm was aching to buggery and he rubbed it vigorously to try and get rid of the tingling. He wasn't due another pill for four more hours but decided he would have to bring the dose forward a bit, and he was looking forward to a glass or two of Bordeaux Superieur with his lunch, which always helped. His phone rang and he fished it out of his pocket, scanning the display. He smiled and put it to his ear.

"How's my favourite lawyer?" he said. Michael, calling on a Sunday? Must be a personal matter.

"We found her." A statement. All he needed to say. The colour drained from Peter's face as his eyes widened like saucers and his mouth dropped open.

"Michael? What?"

"We found her and she's okay," said Michael.

"But … but …" Peter was stammering and he knew it, and although he had a thousand words in his head, none of them would come out in a coherent fashion.

He sat down on the old wooden bench next to his vegetable patch. Four years. Four years since he had given the instruction. It was barely credible. He had never forgotten, and in the first few months, Michael had reported back on progress regularly, even if there had been none, and the bills had quickly totted up. But after time there had been little to report, and once the overseas leads had all but dried up, it had been left to a hard core of special services veterans, Jackson and Rutherford, to do the legwork. It had been less expensive but seemingly interminable. Michael was speaking again.

"It's been in the offing for a while," he continued, "but I wasn't sure until I got the call this morning so I didn't want to tell you sooner in case it all came to nothing. But we made the final payment, the deal was done and she's on her way back."

"And are you sure she's okay?" said Peter, desperately trying to visualise what was unfolding five thousand miles away.

"I'm told so. I haven't seen her or spoken to her and, as you can imagine, communications are very poor in these primitive areas. But Jackson's on the ground and his sources assure him she's in good health and in good spirits. I won't be able to tell you anything more for a couple of days, and then I'm afraid it may be two weeks before she gets home."

"Two weeks?" spluttered Peter. "Why so long?"

"Passport," said Michael. "We need to get her a passport. And to get one that quickly will take a little more cash."

"Oh," said Peter, deflated but accepting. "When will I be able to talk to her?"

"As soon as she's back in civilisation."

"But where is she now?"

"I'm not sure, but apparently she's travelled a fair distance already. They came across the foothills. It's about a hundred and fifty miles."

"My God. They walked?"

"It's what they do. There are no roads out there, you know."

"Who's 'they'?"

"Rutherford's with her and they've got a guide."

"Michael. I knew it. I knew it!" said Peter triumphantly and then, suddenly remembering his manners, added, "I can't thank you enough for this. I can't ever thank you enough."

He felt the pain rising in his chest again, exactly the same way he had felt when he was in the Langtang Valley four years ago. The same crushing tightness, the overwhelming urge to cry out, stifled by his emotional discipline and the determination to stay calm, suppressing the waves of fear and darkness; but this time, instead of dark, finally there was light.

"It's okay, old man. You have lots of others to thank. Go and have a stiff drink. I'll call you the moment I know more." And he hung up before Peter could say anything else.

Peter sat for a moment, stunned, trying to make sense of the conversation he had just had, barely believing it to be true, but knowing, having always known, that one day it would be.

But now, other thoughts moved in to occupy his mind. He had to weigh up the consequences of what he had done and the ramifications that would follow. He began to question, with mounting concern, whether he had done the right thing.

But he had had to do it. For her sake. For all their sakes. Yet in the midst of the euphoria, there was a terrible uncertainty, a terrible foreboding. Their lives had been made perfect again, as perfect as they had been before, and now the spectre of change was upon them. Change for the better, he could only pray.

He turned his tired eyes towards the house and in the distance saw Alice and her daughters playing on the grass, and his heart filled with joy at the sight of them, happy and contented, confident and loving.

But what was done was done and there was no going back. He stared out over the fields of wheat that bordered the western boundary of Chalton Manor, the Jeffries family home for over three hundred years, and watched the long yellow stalks swaying in the summer breeze as they had done for centuries. This had always been the Jeffries' home and he had made sure it would remain so in the future. His eyes filled at the thought, and for only the second time in his life, he opened up his heart.

"Oh, Lisa," he said, his voice trembling with pain and fear and joy. "Forgive me. I can't wait to see you again." His left arm was numb and the vice closed on his chest, but before he lost the power to speak, he was able to say that which he had never been able to say before.

"I love you."

***

Alice took Sophie and Lucy by the hand, the girls skipping and squealing and laughing as they set off down the lawn towards where Peter was sitting motionless on the bench. They were still a hundred yards away when Alice stopped. She knew. She turned around and knelt down.

"Sophie. Lucy. Hold hands. Stay there." The girls did as they were told and she turned and took several steps in Peter's direction, her pace quickening, breaking into a run, her fears rising as she drew closer. She got within ten feet

286

and stopped. Peter was indeed motionless, his head tipped forward on his chest, one arm hanging limply at his side.

CHAPTER 33

A dozen of the good folk of Chalton turned out for the funeral of Colonel Peter Jeffries, DCM, MC, DSC and bar, even though most of them hardly knew him. They had certainly known his father, who had been a pillar of the community, and they had all been beneficiaries, directly or indirectly, of his generous contributions to the village.

But when Sir John had died and his reclusive army officer son, his surprisingly young wife and teenage daughter had moved in, things were never quite the same. The Jeffries family seemed perfectly pleasant types but liked to keep themselves to themselves, so the local population had to resort to rumour and gossip in order to fill in the gaps in their knowledge.

They knew of the twin tragedies that had befallen the colonel, of course: firstly, the untimely death of his impossibly beautiful young wife – "She was foreign, you know" – and then the mysterious disappearance of the daughter. But they had kept their distance, limiting their contact to expressions of condolence when they happened to pass him in the country lanes.

Their sympathy for him had been genuine, but nothing could explain the extraordinary arrival, four years ago, of a young woman who bore a remarkable resemblance to his missing daughter. Tongues began to wag, naturally, and while some simply assumed it was a coincidence that the colonel's new housekeeper was a dead ringer for his daughter, there also some vile gossip put about that, having tired of his Latvian girlfriend, he had taken up with a new, young English floosie who could presumably cook more than boiled lamb and potatoes.

There even remained, amongst a few of them, the suspicion that, having conflated the disappearance of one

288

young woman with the arrival of another who was virtually identical, this was no coincidence and indicative of something far more sinister.

But nothing could prepare them for the unexpected arrival of babies, two of them, around nine months after the new girl took up residence at Chalton Manor.

Dismay, outrage and criticism, mainly from the womenfolk, was often expressed privately but never outspoken, as was, from the menfolk, the occasional murmur of admiration that, not only did the old fella still have a few bullets in the magazine, he could hit the target.

So the mourners, if they could be so described, included not only those of a prurient disposition but also those motivated by genuine respect for the departed and concern for the bereaved.

After a simple service, Peter was laid to rest in the cemetery of St Mary's Church, Chalton alongside his forebears whose headstones monopolised a dedicated area of the graveyard purchased by George Jeffries, Peter's great-great-great-grandfather, in 1801.

Alice stood rigidly outside the main church door, Sophie and Lucy by her side, each holding her hand. The twins didn't understand what they were doing there and Alice had not yet had the courage or the opportunity to try and explain, so they had begun to get a little fidgety, kicking their feet in the gravel and twitching their noses in boredom. But Alice held on firmly. It would be over soon.

Michael had been a rock, of course, as had Emma; the only family Peter had. The rest of the congregation comprised people she barely knew, but some she recognised by sight, although only a few expressed their condolences to her personally.

She cut a striking figure, standing there with her beautiful daughters, in black Jaeger cashmere overcoat over a black silk dress and black court Jimmy Choos, with a black velvet hat and lace veil. The twins were equally well dressed

289

considering their age and the good folk of Chalton could tell that the women in the Jeffries household wanted for nothing.

Alice's relationship with Emma had blossomed after Emma had been made aware of the basic facts and, having no children of her own, she took Alice under her wing during her pregnancy and was a tower of strength after the twins were born. It was Emma who broke the awkward silence.

"Come on, Alice. It's time to go," she said. Alice was reluctant to leave this place, leave him behind, but after a moment, sense took hold and she let her body relax. She held her head up and led her daughters, followed by Emma and the rest of the congregation, slowly down the path towards the main entrance gate.

Michael stayed at the back, last man standing, but when he approached the entrance gate something in his peripheral vision caused him to stop and turn. To his right, about hundred yards distant in the corner of the graveyard, stood a figure. He tried to focus, and his eyes were not what they once were but there was a familiarity he couldn't place.

The figure was dressed in a colourful jacket and wore what appeared to be a woollen hat, not normal funeral attire. The figure stood motionless, staring back at him and the others as they filed out. Behind this figure, another emerged from the trees, similarly dressed in informal colourful clothes. A man and a woman, he judged, and suddenly it became clear. He knew who the woman was.

From the other end of the graveyard, the woman, dressed in a red puffer jacket, blue woollen hat with ear protectors and woollen ties dangling down each side, watched as the funeral party left the churchyard.

She recognised Michael Goodman and watched him stop and look at her, and made no attempt to conceal herself. She sensed a noise behind her but stared straight ahead. She felt the hand placed gently on her shoulder and she put her own on top, before turning her head around and smiling at the Nepalese man looking at her fondly, with a deep sadness.

Down the side of her face, she bore the remains of a once hideous scar, still red and angry after five years, and although she returned his smile warmly, the tears flowed steadily down her disfigured cheek.

Lisa Jeffries had clawed her way out of the rubble of the only school in Langtang with her bare hands and, despite serious head injuries and a broken pelvis, had managed to drag her broken body three miles to a trail where she was picked up by a mule train en route to Chumtang, a remote village to the north, near the Chinese border.

The villagers of Chumtang cared for her, and although her physical condition slowly improved, her injuries, together with the psychological trauma of her ordeal in Langtang, had resulted in retrograde amnesia. She didn't know her name or who she was, so the women villagers called her Alisha. Protected by God.

Alisha started a new life in Chumtang, adopting Buddhism, returning to teaching; and as the years passed, fragments of her memory began to return. Word spread of a Western girl who had survived Langtang, and it eventually reached Kathmandu, and the ear of Sujay Bahadur Gurung.

It took Sujay a week to get there, and as soon as he saw her he knew she was the Jeffries girl. He told her about her father's efforts to find her, and the shattered pieces of her lost memory finally fell into place.

Michael took the call exactly one week after Peter had died. He recognised Lisa's voice immediately, but Alisha sounded very different. She had a calmness and serenity that seemed at odds with the girl he once knew.

He gave her the terrible news. She was too late. Alisha remained composed and said she would return as planned. Michael had sensed the danger and the complications that would arise, and thought it would be better if she delayed her arrival until after the funeral. He thought she had agreed to wait. He was wrong.

Alisha took Sujay Bahadur Gurung's arm, and they slowly walked out of the side exit of St Mary's Church.

CHAPTER 34

Alice let herself and her daughters in the front door of Chalton Manor. Lucy and Sophie took off down the hallway, shouting, "Grandad! Grandad!" ever hopeful that their beloved grandfather had finally returned from wherever it was he had been for the last couple of weeks.

Alice closed the door behind her and bit her lip as the girls disappeared into the kitchen, quickly reappeared and chased each other up the spiral staircase, still squealing, still calling for their beloved Grandad.

She would have to explain to them that Grandad was not ever coming back and that would be very hard. She decided she would say nothing to the twins today but sit them down tomorrow and tell them they were on their own now.

She felt lost again for the first time in four years, and the house that had become her home felt suddenly alien and unwelcoming. She felt like an intruder, the figures in the oil paintings of the Jeffries dynasty staring down at her, questioning her legitimacy. As the girls' voices became too faint to hear, a rush of silence filled the void, punctuated only by the rhythmic ticking of the grandfather clock. She didn't know what she was going to do without him.

She needed something to do, so she changed into her work clothes and set about cleaning the already immaculately clean kitchen, mopped the floors in the perfectly tidy bathrooms and hallway, and started preparing an early supper for the twins. The sooner they went to bed, the better.

Lucy and Sophie ate their suppers at the kitchen table as usual and asked only once about Grandad, but Alice changed the subject and told them to eat up. At 7 p.m. she put them to bed. They all still slept together in one room and had done so since they were born, as despite the many bedrooms in the house, Alice wanted them close by at all times and would never let them out of her sight.

She tucked them in, kissed them both goodnight and went back downstairs to the kitchen, carrying the child monitor that she kept with her permanently when they were asleep.

In the last two weeks, Michael and Emma had come round to see her a few times and Emma had even stayed over on a couple of occasions, but tonight was different. Tonight marked the end. Peter was dead and buried and she was now alone with her three-year-old twins in a huge house that didn't belong to her. The silence in the house was almost unbearable.

She sat in the kitchen with the radio on and had a glass of Chablis, Peter's favourite, which she thought may help her; but it tasted bitter and made her feel morose. She had nothing to be angry about. *It's just life and everyone just needs to get on with it.* And although they had never discussed his condition in detail, she knew from the ever-increasing number of pill bottles and capsules in his bathroom that his medication was becoming more and more important.

So, it should have been anticipated and plans made. *What plans?* She shook herself, poured the remains of the wine down the sink and went up to bed. *It'll look different in the morning. It always does.*

She climbed the spiral staircase to the first floor but when she got to the landing, she stopped. She turned left towards Peter's room and opened the door. His smell was still there. The smell of his clothes and his shoes and his shaving foam and his soap. Not a bad smell, just aromas that had been so familiar but would now dissipate and eventually disappear.

294

She looked around the room. It was immaculate, of course, as she had busied herself washing and ironing all his clothes and tidying everything away in the aftermath of his death, just to give herself something to do. She went to the chest of drawers by the bed and without thinking opened the one that contained some of his pullovers.

She lifted out the one she was looking for: a dark green one with brown cotton epaulettes secured by faux brass buttons, and she put it to her face, closing her eyes and inhaling deeply until her breath caught.

She sniffed as her nose began to run and she wiped a hand across one eye and looked again at the open drawer, felt around under the pile of sweaters and withdrew the framed photograph. The mirror.

Janica and Lisa, still smiling, just as they had been when she had first seen it four years ago. Together again. She placed the frame on the chest of drawers and turned it to face the bed.

Alice climbed onto Peter's bed with Peter's sweater clasped to her chest, and cried and cried till she could cry no more.

CHAPTER 35

The next morning, and despite her own best advice, nothing looked different at all. The girls were – mercifully, for once – a full-time job and so she decided that the only thing she could do was stay with them at all times, to act as a distraction.

But she could not dispel the fear and uncertainty which hung over her like a cloud. *You've been here before. Deal with it. And this time you're not alone.* But then that was the point.

Had she been on her own she would have been able to cope much more easily, slip back off-grid, change her name to Emily or some such and set off again. Survive. But Sophie and Lucy needed her and, did they but know it, she needed them more than ever. They were her life and she would give it up for them, but she hadn't worked out how she was going to protect and provide for them from now on.

The sun was out. "Glorious!" she could hear Peter say, and so after breakfast she took the twins outside and walked them down the long sloping field to the river where *Carician* was still moored, now gathering moss and cobwebs, a brown tide mark around her white hull. The girls ran around chasing each other and the butterflies and picked buttercups, and Alice watched them, thankful for them and thankful to Peter for looking after them all. She was so lost in her thoughts she didn't hear someone coming up behind her.

"I thought I'd find you down here." She turned and smiled.

"Hello, Michael. I didn't know you were coming today." She walked up to him and he kissed her on both cheeks. The twins spotted him and ran up to meet them.

"Hello, Uncle Mikey!" they shrieked in unison, jumping around at his feet.

"Hello, princesses!" said Michael, dropping to his knees and taking their tiny hands in his. "Hey, you two, go on up to the house and see Auntie Emma, she's got a present for you!" They shrieked with delight and set off up the field, little legs wobbling and arms flapping like fledgling ducks.

"Don't run!" shouted Alice, "and hold hands with each other." Hand in hand, the twins dutifully slowed their pace to a plodding walk, and Michael and Alice watched them go in amusement. But for Alice, the dark cloud descended immediately.

"What are we going to do, Michael?" her voice already breaking, her arms wrapped around her chest in an instinctive gesture of self–preservation. Michael looked at her fondly.

"May I call you Jess?" he said gently but with the air of authority she knew well. She dropped her head.

"Yes. Of course. Peter told you." She felt embarrassed at the pretence, the deception that had not been a deception at all. Only to herself.

"Yes. He told me a long time ago," he said, and her frustration and fear quickly surfaced. The fairy tale was over.

"Then he must have told you I have nothing but a bad history," she sobbed, berating herself for imaginary crimes in the past.

"You have two beautiful daughters and, I hope, some fond memories of your time here with Peter," said Michael, reasonable, unemotional, incontrovertible. She looked at the twins still plodding up the field and had to agree; these had been wonderful times. But there were practicalities and they were serious.

"But what are we going to do?" she wailed as the tears continued to flow. "I can't stay here. I feel like I'm trespassing already. And I still owe lots of people lots of money." Michael put his hands on her shoulder to steady her and she dropped her head at the shame and humiliation she felt.

"You don't owe anything, Jess. Peter settled it all."

She looked up, startled, uncomprehending.

"Most of the debt was registered at the Crown Court and therefore public knowledge, so that was easy to rectify. Of the rest, shall we say, the unofficial debt, the stuff that was undocumented, we did some research, tracked them down, and cleared it. *Jackson & Rutherford – top men indeed.* There's no history." But Jess still could not understand.

"But … but … why would he—"

"Because he loved you," he interjected, "and he loved his grandchildren. He did it before they were born. He fixed things so you would always be safe." Jess's body sagged as she took in the enormity of it all.

"Oh, Peter." She wiped the back of her hand across her cheek. "I never got a chance to thank him."

"And as far as staying here is concerned," continued Michael, "you, Sophie and Lucy can stay as long as you like. It's what Peter wanted."

"But …?" she had no idea what he meant.

"It's yours, Jess. Peter left you everything." Her eyes widened as she processed the meaning, and she clasped her hand over her mouth to stop herself crying out.

He had done this for her, a complete stranger, a miserable waif and stray with a chequered past, pregnant with twins. He had taken her in, given her sanctuary, provided for her and given her everything she could possibly want and had asked for nothing in return, other than she stay with him and be his companion for as long as she wanted to.

"What?" was all she could say. Her children would be safe. She would be safe. "I never knew," she whimpered.

"He didn't want you to know. He didn't want to you to feel any obligation to stay with him, or for that matter, any incentive. He just wanted you to be safe."

His love had been unconditional and absolute, and she desperately wanted to hold him once more and tell him how much she loved him.

"He was a wonderful father to me."

"And a good friend to me. We're going to miss him." He turned away and looked out over the river. She could tell he was contemplating something, had something to say but unsure of how to say it. Perhaps Michael disapproved? She couldn't tell, but there was more to come, of that she was sure.

"There's one other thing," he said, and she looked up, bewildered. *When you have just been given the earth, what else can there be?*

"At the same time Peter changed his will, he asked me to do something else. Something we thought impossible at the time." She studied him closely. He appeared to be struggling to find the right words, wrestling with a dilemma, and it frightened her. He had given her nothing but hope so far, but there had to be a downside, a catch. But she could take anything. She just needed him to come out and say it. "There's someone here to see you," he said gravely, and turned his head up the slope towards the house.

Jess, still stunned by what she had heard, slowly followed his gaze, and, seeing a group of people up by the house, took two or three steps towards them. Emma, standing. Sophie and Lucy next to her, gripping her skirt. Emma's hand on the shoulder of another figure she couldn't identify.

She strained her eyes to see. And then it hit her. She knew who it was. It was the girl in the photograph. Her battered, crumpled photograph. Older, taller, still beautiful, in colourful Asian dress, smiling. Jess's mouth opened, the scream emerging as a hoarse whisper.

"Leila!"

She broke into a run, an uphill sprint, arms pumping, legs straining, hair streaming backwards, voice screaming, "Leila, Leila!" and she covered the distance between them rapidly and then Leila was running to her, "Mummy! Mummy!" and Jess dropped to her knees as they collided and she lifted her daughter up high and hugged and kissed. And then the twins jumped on them both and they all fell on the grass in a heap, laughing and crying. A new beginning.

THE AWAKENING

The sequel to Good Girl

... the pathway to truth is lit only for the enlightened to see.

Why did Mohammed Khalid take his daughter Leila with him when he fled the UK for Pakistan, and what happened to her there?

How was Leila eventually found and returned into the arms of her mother Jess?

What really happened to Lisa and why did she disappear so soon after her father's funeral?

What does the future now hold for Jess and her three young daughters?

And, crucially, will Jess ever find true love?

The Awakening, the latest novel from Norman Hall, will be published summer 2019.

Printed in Great Britain
by Amazon